First One Missing

www.transworldbooks.co.uk

Also by Tammy Cohen

The Mistress's Revenge
The War of the Wives
Someone Else's Wedding
The Broken
Dying for Christmas

First One Missing

Tammy Cohen

Doubleday

LONDON · TORONTO · SYDNEY · AUCKLAND · JOHANNESBURG

TRANSWORLD PUBLISHERS
61–63 Uxbridge Road, London W5 5SA
www.transworldbooks.co.uk

Transworld is part of the Penguin Random House group of companies whose
addresses can be found at global.penguinrandomhouse.com

First published in Great Britain in 2015 by Doubleday
an imprint of Transworld Publishers

A CIP catalogue record for this book
is available from the British Library.

ISBNs
9780857522788 (tpb)
9780857522771 (hb)

Typeset in 11/15pt Sabon by Kestrel Data, Exeter, Devon.
Printed and bound in Great Britain by Clays Ltd, Bungay, Suffolk.

Penguin Random House is committed to a sustainable
future for our business, our readers and our planet. This book
is made from Forest Stewardship Council® certified paper.

1 3 5 7 9 10 8 6 4 2

For *las guapas*: Rikki, Mel, Juliet, Fiona, Roma

This time yesterday none of this was real. This time yesterday she was only missing. Hope and possibility still breathed inside me like a thing hiding in the dark.

This time two days ago, none of it had happened. The sun rose on a world that was still normal, and she was standing by my bed whispering, 'Get up, Mummy, Mia is crying,' and because the world was still normal and none of it had happened, I felt tired and impatient for my lost sleep.

This time a week ago I went with her on her school trip to the city farm in East London, and I watched her sitting with her friends eating the lunch I'd packed carefully into different-sized plastic boxes decorated with cartoon characters and realized for the first time that she had a separate life now, that she would never again be fully known. Just one week ago, her life stretching tantalizingly ahead, as she sat on a blanket on the damp grass eating honey sandwiches with the crusts cut off.

This time yesterday, I was still me.

1

Thursday is rubbish day, make sure the recycling box is outside the gate or they won't take it. Jemima? Rounders today, PE kit washed and next to her school bag (shirt getting far too small, must order a new one), ingredients for food tech neatly stacked in the fridge. Damn, Caitlin's violin needs a new string. Must remember to pick one up at Maitland's and drop it into school before her lesson. What time is it? 4? 4.30? Nancy's turn to pick up from ballet, thank God, so there'll be time to do a proper dinner. Roast chicken? Or what was that thing Jemima had at her friend Violet's last week that she said she liked? Tagine of something? Could try that.

Lost in her litany of thoughts, Emma was only vaguely aware of the alarm sounding.

'Can you turn that *fucking* thing off?' said Guy's back. He emphasized the 'fucking', like a child self-consciously trying out swearing for the first time. Funny how his back seemed to have taken on a personality all of its own now Emma saw it so often. It was intractable, solid, unyielding – she imagined it to be like Marlon Brando in A Streetcar Named Desire, all brooding muscle and tense resistance. Unlike Guy himself whose presence settled around the house like fine mist, everywhere and nowhere at the same time.

She swung her legs over the side of the bed and levered herself slowly upright as though being winched. Could there really have been a time when she threw back the covers and leapt headlong into the oncoming day? She tried to think back but her mind was blank.

Perched on the edge of the bed, she picked up the neatly folded pile of clothes from the creamy sheepskin rug. The wool felt soft and soothing against her fingers and she had an urge to put her face to the floor to bury her nose in it.

Instead, with minimal movement, she shrugged off her pyjamas and wriggled into her clothes. Her back was to Guy – if he had turned round all he would have seen was a ridge of spine, a sharp angle of shoulder blade, before the shroud of her loose-fitting grey cotton-jersey top descended over her wide-legged white linen trousers. 'The Western equivalent of a burka', is how Guy once described the clothes she wore nowadays. His tone was sarcastic, but his expression sad, as if he were recalling someone who'd died, someone he'd known well but hadn't seen in a long time.

Although it was early, the sunlight was already burning through the white curtains, illuminating the distressed French-armoire-style wardrobes and the calico-covered armchair with the cream embroidered cushions. In the opaque frosted-glass morning light, it seemed as if Guy, lying on his side in the king-sized bed in a nest of white pillows and duvet, was floating on a cloud, like an overgrown cherub. Only his back, tense and scowling, told her he was awake.

Padding softly along the landing, she nudged open the door to Caitlin's room and lingered for a moment in the doorway. When Emma gently shook her foot, Caitlin's eyes shot open, the exact yellow-brown of mulched autumn leaves, and she blinked rapidly, although Emma knew she couldn't yet see her. She was still back in whichever place she visited in sleep, chasing her dream down echoing corridors in her mind. Finally she began to focus and Emma knew she was coming back to her. It was this moment she relished most of all – when Caitlin returned from wherever she had been, becoming, briefly, hers again.

'Hello, pudding,' she greeted her, neutrally, sitting on the edge of her bed and grazing the soft cushion of her cheek with the back of her fingers. Of course, what she really wanted to do was crush her youngest daughter to her chest, climbing in beside her and snuggling under the duvet. But, a short time before, she'd sensed those morning cuddles were making Caitlin uncomfortable. 'I'm too hot,' she'd complained, making her still-soft body go stiff and resistant. 'You're boiling me up.'

On this particular morning Caitlin seemed to shrink back even from the mere touch of her mother's fingers.

'Did you get the string for my violin?' she wanted to know, her gaze direct and unblinking.

'Sorry, darling, I forgot. Silly Mummy will have to bring your violin to school.'

Caitlin frowned, her still-flushed cheeks dimpling with displeasure. Not so long ago, she would have joined in with the game of mock chastisement. 'Yes, *silly* Mummy.' But now, at nine, she was merely cross. 'You *always* forget things.'

The reproach stung – more so for being well deserved. Emma tried to recall if she had always been a Mummy Who Forgets Things. Fleetingly, she was allowed a glimpse, before the shutter slammed down, of a life marked out with highlighter pens and colour-coded calendars and little brightly coloured notepads with 'Note to Self' stamped across the top. But had these really been her? Perhaps at heart, despite the Post-its and the calendars, she had always been a mummy who forgets – the kind who bursts in late and sweating into a near-empty classroom to collect an angst-ridden child on early-finish Friday, the kind whose daughters turn up empty-handed on cake-sale day.

Down a short flight of stairs on to the next half-landing, she hesitated before knocking gently on Jemima's door. Jemima was so prickly these days, with her newly acquired thirteen-year-old attitude, so at odds with her still childlike body.

Jemima was already awake. Emma could hear her muttering savagely behind her door. She would already be yanking clumps of clothes out of drawers, sifting through them for that one elusive thing that was going to make her friend India seethe with jealousy, or Finn from the other class notice her. Later Emma would go into her room and pick up the discarded clothes, folding them neatly back into drawers. Guy hated her doing that. 'How will they ever learn if you do everything for them?' he'd snap, not understanding that she did it for herself, not them. To feel closer.

By the time she got downstairs, Caitlin was already at the kitchen table, hunched over a bowl of cereal, her mass of dark hair concealing her face. Next to her on the table was a box of loom bands, and Emma's heart sank in anticipation of the tiny plastic elastics she'd be picking up from the floor later on.

'I *hate* Thursdays.' Jemima had thrown herself into a chair and was glaring at her mother as if Emma bore sole responsibility for Wednesday not flowing seamlessly into Friday. 'Double maths, double French *and* ethics.'

From the way she was still glowering, Emma understood this too to be her fault.

She switched on the radio, wishing just for once they could listen to something other than Radio 1.

'Are you sure those shorts are really the right thing for school?'

She made her voice deliberately casual but even so it was the wrong thing to say. Jemima's chin wobbled and her green eyes were immediately stretched wide with affront.

'Well, if I *had* some clothes to wear, then maybe I could pick

12

and choose, but seeing as you never buy me anything, I don't exactly have much choice, do I?'

When did she become so angry, this daughter of hers? How could Emma have gone so quickly from being the centre of her world to Enemy Number One?

She turned away so as not to show that she minded. Shows of weakness only enraged Jemima more.

Trying to ignore the denim shorts over black opaque tights combo that Jemima had decreed appropriate for a day at school, Emma pulled out an obscenely thick butcher's block from a special alcove within the wall of sleekly fitted cupboards and started preparing the packed lunches. As ever, she had to prepare two completely separate meals – Caitlin liked butter but not mayonnaise, ham, tomato but not cucumber ('uck, slimy'). Jemima was houmous (she took Emma's refusal to follow her into vegetarianism as a personal slight) with lettuce (but not the crunchy, white inside leaves). One liked green apples, the other seedless clementines. One favoured salt and vinegar crisps, the other would eat only ready salted. On rare occasions when Emma got the lunchboxes mixed up, her daughters' condemnation had been absolute. 'Thanks a *lot*! I had to *starve* all day.'

This morning Emma was careful to keep the lunches separate, using the colour-coded lids of their Tupperware boxes. Jemima: green; Caitlin: blue.

On the radio, the presenter made a joke about the weather, which had finally turned warmer and brighter after months of sluggish grey mornings, the sun already pooling on the decking in Emma's back garden. For a moment, she gazed out on the neat strips of wood in their rigidly regimented rows, which had re- placed the wild and formless garden that was here when they'd bought the house (could it be nearly ten years ago? When did time start passing in decades rather than days and months?). All the houses in their North London street – large red-brick Victorian

13

terraces, with stained-glass panelled doors and newly restored tessellated front paths – had the same decked back gardens. In Emma and Guy's neighbourhood people had become expert at covering over their rough, unsightly patches. Of course it hadn't been completely the same since it was pulled up during the search. Emma knew she shouldn't blame Guy for that, yet she did.

'Mummy, isn't it true that Frannie said I'd be ready for a *massive* part in the play next year?' Caitlin asked, insistently.

Even though she'd had years to get used to it, Emma still found it strange to hear her children addressing their teachers by their first names. At the progressive private school both girls attended, its rolling green lawns within stroking distance of the vast open space of Hampstead Heath, it was felt first names broke down unhelpful barriers between staff and children, but for Emma it just seemed confusing, and only by careful study of the context could she ever tell if her girls were talking about adults or their peers.

'They might let you be a tree or something,' Jemima sneered, carefully sifting through her muesli, separating off the unwanted bits of dried fruit into a small mound by her bowl.

'Mummy, tell her I'm not going to be a tree.' Caitlin's expression was one of wounded indignation. 'Tell her what Frannie called me. She said I had a lot of vi . . . vi . . . vi . . .'

'Vision.' Emma came to her rescue. 'She said you had tremendous vision for someone so young.'

'Yeah, but what does *Frannie* know?' Jemima interjected. 'Aside from being a teacher she's only ever been in some Andrew Lloyd Webber thing. It's not like she's *famous* or anything.'

As far as Jemima was concerned, famous was being on *The X Factor* or *Made in Chelsea*. Everything else was hardly worth bothering with.

Caitlin already looked close to tears. She was so easily upset these days, wearing her emotions on the surface like an extra skin.

'You're just jealous because you never get picked for anything,' she told her sister, her voice perilously high. Emma longed to squeeze in next to her at the table and enfold her in her arms and press and press until all her worries disappeared. But she knew Caitlin would squirm free of her embrace, and Jemima would triumphantly add it to her ever growing dossier of evidence that Emma favoured her youngest. So instead she stayed anchored to the kitchen worktop spooning ground coffee into the cafetiere as Jemima responded with an infuriatingly sarcastic laugh. In the background, the exhaustingly upbeat radio presenter bantered with the newsreader who was about to read the headlines.

Caitlin's face had now become blotchy with frustration. Finally she let loose with a volley of angry phrases which Jemima countered with equal vitriol. Emma hesitated, wondering whether to intervene, knowing if she did she risked becoming the focus for their combined discontent. Then over the top of the girls' high-pitched voices, she heard on the radio a name that cut right through the cacophony of sibling anger, through the whirring of the microwave as it heated milk for the coffee.

Tilly Reid.

At that same moment, Emma's mobile phone began to ring. Jemima had set it to blare out a ubiquitous pop song which increased in volume with each passing second until it filled the room.

Even without looking at the display she knew the name that would flash up there. *Leanne Miller.*

Conscious that the girls had halted hostilities mid-fight and were listening in silent anticipation, Emma pressed the green phone symbol to answer the call.

'Emma? I'm so sorry,' began the voice she hadn't heard in nearly a year, the voice of all her nightmares rolled into one.

Emma didn't wait to hear what Leanne was sorry about. She didn't need to.

'There's been another one, hasn't there?'

2

There were some parts of the job that got you down, no two ways about it.

Leanne wasn't just talking about the emotional stuff. You expected a bit of angst when you were dealing with families suddenly plunged into a living hell. Anyway, she was supposed to be trained to deal with that sort of thing. 'Stress management' was something they were very big on in those Family Liaison Officer training sessions. Yeah, right! She remembered going to her first assignment equipped with all these strategies and techniques for dealing with the pressure, keeping her emotional distance, blah blah blah. She'd felt nervous, but prepared, quietly convinced she was ready for whatever she might encounter, the commendations of her supervisor still ringing in her ears. Now she cringed to think of how naive she'd been – as if stress was something that could be managed, like accounts or office admin. As if human emotions could be neatly packaged up and kept at a nicely appropriate distance.

Leanne hadn't been there five minutes before she realized there was no training for dealing with grief. You could only witness it and absorb it. Course she was careful not to use that word 'absorb' at the debriefing sessions with Occupational Health. You couldn't really – not if you wanted to stay doing this job. Instead, she might say 'empathize', as in 'I empathized with the family's feelings'. But she was always quick to add that she remained objective. *I know my first job is to investigate and never to counsel*, she told them. She knew all the jargon. She'd been doing it off and on for nearly eleven years.

Training or no training, some days it could really get you down, and today was one of those days.

She'd been woken up shortly after six by a call from Desmond. As soon as she'd seen his name on the screen, her heart practically hurled itself up through her mouth. Detective Chief Inspector Desmond wasn't the type to place an early call to wish you a good morning or to check you'd done your positive affirmations for the day.

'We have another murder on our hands,' he told her. No pre-amble. No pleasantries.

As Leanne snapped her phone off, Will raised himself up on to his elbow and gave her the quizzical look that could still melt her, with his right eyebrow arching up into his floppy brown hair. Will knew better than to talk to her after she'd been woken up by the phone. Well, after she'd been woken up, full stop. 'You're like an old motor,' Leanne's ex-husband Pete used to say. 'Need a lot of warming up in the morning.'

Leanne sat back against the pillows for a while, trying to take in the implications of what had just happened, but her brain seemed to be operating a half-hour delay behind the rest of her.

After a while, Will got up, wrapping Leanne's old towelling dressing gown around his skinny frame, and padded away to make the tea. Leanne still couldn't really get her head around someone making her tea in the mornings. She couldn't remember Pete ever bringing her up a drink to bed throughout their entire twelve-year marriage. And he'd rather have gone downstairs stark

naked than wear something of hers. He'd have called it 'emascu-lating'.

Leanne lay back in the bed that used to belong to her and Pete but now belonged just to her (and Will sometimes), on top of the worn blue and white gingham duvet she and Pete had got as a wedding present, as Will clattered around the kitchen down the hall.

She tried to focus her thoughts on the conversation she'd just had. Or, more to the point, the conversation she was going to have to have now that she'd had the conversation she'd just had.

It was fair to say Leanne was not looking forward to calling Emma Reid.

Desmond had assured her there had been no leaks to the media. *Yet.* Was ever a three-letter word so weighted with unspoken pressure? Leanne knew that dead children were gold dust to the media. When she'd first started doing the job, she'd been shocked by the lengths to which reporters would go to get a story, trotting out the same old lines: 'People find it cathartic to talk about it.' 'Maybe your story will prompt someone who knows something to break their silence.' And the odious last resort, 'If you don't talk to us we'll still write the story anyway. Wouldn't you prefer to have some control over what we say?' That awful *Chronicle* journalist Sally Freeland being a case in point.

Since getting together with Will, she'd become much more cynical. Not that Will was exactly the archetypal hard-bitten hack. As features editor on a small-circulation marketing maga-zine he was far more likely to be writing about the latest perfume campaign than a crime investigation, but still he knew how the business operated, and as a result Leanne liked to believe she was now less shockable. She knew it was only a matter of time before someone from the media called Emma Reid asking for her reaction to the news. It was imperative that she got in there first. *Imperative.* Already she was talking like Desmond.

When Will came back into the room, carrying two mugs of steaming tea, Leanne was still exactly where he'd left her.

'Yours, I believe.' He extended the mug she always used, the one that had 'Diva' emblazoned across the side – a present from Pete in better times.

As Leanne blew across the surface of the tea, Will studied her face, looking for clues as to what was going on.

'All right,' she conceded. Although he hadn't said a word, Will's endless, exaggerated patience was always guaranteed to push her towards indiscretion. 'One of my old cases has, well, come to life again.'

'Tilly Reid?'

Leanne looked up sharply. Then she made a face. The kind of face that says, 'You know I can't possibly talk about this.'

It was at times like this she felt like she might actually miss Pete. Not because Pete was so emotionally supportive or anything, but because he was on the force, so at least he had some idea of what she was going through.

'Something's happened that means the media are going to be raking everything up again,' she told Will, as cryptically as she could. 'So I've got to get back in touch with the family. Like, right this minute.' Still she made no attempt to move.

Will continued to gaze at her levelly. The towelling dressing gown, faded purple with stains that told a hundred stories, was gaping open at the front to reveal his pale, almost hairless chest and she averted her eyes as if it was indecent.

'And, let me guess, you really, really don't want to,' he said softly, stroking her arm.

Leanne almost allowed herself to relax, but then she stopped herself short. Even though it sometimes seemed like Will could read her mind, in this instance he couldn't possibly know just how much she really didn't want to make that call.

'It's the same every time,' she blurted out. 'I let myself believe it's the last one. And then it happens all over again. And there I am again, ringing on that bloody doorbell . . .

'She hates me, you know,' she told Will, not even bothering to pretend he didn't know exactly who 'she' might be. 'I'm the Grim Reaper in a skirt as far as she's concerned.'

'Can you blame her?'

'I suppose not.' Leanne was grudging, but the truth was, obviously she couldn't blame Emma Reid for the way she tensed up whenever Leanne came within a foot of her. When Leanne last appeared, it was because another little girl had died. Someone else's daughter, someone else's sister/niece/grandchild. Two more dead now since Emma's Tilly, and of course before Tilly there'd been Megan Purvis, the original 'angel', as the tabloids had dubbed them all. And still Leanne kept popping up, the uninvited fairy at the christening – and never with the one thing Emma most wanted to hear. That Tilly's murderer had been found.

While Will went off for a shower, Leanne leaned back against the headboard, both hands clasped around her mug. If her eyes had been focused, she might have found herself staring at her own reflection in the mirror propped up against the wall opposite the bed, or at the overflowing laundry basket next to it. ('Those clothes will get up and walk away of their own accord if you leave them much longer,' is what Pete would have said if he'd seen it, like the washing was somehow her responsibility alone.) But that morning her surroundings failed to register.

Instead she was picturing Emma Reid, as she'd first seen her – shiny caramel-coloured hair pulled back into one of those styles certain women can do where the hair is kind of tied up messily, with some strands artlessly coming loose. It was one of those styles that looks really casual, but Leanne had tried it herself often enough on her own wayward light-brown hair ('beige', Pete had teased her) to know that it was nowhere near as careless as it appeared.

The loose strands of hair framed a small, pretty, flawlessly complexioned face. She was the kind of woman who knew how to do make-up so that it looked like she wasn't wearing any. Leanne remembered she'd been wearing tight faded jeans tucked into knee-length leather boots and Leanne had thought about her own boots that barely fitted around her calves and wondered how many inches she'd have to lose off each leg to get them to slide on over thick denim jeans. And then she'd felt bad for thinking about something so trivial. She didn't get that so much these days, the guilt. She understood now there were no rules for grief. or grieving, no restrictions on how you should or shouldn't think. One minute you could be facing something so terrible it made you question everything you knew about the world, and the next you'd be reminding yourself to pay the gas bill. It was just how it was.

When she first met Emma Reid, Tilly was only missing. Guy, Emma's tall, strong-jawed husband, had been in full motion, striding around the house. There's lots you can *do* when a child is missing – people to ring, searches to organize – and Guy Reid was a *doer*. So he was in full flow, working out strategies, thinking of solutions, of 'best-case scenarios'. He was some kind of trouble-shooter in the City as far as Leanne could make out, one of those people who spend their lives bandying about phrases like 'best-case scenario'. That was before there stopped being anything for him to do, when all that 'doing' energy inside him turned to something else and the best-case scenario turned out to be worse than anything he could have imagined.

Emma had clearly been used to her husband achieving those best-case scenarios. She didn't seem to have quite taken in the seriousness of the situation – hadn't even made that link to the death of the Purvis girl two years before. She'd had that look of someone waiting for a misunderstanding to be cleared up, as if the shop assistant had given her change from a ten instead of a twenty.

Leanne was the one who'd had to break the news to them when they found the body two days later. It wasn't something you'd wish on your worst enemy. The SIO had offered to be with her while she did it, but he'd done so in a way that left Leanne in no doubt that he'd rather pull his own toenails out without anaesthetic, as she'd told Pete later on.

So she'd done it on her own, leaning forward on the Reids' brown leather sofa to touch Emma's knee across the coffee table. They were taught about body language and comforting gestures. They weren't taught about how it looks when the life drains out of a person right in front of your very eyes, or how it feels to be looked at as though you yourself were responsible for the very thing you were describing. They weren't taught how inadequate the word 'sorry' can seem.

By 7.45, Leanne still hadn't called her.

At least she'd started to get dressed by then. Normally she'd just pull on the first things out of the 'work' side of her wardrobe but today she chose more carefully. Clearly this was not going to be an ordinary day and she wanted to be armoured up, by which she meant wearing clothes that didn't look like they'd been scraped out of the bottom of the dirty-laundry basket. One thing about Emma Reid – even in the depths of her grief, she still matched her socks to her outfit. Leanne was lucky if she even matched her socks to each other.

Leanne was just digging through her underwear drawer in search of a pair of tights without a hole when her phone rang again. Desmond.

'I hope you've called her, because we've just found out the news is already out.'

Shit.

'I was just ringing her now.'

Desmond was unimpressed.

Hanging up, Leanne scrolled immediately through her contacts list. *Reids* was the landline number, she remembered that much. Scrolling down one further to *Reid Emma*, she pressed the green phone key.

While waiting for Emma to pick up, Leanne tried to remember the stress-management techniques they'd been taught during training. *Deep breath, concentrate on your breathing, not on what's around you.* Not on the crack in the ceiling above the bedroom window which, come to think of it, appeared to have got wider in the last month, not on the fact that the tights she'd chosen turned out to have a ladder near the top (she made a quick judgement call that the skirt would just about cover it), not on the image of Emma Reid going about her morning business serenely unaware, or of Jemima Reid's face, blotchy with fear and frustration.

'Emma? I'm so sorry . . .'

3

'Quite frankly, I don't give a fuck about your profit margins, Mr Bellows. When one commissions a water feature, one expects it to feature water. Not just a few drops here and there, but a great big fucking cascade of water.'

Sally Freeland noticed the man sitting across the table from her on the crowded train was nudging his wife but it didn't bother her. What did bother her, however, was Mr Bellows trying to tell her it was her own water pressure that was to blame.

'I'm a journalist, Mr Bellows. If I tell my editor I'm going to write fifteen hundred words on "MPs on the Make", and then I turn in a thousand words instead, and say, "Oh, but my desk was a bit rickety so I couldn't write as much," he's not going to be very fucking happy, is he?'

Mr Bellows didn't see the analogy, apparently. Frankly Sally doubted if Mr Bellows would recognize an analogy if one punched him in the face. Pressing 'end call', she yanked aside the mouth-piece of the hands-free headset.

She was having a pig of a day already, and it was barely ten o'clock. She'd *kill* for a cigarette.

'I am a person who doesn't smoke,' she reminded herself, trying to remember the exact wording Sebastian the hypnotherapist had used. 'I can *think* about having a cigarette but I make the choice *not* to have one.'

It wasn't working.

Sitting back in her seat, she looked out of the window at the green rolling East Sussex countryside, trying to let go of her anger, as her life coach, Mina, kept telling her to do. Shift focus, she told herself sternly.

She picked up her Mulberry bag from the seat next to her and started to rifle through it, frowning as she spotted the Mulberry wallet which, being a totally different shade of brown to the bag, never failed to jar. Really, she'd been right to end things with Noel. What kind of person bought you a tan Mulberry bag for your birthday and then a chocolate-brown Mulberry wallet for Valentine's Day? Not that that had been the main reason for the split. A symptom rather than the whole malaise, she'd told Mina.

She wouldn't listen to the little voice that pointed out it had been Noel who'd broken up with her, and she certainly wouldn't dwell on that awful scene when she'd turned up on his doorstep drunk and sobbing and he hadn't let her in, just called a cab and waited with her outside until it arrived.

Pulling out a red crocodile-skin case, Sally extracted her reading glasses before opening up her laptop decisively.

Focus, focus, focus.

It was only six months since she'd last revisited the Kenwood Killer case – that awkward interview with Fiona Botsford, the mother of the third victim – but a full four years since the whole thing started with the death of Megan Purvis. Of course, it hadn't been a serial killer then, just a seemingly random stand-alone murder of the type that happened sometimes. A body had been found in woods to the east of Hampstead Heath. Though Sally had lived in London at one time, she was a Fulham girl and hadn't ever ventured to the vast expanse of grass and woodland to the north of the city, so had been taken aback to find that what was almost a wilderness existed so close to civilization. The scale of the Heath had unnerved her, with its hidden glades and miles of footpaths where you could walk without seeing another person and end up losing all sense of direction.

That first time she'd driven up to North London, cursing her stupidity when she became completely gridlocked in traffic around Croydon. She'd spent nearly a week hanging around the Purvises' house, talking to anyone who went in or out, offering money around like it was going out of fashion and clocking up thirteen parking tickets. Persistence had paid off though. It nearly always did as far as Sally was concerned. She'd hit the jackpot when she'd offered a massive donation to the charity of Helen Purvis's choice, and convinced a close friend of hers that giving an interview was the only way to get the rest of the press pack to back off.

She'd been proud of that interview, not to mention relieved. There was a time back in the 1990s when she'd been nicknamed the Queen of the Exclusives, dispatched here and there with what was basically a blank chequebook and a hefty expense account, but those days were long gone. Nowadays everyone was too afraid of losing their jobs to sign off on any payments over a hundred quid. Everything was done by committee so no one's head would end up on the block. Thank God she wasn't based in an office any more, all of them tiptoeing around eating salads at their desks that they brought from home in plastic containers. The last time she'd been into the *Chronicle*'s offices, it had been like walking into a library it was so quiet, and all those earnest interns being so self-important even though they weren't being paid a bean. She'd felt like a den mother or something. So depressing. Of course there were still a few of the old crowd around, but mostly they'd either been promoted to some sort of executive position where they sat in an office making pie charts on their computer, or else they were dribbling in a corner in their shiny suits, stinking of last night's Jameson's. Well, apart from the odd one in prison.

Nothing was as it used to be. Still, as Mina always said, nostalgia was for losers. Onward and upwards.

Peering at her computer screen, she called up the folder marked 'Purvis'. It had been a while since she'd read that interview, but now that there'd been another murder she wanted to refamiliarize herself with the facts. Sally took her ginkgo religiously every morning to boost her memory, but frankly she was fucked if she could remember her own name some days, let alone facts from a case she first wrote about four years ago.

When she double-clicked on the PDF file titled 'Purvisinterview1', a double-page newspaper spread opened up on the screen. The main photo showed a woman, with a mass of frizzy brown hair, tied back in an ill-judged ponytail, and watery blue eyes, gazing sadly out of a window. Sally instantly remembered the moment that was taken. Helen Purvis had seemed so self-controlled up to that point, yet when the photographer asked her to press a hand up to the glass, it was shaking so uncontrollably she'd ended up putting it in her lap instead.

The headline of the feature was: NOT A DAY GOES BY THAT I DON'T THINK ABOUT MEGAN. Very original. Not. The sell was equally uninspiring: 'Nine months after her daughter Megan, 7, was murdered, Helen Purvis talks to **Sally Freeland** about coming to terms with every mother's worst nightmare.' At least her name was in bold. That was something.

She read on.

Little Megan Purvis's bedroom is like any other 7-year-old's. Her duvet cover and pillow are covered in pink and orange flowers, to match the pink fluffy rug on the floor. Megan's soft white fleecy dressing gown hangs on the back of the door, and her pink fluffy slippers are tucked neatly under the bed. Everything is just as she left it when she got up on 3 May 2010. Except Megan Purvis is never coming home again.

Sally frowned as she read that intro. Almost immediately after that feature had come out, she'd been called up by the *Chronicle*'s deputy editor and told, 'No more dead kids' bedrooms.' Apparently it was hackneyed. He'd clearly never heard the phrase 'setting the scene'.

Helen Purvis, a Special Educational Needs Adviser, is a petite, softly spoken 44-year-old. When I met her at the family's £1m home in the desirable Crouch End area of North London, which she shares with her partner Simon Hewitt, an Account Executive, and her son Rory, now 13, she was still evidently grieving for the little girl she lost 9 months before.

Reminders of Megan are everywhere in the comfortable light-filled 5-bedroomed Victorian home. A photo of the cherubic-faced little girl, with her mop of blonde curls, smiles out from the mantelpiece. A framed finger painting, completed in her reception year, takes pride of place on the wall. Her pink coat, embroidered with flowers, still hangs on the coat-stand in the hallway. It has the expectant air of a house in limbo.

'It's true, in many ways I'm still waiting for her to come home,' Helen admits. 'Of course I know in my heart that she won't be coming, yet still there's a big part of me that can't accept that as a possibility.'

The whole family has been crushed by Megan's murder. 'Simon had been in Megan's life since she was four and was like a father to her,' Helen explains. 'And of course Daniel, her natural father, has been completely devastated. Poor

Rory is having to come to terms not only with the loss of his sister, but also the completely unfounded feeling of guilt that he is partly to blame.'

It was Rory who was charged with picking Megan up from her maths tutor the evening she died. Helen was at a late school meeting and Simon was having dinner with clients. Rory, 12 at the time, walked the 15 minutes through the park to pick up his sister after her class finished at 6.30.

'It was quite a fresh night, but dry, and as they entered the park gates, Rory saw some of his friends playing football on the grassy area in the middle,' Helen recalls as if remembering a speech by rote. 'They were friends from primary who'd gone on to different schools, so he was glad to see them and told Megan to go and play in the playground for a bit while he joined in the football with his mates. There were a few other people in the playground when she first got there, and he checked on her a couple of times, but when he looked over the third time the place was empty.'

Megan Purvis had simply disappeared.

Who can imagine the panic of a brother whose little sister vanishes? Who can conceive of the agony of returning home empty-handed?

For Helen Purvis, the dreadful moment of truth came when she walked through the door after her meeting finished.

'My phone needed charging so I hadn't received any messages, but as soon as I set foot in the house I just knew something was wrong,' she relates in a whisper, clearly struggling with reliving the memory. 'Usually there was noise and an atmosphere of activity in the house, but on this evening it was silent. It has been silent ever since.'

The police were already in the house, waiting with Rory. He'd run home from the park, convinced he'd find Megan on the doorstep, and already rehearsing the telling-off he'd give her, but when he'd found the house empty, he'd called 999.

'He kept saying, "I'm sorry, Mum, I'm sorry,"' Helen recalls now. 'As if I would somehow blame him.'

After Simon returned, the family had waited up together most of the night, while the police came and went, taking statements and following up leads, but the little girl seemed to have disappeared into thin air.

Then the next morning, a couple out walking their dog on the Heath in the wooded area around the poignantly named Vale of Health came across a grisly discovery. Megan Purvis's body was found wrapped in a plastic sheet. She'd been strangled.

'People say time is a healer, but it isn't,' says Helen sadly. 'Time just seems to increase our sense of bewilderment and isolation. The problem is, when something like this happens to you, there's no one else you can talk to. People tell you they understand what you're going through but they don't. We have met a couple of other parents of murdered children, but they have their circumstances and we have ours. No one knows what we're going through. It's the loneliest place in the world.'

The only thing now keeping Helen going is her need to find out who killed her daughter. 'I have to know who did this thing,' Helen says. 'I have to know why he took my baby from me, and how her last hours were spent, and I want the opportunity to explain to him just what he's done to my life and my family's life. It's like he's taken the light away from us. Now we are living in darkness.'

Helen Purvis has not received any money for this interview but asked that a donation be made to the Society for the Parents of Murdered Children.

Sitting back in her seat, Sally gazed through the window at the suburban stations the train rattled past. Soon it would arrive at Victoria, from where she would walk the ten minutes to New Scotland Yard for the press conference. She'd have preferred to go straight to the hotel in North London, where she was booked in, but there wasn't time. The hotel was in Highgate. All four of the murdered girls had lived within two miles of there. She started running through them all: Megan Purvis first, then a two-year gap before Tilly Reid. Then fourteen months until Leila Botsford, and now, less than a year later, Poppy Glover.

Whoever he was, he was getting greedier.

To take her mind off her nicotine cravings, and off the image of Simon Hewitt that had suddenly lodged itself, unwelcome, in her brain, Sally went back into the folder marked 'Purvis' and double-clicked on a different file, 'Botsfordinterview1'. This was a much shorter piece, illustrated with an old family photo of a smiling young couple showing off their frilly-hatted baby. She remembered how much wheedling it had taken before Fiona Botsford agreed to meet her for a coffee – in the end she'd had to lean on Helen Purvis to talk her into it. But Fiona was a very different kettle of fish to Helen. A very prickly character – although, if one was being charitable, it *was* only four months after her daughter's death.

They'd arranged to meet in a pergola at one of the outer edges of the Heath. It had been Helen's idea to do it there. She said it was a peaceful place that she came to when she wanted to feel closer to Megan. By that stage they all knew they were dealing with a serial killer with a thing about north-west London. Two years after Megan's body had been found in the heart of the Heath, the second body had been discovered on the West Heath, a separate enclave, not far from where they gathered for the interview, divided from the main Heath by a busy intersection. That was Tilly Reid who'd disappeared while walking alone to the local shop for the first time. And then, just over a year later had come Leila Botsford, who had been found on an offshoot of the Heath that bordered a quiet side road to the east. It was Sally herself who'd coined the term Kenwood Killer initially, and then Kenwood Killings. Even though none of the girls had technically been found near the former stately home to the north of the Heath that now housed a museum and a café and staged summer concerts on its sloping lawns, there was always something satisfying about alliteration, Sally couldn't help feeling, and most of the *Chronicle*'s readers couldn't care less about the precise geography.

Sally had found the pergola, apparently hailed as one of London's hidden gems, to be rather gloomy. Creepy even. Fiona had arrived late, already looking at her watch, which was never a good sign.

Sally had already been worrying about this interview because of Helen Purvis's insistence on being there in person to 'facilitate', as she put it. Now she began to have serious doubts.

'If sorrow wears a face, that face surely belongs to Fiona Botsford,' was how she'd started the feature. She'd actually written that first line before even meeting Fiona, and though she could tell immediately that it didn't really fit, she refused to change it. She liked the flow of the words. Rereading it now, she still liked them.

Three months ago, this loving mother from North London dropped her only child Leila off at school, just half a mile from the £1.1m family home. Like all the parents in this area, she was horribly aware that there could be a serial killer at large, preying on young girls just like 10-year-old Leila, so she made sure to drive her car as near to the school gates as possible, so she could watch Leila going through. She could have had no clue, as her happy, outgoing daughter

32

turned to wave, that this would be the last time she'd see Leila alive.

Over the course of that day, she went about her normal business – going to the supermarket, the gym, the charity where she works as a fundraiser – but it was only when she went to call her husband, Mark, a £400 per hour lawyer, that she realized her phone was missing. Irritated but not unduly worried, she went off to pick up Leila from school at the usual time, 3.45.

As always, the main school gates were awash with children streaming in and out of school, meeting parents, going back inside for forgotten coats and books, loitering to say good-bye to friends. But as the hordes cleared, Fiona started to grow concerned. Normally Leila was one of the first through the gates, bursting to share with her mum some little piece of news from her day, but today there was no sign of her.

Anxiously, Fiona entered the school and looked through corridors that were eerily silent. The school secretary joined her in her search, but Leila was nowhere to be seen.

'It's the worst feeling in the world,' shudders Fiona, 34. 'When every avenue is closing to you.'

Trying not to panic, Fiona and a few lingering staff members called Leila's classmates, hoping that maybe the normally conscientious little girl had decided to get a lift back with a friend, but nobody had seen her. Then Leila's friend Natalie remembered something that sent a chill down Fiona's spine. Leila had received a text on her mobile phone as they were getting ready to leave school, Natalie told her. It was from her mum saying she was to meet her by the back entrance to the school rather than the front where she normally went.

Fiona's nightmare was about to begin.

When you write a lot about people being murdered, as Sally did, certain words tend to be overused and 'nightmare' was one of those. It was convenient shorthand for anything catastrophic (although, to be fair, she'd also used it when describing a minor cosmetic-surgery glitch and a dispute over a leylandii hedge).

Fiona Botsford had one of those faces that was born middle-aged. She was in her mid-thirties when Sally met her but her face had that pinched quality that hardens with age like slowly setting concrete. Naturally Sally made excuses for grief, but she nevertheless suspected that Fiona was not, even in the best of circumstances, one of life's sunnier characters. She had been wearing skinny jeans that accentuated her pipe-cleaner legs, giving them the appearance of twigs that could snap at any moment.

It was a mild autumn day, as Sally remembered, but Fiona Botsford was wearing layers and layers of clothes, a short-sleeved T-shirt over a long-sleeved one, a padded down gilet over a fleecy zip-up top. It had been as if she was trying to bulk herself up to give the illusion of substance. Because Fiona Botsford was horribly thin. Of course Sally was perfectly well aware she'd only just been through this nightmare (there she went again), but even by the standards of the famous Grief Diet, she was minuscule.

Helen Purvis was up off the bench she'd been sitting on like a bloody rocket. She was one of those laying-on-of-hands type of women who have to touch you when they look at you, so she'd been positively pawing at Fiona Botsford as she sat down. The two of them had obviously been in quite close contact in the lead-up to the meeting and had sat huddled together with Helen's hand even resting protectively over Fiona's as the younger woman spoke.

'There's a phrase for people like Mark and myself,' Fiona told me. 'Childless parents, that's what we're called. After Leila was born, people always asked us when we were going to have another child, but the truth is we didn't feel the need to. To us, our family was complete. She was such a special child, so vibrant and energetic. And now she's gone, we still have all those feelings. Yet there is no child to lavish those feelings on. Instead they're just building and building inside us, without an outlet. One day they'll surely explode.'

Written down, it looked like Fiona Botsford had just come right out with this eloquent, impassioned little speech, but in reality it was built up of false starts and little prompting questions. The truth was, Fiona Botsford was guarded and as spiky as the hair clip that held her fine, mousy hair out of her eyes.

It didn't stop Helen Purvis from being overcome with emotion though. Throughout the interview, her eyes welled up regularly and she'd nod fervently and make this sort of humming noise of agreement. When Sally had transcribed the conversation from her recording, she'd wondered at first just what that sound was.

During the course of the very awkward interview, Sally asked Fiona whether she'd bonded with Emma Reid, the mother of the second victim. Emma was the one Sally was most interested in – mostly because she flat out refused to have anything to do with her, but also because she was, not to beat about the bush, the looker in the group. Obviously one wasn't supposed to think about that in situations like this, though everyone did. Only Sally actually dared put that thought into words. Not that she'd ever say those words out loud.

Helen had tried to put in a good word for Sally with Emma Reid. Sorry, *facilitate*. But nothing doing. 'She's a very private person,' she'd explained. Even better, thought Sally. Private people always have the most secrets.

But Fiona Botsford had looked at her like she was bonkers when she'd mentioned Emma Reid.

'It's not exactly a social club,' she'd said in her dry, curt voice.

Gathering all her things together as the train drew into Victoria Station, Sally noticed that the man opposite her had a packet of Marlboro Lights clasped in his hand, ready to light up as soon as he stepped out of the station.

I choose not to be a smoker. I am a person who doesn't smoke. It wasn't working.

4

'I don't know why you don't just go into work. It's not as if you're *helping* anything, just lurking around the place.'

Emma Reid turned away and busied herself filling the kettle, so Guy couldn't see her sudden confusion. Until the words tumbled out, she hadn't been aware of feeling resentful. Until a split second ago, it hadn't occurred to her to question her husband's decision to stay at home. Any bereaved parent would do the same in the circumstances. But then she'd opened her mouth and a lump of undigested bitterness had fallen out.

'Right.' The word shot, bullet-like, from Guy's mouth. 'So it's fine for the mother to sit around all day glued to the news reports – not that this particular mother has done very much else for the last two years, mind. But if the father decides, just for once, it would be too *fucking* painful to drag himself into work and face all the oh-so-tactful questions and the *fucking* sympathetic looks, that's *fucking lurking*, is it?'

Guy was getting slightly better at this swearing thing, Emma decided. He'd stopped tossing the expletives out gingerly like a small child with a new ball.

This was the point where she ought to apologize. She was fully aware of it. She knew she had been inexcusably unreasonable, cruel even. The apology was inside her, fully formed, but it couldn't fight its way through that backed-up bitterness in her throat. Instead she countered affront with affront, fixing on the one point where she felt sure of the moral high ground.

'Any excuse to throw in a dig about me not working, hey? Our daughter's killer strikes again, but let's not lose sight of what's *really* important here, that your wife sits around painting her nails all day.'

Guy glared at her without speaking, and she noticed suddenly how sorrow had dulled his once green eyes to the colour of sludge. When, finally, he turned away in disgust, she claimed it as a victory. Of sorts.

Guy went upstairs to his study. Emma heard his heavy, accusing footsteps on every step. Dead man walking. She had no idea what he did in his study. Certainly she never heard any signs of activity from there whenever she crept past, padding softly from room to room in search of what was no longer there.

One time, she'd entered his study while he was at work and had sat in his black leather swivel chair, trying to imagine what it was like to be him, to inhabit this room in his own right. She imagined his hand on the computer keyboard, the hand whose strong, blunt fingers she'd once adored, whose plain gold ring she once awkwardly slipped on in front of eighty-five of their closest family and friends. She'd slid open the drawers of his oak desk, imagining how it would feel to be this man, trying to experience his grief from the inside – as if sorrow were a woolly jumper that could be tried on for size.

The top two drawers held papers and stationery, the usual detritus of a purposeful life. The bottom drawer was deeper, its contents less orderly. On top of the heap of assorted letters, bills, invoices and receipts was a loose pile of photos, edges slightly worn away through over-handling. She'd spread them out in front of her on the desk.

Tilly had looked up at her, taunting, teasing, from all the shiny surfaces. There she was wearing a yellow and white ski suit, her red-brown hair, so much straighter than either of her sisters', hanging down in fat, gleaming plaits beneath her white woolly hat. Now, she was in a witch's costume, standing sandwiched between her identically dressed sisters, in a simulation of the natural family order. Her left hand, with its black-painted finger-nails, was outstretched, and her black-lipped mouth contorted in what she clearly intended as an evil rictus.

In a third she was sitting at the blond-wood kitchen table, with her painting overall on, and a pristine sheet of white paper in front of her. She had a plump brush in her hand, its tip slicked thick with crimson paint, but it was her expression that held Emma's attention. Her lips were opened in an 'O' shape as though caught mid-sentence, her eyes burned with purpose, intent on whatever she was saying. Emma gazed at the photo mesmerized, as if by keeping sufficiently still, she might be able to hear whatever it was her daughter was trying to say.

In the months after Tilly died, Emma had struggled to keep her daughter's voice alive in her head, holding conversations with her in which she'd answer in that clear, deliberate way she had, her 'o's particularly over-emphasized as if there was a 'w' at the end of them. Then one day Emma had forced herself to watch, for the first time, one of the hundreds of home videos she and Guy had taken of the girls over the years. The short footage showed the aftermath of Caitlin's fifth-birthday party, and the wide oak floorboards of the living room were strewn with the remains of pink streamers, party poppers and spent balloons. Caitlin, completely overwrought, was hunched in a corner of the pewter-coloured L-shaped sofa, her still-babyish face blotchy with tears, a plastic tiara perched lopsidedly on her clammy curls, her plump hands clutching the new doll that either she didn't like, or which didn't make the sound she wanted it to, or which was too much like the one she already had (how easily one forgets the details of childhood). Tilly, sitting next to her in protective older-sister mode (although at only seven, she was barely past such tantrums of over-tiredness herself), was doing her best to cheer Caitlin up.

'You mustn't mind that your party is finished,' she was saying. 'Think of all the nice presents you got and remember it's only three hundred and sixty-*five*' – here she broke off momentarily and looked directly towards the camera for corroboration – 'days until your next birthday.'

Watching that video Emma had been shocked to discover that the clear voice which came from Tilly's childishly lipsticked mouth didn't bear any resemblance to the one she'd been hearing inside her head all this time. She remembered feeling almost sick with horror listening to her, as if all those months she'd been betraying her dead child. To whom had that high-pitched disembodied voice belonged then? Whose child had spoken to her through those sleepless early mornings when the grey light trickled in through the chinks in the curtains?

She remembered that then, sitting at Guy's big solid desk, gazing at the photo of Tilly, struggling to conjure up her voice, to hear what it was she was trying to say. All Emma's powers of concentration were focused on Tilly's eyes and her mouth, willing them to set free whatever secret they were holding, desperate to hear her speak once more inside her head, unlocking what had been so tightly shut.

There was nothing. Of course.

Now, listening to the sound of Guy moving around upstairs, she found herself filled with a fierce longing to see that photo again. With the image of Poppy Glover that had featured on every news bulletin still seared across her mind, she was seized once more by the ludicrous notion that Tilly had something she needed to tell her, something important. Again she was hit by a wave of irrational anger that Guy should be there at all, inhabiting the space that during the day was rightfully hers. The house was her kingdom, her territory. It felt as if he were keeping Tilly from her. Emma paced up and down in front of the folding glass doors that opened out on to the back garden, remembering how the police had swarmed all over there in the days when Guy was a suspect, pulling up the decking around the apple tree. Jemima had gone to pieces then, all the feelings she had been bottling up about her missing sister erupting into a wail of outrage – about their long-dead cat, of all things. 'But that's where we buried Muffin!' she screamed, and Emma would never forget the contortion of her face. 'Don't let them dig up Muffin, Mummy!' That was Guy's doing. A neighbour reported having seen him in the garden around the time Tilly died, lurking in the darkness. Only later did he admit he'd been sneaking out for a cigarette, knowing how disappointed Emma would be if she found out he'd started smoking again. So as a result of his weakness they'd had to watch their garden being ripped up piece by piece. Anger mushroomed inside her, and she chewed furiously on the already jagged skin at the base of the nail on the index finger of her left hand. The blood, when it came, was a release. She squeezed the top of her finger savagely, enjoying the sight of the growing bulb of red, still faintly throbbing with her own angry pulse.

Suddenly Guy appeared in the doorway. Emma was surprised to see he had his jacket on, a black leather biker-style one he wore with the self-consciousness of a girl in her first pre-teen bra.

'You'll be pleased to know I'm going out,' he said coldly, and Emma didn't dare look at him for fear he'd see the jolt of joy that shot through her, followed almost immediately by an irrational sense of abandonment.

Slowly, she made her way upstairs, pretending to herself that she might be going to take a midday nap, or collect the washing, retrieving socks from under beds and behind beanbags.

She entered Guy's study as if on a whim, and sat for a while in the black chair, swivelling it slowly from side to side. Only now did she allow herself to open up the drawer and once again pick out that photo of Tilly at the kitchen table.

Immediately, she was disappointed. She had no idea what she'd been hoping to find, but whatever it was, she didn't recognize it. There was Tilly again, there was her little mouth in its plump 'O', but whatever she was saying was still lost. There was nothing new. What had she been expecting? Emma felt angry at herself for indulging in a cruel and ridiculous fantasy.

And yet . . . as she gazed at the photo she was struck by Tilly's hair, pulled back into low bunches behind her ears by two thick elasticated bands – red, with a pattern of yellow and orange flowers. And now, suddenly, Tilly's voice did come to her. Not speaking through the photo but in an echo of a conversation from around the time it was taken, when she'd been standing in front of the hall mirror, with its ornate white frame, endlessly adjusting her plaits while Emma waited in the doorway impatiently jiggling her car keys.

'For heaven's sake, Tilly, your hair looks fine.'

But Tilly hadn't been satisfied. 'They have to match, Mummy.' She'd frowned, tugging at the hair bands until they were exactly the same level on both sides, her little fingers inching the left one down fractionally to mirror the right. She'd always been so particular about matching pairs of things, Emma remembered. 'Clearly on the spectrum,' Guy used to joke. In the days when Guy knew how to joke. And Emma knew how to laugh.

'If things don't match I feel funny all day, like there's a worm wriggling around in my tummy.'

Now, something was nagging at Emma. Something she couldn't

quite pinpoint, a word dancing tantalizingly on the tip of her tongue.

'What?' she asked out loud, glaring at the photograph as if it were deliberately withholding information. '*What?*'

'Who are you talking to?'

Something lurched inside her. Guy had come in without her noticing. What did he mean by sneaking up like that? Men oughtn't to sneak. Men ought to make proper noises, solid sounds by which their progress through the house could be tracked. Men ought to announce themselves, not waft through rooms like ghosts, vaporizing through outside walls so there was no click of a key turning in the lock, no thud of a door closing.

'You scared me.'

She made her voice accusing to quash the guilty feeling that it was she who was in the wrong, sitting here at Guy's desk, the drawer open beside her, his secrets bared to the elements.

'Why are you in here, going through my things?'

'They're not your things. This is a photo of Tilly. You shouldn't have it shut away in here where I can't see it.' Emma's voice grew higher, shriller. On a level completely outside of herself, she listened to it in fascination. That voice wasn't hers. That horrible, grating noise. Even so, she continued: 'I've been looking for this photograph, and all the time it was right here where you'd hidden it.'

Framed in the doorway with the glow from the skylight behind him, Guy seemed enormous, an imposing dark shadow of a man. For a second she felt a prickling of fear. Then it was as if the air went out of him and he slumped to the right, leaning his forehead on the wooden door frame.

'For God's sake, Emma.' His voice was sad and tired. 'Do we have to argue about *everything*? I'm not the enemy here.'

He looked so utterly defeated standing there, she almost got up to go to him, obeying some impulse born from years of habit, but then she glanced back down at the photograph, and immediately understood that the thing she'd been on the verge of remembering, the message Tilly was trying to tell her, had been lost, the spell broken. Tears of frustration pricked her eyes, and she wiped an angry hand across them.

'I'll leave "your things" alone then,' she said. 'But I'm keeping this.'

Waving the photograph in front of his face, Emma pushed past her husband as if he wasn't even there.

5

The photos were all over the television news, but Jason didn't look at them. If he didn't look, he might save himself from those terrible flashbacks that sent his pulse racing, sweat breaking out all over his body. *Give yourself permission to block out what upsets you.* He repeated it to himself like a mantra, until he could almost hear Dr Ancona's voice in his head. It calmed him and he realized from the twinge in his jaw how tightly he'd been grinding his teeth together. Mrs Charlton, the bad-breath dentist, had told him at his last appointment that he'd been grinding them so much in the night he'd cracked one of his back teeth. 'You'll be needing root canal soon,' she'd warned him, leaning right over so that her breasts were practically smothering his face. She must be well into her forties too. Gross. He'd bought one of those plastic mouth-guards that mould to the shape of your teeth and he wore it at night even though the hygiene aspect of it bothered him. It had its own light-blue plastic case that he washed out every day with a mixture of bleach and water, but still he worried about the germs. Mouths were disgusting when you thought about it. The things that went into them.

After he finished dinner – a bowl of cereal, he never ate much in the evenings – he still had half an hour before he had to leave for the club. Some of the other bouncers didn't like working nights but Jason preferred it. It left the days free for other things.

Pulling his laptop out from the bottom drawer in the kitchen, Jason carried it to the table in the living room. The kitchen in this flat was tiny, a galley kitchen it was called, so the dining table was in the living room, but he preferred it that way. He could sit at the table and see everything he needed to see – the television, the street outside. He had never understood the fuss people made about eat-in kitchens. Why would you want to eat in the place where the bin is? Or where you chop raw meat?

The table was a squarish white one from Ikea pushed against the middle of the wall exactly halfway between the twin living-room windows so that if you folded the room in half it would all match up. It felt important to him, that line of symmetry. The flat, which he got at a cheaper rent on account of it being above a laundrette, was purpose-built and all the rooms were like boxes, no feature fireplaces or alcoves. People always went on about original features like it was so great to have cornices on the ceilings and picture rails but for Jason it was all about clean lines and neat corners. No nooks and crannies where dirt and germs could hide.

Lining up the edge of the laptop with the edge of the table, Jason noticed a smudge on the glossy black surface of the machine's casing. Cursing, he made his way back to the kitchen to get the computer cloth from the drawer.

Logging on to matchmadeinheaven.com, he saw he had only three unread messages in his inbox and a hard ball of disappointment formed in the back of his throat. Normally he got at least five or six overnight. He glanced at his profile photo again. Nothing wrong there. It was a studio photograph taken a couple of years ago (not ten years ago, not like some of those you got on dating sites. 'In my late thirties,' they said, and you knew they actually meant fifty-something. So many liars out there. People had forgotten how to tell the truth). His blond hair was a bit shorter in the picture than now, but his physique was still the same. You could tell here was someone who took staying in shape very seriously indeed. In the photo Jason was wearing a crisp white T-shirt, not queer tight, but tight enough that it stretched across his biceps, and he had a very small neat blond goatee beard. He was looking directly at the camera (he never trusted profile photos where people were looking away or, even worse, wearing sunglasses. You could tell a lot from a person's eyes). His avatar was ToughButSensitive. Not very original, but it did the job. Jason was aware that many people tried to make their names funny but it was a mistake as far as he was concerned. Women said they wanted funny, but they didn't really. It's like when they said they wanted equality, but that was a lie too, because really they wanted you to take them out and buy them things and tell them they looked fantastic, but they didn't want to do the same things for you. Oh no. So how was that equal then?

Double-clicking on his inbox, Jason noted that one of the three messages was from Suzy, aka ButterfliesInMyTummy, and his mood lifted. It was the fourth or fifth message they'd exchanged, and they were just starting to move beyond the tedious small-talk stage. He skimmed through the message, growing increasingly impatient. Suzy favoured those little face icons. The whole page was littered with them – smiley faces, sad faces, surprised faces, embarrassed faces. Why couldn't she just use words like everyone else? She also put five or six exclamation marks after a sentence, or added extra vowels to words, so everything was soooooooooo much fun or soooooooooooo boring. It wound Jason up when people couldn't write properly. He wasn't asking for brain of Britain, but he liked a woman to be able to write a sentence that started with a capital letter and ended with a full stop and at least made an attempt at the Queen's English. At least it wasn't in text speak. He refused to answer the messages that spelled thanks 'tnx'. Britain didn't go through two World Wars so that the English language could be mutilated beyond recognition.

Suzy wrote about her job as a credit controller (bored-expression face) and how she had thought she'd never want another relationship following the painful break-up of her marriage (crying face) but now she felt she might finally be ready to 'dip a toe back in the water' (smiley face). She went on to talk about what she did at the weekend (not a lot). She kept stressing how she went to the gym, obviously because she'd read his profile and knew he liked to keep fit. Jason saw loads of women like Suzy at the gym. They came in wearing their matching pink designer shorts and tops and their trainers that they'd bought because they liked the style not because they actually did the job they were supposed to. They walked on the treadmill for forty-five minutes while watching *Loose Women* on the TV and barely breaking a sweat. Then they went on the machines to do their abdominals and their biceps. And that was them done. Might as well save their money and their time and stay home and get fat. They would anyway.

Finally, near the bottom of the message, the name Bethany came up. Jason stopped skimming and began to read more intently. Suzy had already told him how she'd struggled at first with being a single mum and having to make decisions without anyone else to bounce them off, and to lay down the law, even though being strict didn't come naturally to her. Bethany's birthday was coming up, Suzy now informed him (smiley face plus scared face). She'd been driving her mum mad coming up with different plans, each one more extravagant than the last. Finally Suzy had had to put her foot down, and it was decided that Bethany would just have a few friends over to the house to watch DVDs and for a sleepover.

Jason closed his eyes for a moment. Suzy's words had conjured up an image that he was reluctant to let go of. They'd already exchanged photographs so he knew exactly what Suzy's daughter Bethany looked like. Suzy had sent him one with her very first message showing the two of them squashed into an armchair together. Jason reckoned it was supposed to show what a fun, 'bubbly' mum Suzy was, but it was Bethany who had captured Jason's attention. Thick, wavy blonde hair, hanging down over her shoulders, big clear-blue eyes gazing out over smooth, rounded cheeks. Jason thought she was younger, but Suzy said she was ten, almost eleven. Though she'd described her as 'very young for her age'.

Jason imagined the preparations Bethany would be making for her sleepover, the spare duvets – a heart pattern, he decided, or flowers maybe – the odd pink sleeping bag, a couple of blow-up mattresses, all heaped in a corner of her room, awaiting the big day. He envisaged her labouring over the invitations, the tip of her pink tongue protruding from between her lips. He imagined her friends talking about it at school, shiny heads bent together as they discussed which DVDs to watch.

'It's still two and a half weeks away, but she's already counting down!!!!!!!' Suzy had written. So. He didn't have long to get his feet under the table and insinuate himself into the lives of mother and daughter. It was doable though, he thought. But he'd have to move quickly. Women like Suzy were ripe for the big dream, the whirlwind romance. They wanted love at first sight – and half the time they'd already decided you were it before even meeting you. Because love at first sight leads to happy ever after. It was amazing how many intelligent women actually thought like that.

Suzy was in the market for being swept off her feet. You could always tell. Jason glanced at her profile photo again with indifference. She wasn't bad-looking – teeth a bit too large for her mouth maybe, chin a little weak, but he wouldn't mind too much, doing what he had to do. He'd done a lot worse, that was a fact.

Jason clicked open the photo of mother and daughter sitting on the armchair. Suzy was slightly to the back of the photo, while Bethany was sitting on her lap, but over to one side, leaning in towards the camera. He cringed when his gaze passed over Suzy's feet, which were crammed into a pair of those awful sheepskin boots. What would possess a woman of that age to go around in things that looked like elephant's feet? He put his hand over the boots, and then moved it so that it covered Suzy up altogether.

On impulse he went back to the kitchen and brought out the printer he kept in the cupboard in its original box. Once he held the printout in his hand, he gazed at it critically. The skin tones were a bit orange on account of the inks being low, but no way was he shelling out for another cartridge. It would have to do. Suzy smiled out at him with her florid face until he had a stroke of genius and folded the paper down the middle of the picture. He ran his thumb and fingernail down the crease until it was razor sharp. When he'd finished Suzy was safely on the reverse and only Bethany was visible. That was better. Now he was getting somewhere.

Everything was taking shape.

6

The women reporters were definitely worse, Leanne decided. At least the blokes didn't bother to try to put on an act, but the women? They had these fake sad eyes and these fake shocked expressions and then they put up a hand and asked a question so brutal it took your breath away.

'Was she raped?'

'Was she naked?'

Leanne wasn't one of those police officers who nursed a blanket hatred of all reporters, it would be hypocritical, wouldn't it, seeing as she was going out with one. They had a job to do, just like she did, and like her they were the lucky ones, hanging on to their careers when there were so many out of work. Doing liaison work meant she occasionally formed quite close relationships with journalists, and one or two had even become friends. She remembered working on the case of a missing teenager. She'd been in Wetherspoon's with a woman writer from one of the nationals when the news came through that a body had been found, and the two of them had both ended up in tears. But sometimes at these press conferences she found herself thinking, as she knew some of her colleagues did, *Scavengers.*

'What was the mother's reaction, DCI Desmond?'

The mother, mind, not even *her* mother. What did she think *the* mother's reaction was going to be on hearing that her seven-year-old daughter had been found strangled? Did she think she maybe shrugged and said 'never mind' and invited the officers in for tea? The truth was that reporter knew exactly what the reaction would have been but she wanted to see the spilled guts for herself, like a rubbernecker at a motorway pile-up. She wanted *the* mother delivered up with her heart ripped out and smeared all over the plate like so much ketchup.

'We'd ask that the Glovers' privacy is respected at this most difficult time.'

Desmond was in his element of course. Sitting there with three huge microphones on the table in front of him and sporting his Solemn and Dignified Look. Desmond had a limited repertoire of looks, which he selected like jackets from a rail, and over the years Leanne had seen them all. He had this way of picking out individual reporters who were waving their hands around in the air and fixing them with his eyes and waiting for a fraction of a second before nodding at them to ask their question. It was a one-man show.

'Is it definitely linked to the others, Detective Chief Inspector Desmond?'

Again, Desmond did his deliberate hesitation thing, so it looked as though he was weighing something up in his head before he answered. As if he hadn't been waiting for this question since the moment he got the news.

'It's too early to say at this stage whether this tragic murder is in any way connected to the deaths of Megan Purvis, Tilly Reid and Leila Botsford. However, naturally, that's one of the theories we will be investigating.'

When he said the word 'tragic', Desmond closed his eyes momentarily.

The woman in the orange flowery top who'd asked the question about Susan Glover's reaction had her hand up again.

'The public is going to be asking where the police were in all of this. The killer has struck four times now and each victim has been found on or around Hampstead Heath within a few days of disappearing. Why were the borders of the Heath not adequately patrolled? Why hasn't he been caught?'

Desmond fixed the woman with a long, steady look.

'I'm glad you brought that up. Those of you who are not from London might not be aware of just how large an area we're dealing with. Hampstead Heath is getting on for two square miles and much of its border is unfenced. It is not a park where there are only so many gates which are closed overnight. As you'll remember, Tilly Reid was found in woodland in the West Heath, which is a separate area. And this most recent victim, Poppy Glover, was found on the Heath Extension, which is in a completely different location altogether. Even the two victims who were found on the Heath itself were a long way apart. Be assured there was a very strong police presence in the general Heath area last night, not just our people, but also officers from the dedicated Hampstead Heath Constabulary. Cars were routinely stopped and drivers questioned but there was simply no way of closing off all the roads within a two-mile radius. As you know a couple of the victims – Tilly and Leila – were found some days after they disappeared. Unfortunately there was no way of second-guessing the killer's intentions.'

Ms Orange Top wasn't satisfied. 'But surely you must have captured something on CCTV? Aren't we always being told we live in the most Big Brother country in the world?'

Desmond made that face people make when they're trying to swallow a big sigh.

'We will of course be studying any CCTV footage. However, it must be stressed the areas where the bodies have been found are very quiet. Some of the most expensive real estate in the country is around there, so of course there are security systems, many of them privately operated, but the cameras tend to be positioned to keep watch on the properties themselves, rather than the roads, particularly the quieter parts of the roads where there are no houses. Nevertheless, I can tell you we are following some active lines of enquiry resulting from existing CCTV footage.'

It wasn't completely a lie.

Two of the investigations into the murders – Megan's and Leila's – had yielded CCTV footage of a vehicle most likely to have been used by the killer, but in the first case, the number plate of the car, a black VW Golf, had been obscured, and in the other the picture had been too grainy to make out any details at all, only that it was a dark-coloured estate. Calling up data on every black Golf in the area had practically brought down the entire computing system.

Leanne looked around the crowd of assorted police and reporters. There was a young lad a few rows from the front with a phone in one hand and an apple in the other. He looked in his early twenties, face still pockmarked with faded acne, and he had a half-bored expression. The young man raised the apple to his mouth and took a huge bite, leaving a string of saliva stretching from his lower lip to the flesh of the apple, and she looked away.

'Has there been any contact between Mr and Mrs Glover and the other parents?'

Instantly, Leanne recognized the clipped, slightly too-loud voice and her heart sank. Trust Sally Freeland to be straight on the scene. The woman sought out tragedy like a pig truffling. Hearing Sally's voice transported her straight back two years to the time of Tilly's murder when her marriage to Pete was in its final death throes and she was shuttling between a home full of loaded silences and the Reids' house where the initial fear surrounding Tilly's disappearance was fast superseded by horror and then a tidal wave of sorrow. Leanne remembered it as the worst period in her life. Worse even than when she'd had all those tests only to be told by a doctor, who hadn't looked much older than the apple-eating reporter over there, that she was unlikely ever to have children, and who urged her not to keep on looking for causes, because sometimes there just weren't any, but simply to accept it as one of those things, and besides, had they ever thought of adopting? She remembered Pete's face – as if he'd just been punched in the gut – as the future she'd imagined for them unravelled in an overheated consulting room with a view of the hospital bins.

'Of course there is a wide range of support available to Mr and Mrs Glover, if and when they should need it.'

Had Desmond been taking actual classes in smoothness? Leanne leaned forward so she could get a good look at Sally Freeland. She was sitting in the second row, scribbling furiously in a notebook.

Sally looked up suddenly, before Leanne had a chance to react, and the two women locked eyes. A puzzled look passed across the journalist's face, as if she was trying to place her, but she quickly lost interest and her gaze slid away. Leanne wasn't altogether surprised. At thirty-six she was big enough and old enough to accept that she had one of those not-terribly-memorable faces.

It was weird to see Sally Freeland again, though not unexpected. She'd poked her nose in all over the place at the time of the last murder. Awful to think it wasn't even a year ago. She made herself very unpopular, from what Leanne could tell. Emma Reid had refused to have anything to do with her, luckily. The Botsford mother had been persuaded into giving an interview and had apparently gone ballistic when it appeared.

Something occurred to Leanne. Wasn't there some kind of funny business involving Sally Freeland and Megan Purvis's stepfather? Rumours of some kind of affair. She pictured Simon

Hewitt – there was something a little *womanly* about him with his soft, blurry features and wide hips. As the stepdad, Simon was top of the initial list of suspects for Megan's murder. But he'd had a cast-iron alibi – a dinner with the CEO and marketing director of a big insurance firm – so he'd been in the clear. You had to wonder, didn't you, though, what kind of man would get involved with someone like Sally Freeland.

Leanne turned her attention back to Desmond, who was gracing the room with his best Steely Look. He must have been really working on that over the last few months. It was pretty impressive. She'd have to memorize it so she could re-enact it for Pete later on. Oh. No. Scratch that. She wasn't with Pete any more. Sometimes even now, nearly two years later, that fact could still come as a shock. Not that Will wasn't enough for her. It was just that he wasn't force, so there was a massive part of her life she'd never be able to share with him.

She supposed she'd be seeing Pete again soon enough. He'd become the Botsfords' FLO when their daughter was killed last year. He'd been an obvious choice, having been involved in the murder investigation since day one, like her. Still, she'd been upset when Desmond first told her. Everything had been so painful back then. When Pete had had himself transferred to a station a couple of miles away following their split she'd been glad of the distance. But his position as FLO for the Botsfords meant he was regularly in and out of the main office. Unlike her own experience with the Reids, he'd bonded with the grief-stricken couple to the extent that he'd even joined them for a meal out in honour of Mark's fortieth birthday. It hadn't been much of a celebration, from all accounts. And now there'd been another death, Helen Purvis would no doubt hold a get-together of the support group the press had cloyingly nicknamed Megan's Angels, at which she and Pete would meet. The thought of being in the same room as Pete did funny things to Leanne's stomach.

Leanne didn't relish meeting the Botsfords again. She didn't think she'd ever seen anyone look quite as raw as Fiona Botsford had in the weeks following their daughter's death. Leila had been the Botsfords' only child. That was a particular kind of grief, Leanne always thought. All of the families had lost children, but the others were still technically parents. How must it feel to be a childless mother? She couldn't imagine it. It was hard enough to imagine being a mother, full stop. At the last Megan's Angels meeting Fiona Botsford had seemed like someone flayed.

People always expected the families to be a harmonious little group, bound together by tragedy, supporting each other through the nightmare they'd stumbled into. But they were just like everyone else. Some were prickly (Fiona Botsford), some over-bearing (Simon Hewitt). They didn't stop having personalities just because of what had happened to them – they could still get right up each other's noses, despite the horrible thing that had brought them together. They could still bicker and snap and wind each other up and say the wrong thing. Being tragic didn't suddenly make you world experts in diplomacy, Leanne had discovered. You didn't become a nicer, kinder, better person simply because your daughter had been murdered.

Still, she felt for them. Emma Reid had once told her that when Tilly died it was as if someone had turned out all the lights. Life still carried on, but you were just stumbling about in the dark. Like veal, she'd said. Leanne had thought it such a strange thing to say.

The press conference was held in New Scotland Yard – very convenient, Leanne didn't think, seeing as she'd have to travel all the way back up to North London afterwards. As soon as it was finished she went to find Desmond. He'd told her to check in with him (Desmond loved phrases like 'check in' and 'touch base') before she visited the Reids. She located him in a corridor outside talking urgently to the Met's head of press.

'Sir?' Leanne hated the way her own voice automatically turned obsequious in the vicinity of her über-boss.

'Ah, Leanne.' Desmond gave an apologetic shrug to the head of press, who smiled in a knowing way Leanne didn't altogether like before inclining his head slightly and bustling off, tucking folders under the arm of his grey suit jacket as he went. 'I just wanted to get you completely up to speed before you drop in on the Reid family.'

Desmond had a weird flap of loose skin on one of his eyelids that drooped over his eyeball, making his left eye look considerably smaller than his right. Whenever she talked to him, Leanne found herself transfixed by that flap of skin, wondering how it felt to look out on the world past a blur of pink flesh.

'We'll just wait a couple of minutes for the others to join us.'

'Others, sir?'

'The other FLOs assigned to this case.'

Oh. So that meant . . .

Hearing Pete's voice was like rediscovering a long-forgotten favourite jumper at the back of the wardrobe. Leanne took a deep breath before turning to face him.

'All right, Pete?' she said, allowing her gaze to slide off his cheekbone, so as to avoid meeting his eyes.

'Not bad.'

Leanne's determinedly downcast eyes watched Pete's feet, in their black slightly pointy lace-up shoes (he always did have such terrible taste in shoes), shuffling nervously. How bizarre it was that they'd shared all those things – breakfasts in bed, vomiting bugs, weddings, funerals, quarrels, makings-up, bad sex, good sex, rushed sex in public places that had ended with both of them laughing too much to go on – and yet here they were meeting as virtual strangers.

'Right, why don't you two come with me. Jo Barber – she's the Purvises' FLO, as you know – is already waiting for us.'

Oh, this isn't awkward at all, Leanne thought as she and her ex-husband followed Desmond along the corridor in agonizing silence.

Jo was waiting for them in a small, windowless room with a desk in one corner and five plastic chairs arranged in a cramped circle in the centre. Whatever perfume Jo was wearing rose to meet them like an extra person as they entered the room. She was a small, plump woman with a curiously blank, round face, like someone had over-polished it and smoothed out all the features. Leanne remembered that she worked in dog training when she wasn't acting as FLO. 'You know exactly where you are with a dog,' she said once, and Leanne and Pete had laughed about it afterwards. She felt that churning sensation in her stomach again. Leanne hoped this wasn't going to continue all through the investigation, this unsettling feeling of things shifting around inside her.

'Hi Jo, how—'

Desmond cut right in, his hand raised. 'No pleasantries, Leanne. The demands on my time are, as you can guess, consider-able. I just wanted to keep you all in the loop with what's going on in the investigation, before you go to see the families.'

In the loop. Where did Desmond get this stuff from?

'Just to recap, there's been another murder. Same MO. Definitely our perp.' *Perp?* 'Victim is Poppy Glover, aged seven. She was on the Heath with her parents, by one of the ponds. Begged her parents to let her go to the ice-cream van on her own. Ice-cream van was on the road but just visible from where they were sitting. Beautiful day, lots of people around. Poppy was standing in the queue, then there was a commotion. Someone's bag was stolen. Everyone shouting and people darting about all over the place. When Oliver Glover went to find Poppy a minute or two later, she'd disappeared.'

'So you think he had an accomplice this time?' Pete asked.

Leanne had heard all this in the press conference and had the same reaction as Pete – that someone had created a deliberate diversion, but Desmond didn't seem convinced.

'It's a possibility. Or it's a coincidence, and our perp saw an opportunity and took advantage. Anyway, what's important is it's the same MO. No sign of a violent struggle. It's too soon to be definitive but early indications are she was drugged and then suffocated while asleep. Same as the others.'

'Apart from Megan.'

It was the first time Jo had spoken and Leanne had forgotten about her strange, high-pitched, girlish voice.

Desmond looked irritated and glanced pointedly at his watch to show he considered this time-wasting.

'As we all know by now, our profilers believe Megan Purvis was almost certainly his first victim. The theory is he was more reckless back then and less controlled and probably panicked in disposing of the body. That having been said, there are too many similarities between all the cases for it not to be the same perp.'

'But Megan Purvis was also semi-naked,' Jo continued, un-perturbed by Desmond's brusqueness. 'And traces of semen were found on her clothes. So far that hasn't been the case with any of the others.'

Desmond stared at her, as if weighing something up in his mind.

'Actually – though this info is strictly classified – this body also was partially unclothed and there was a semen sample recovered from the scene of this latest murder. Not on the body itself, but on plant matter nearby.'

Leanne was almost too intrigued by this fresh information to mind him saying 'plant matter' instead of 'grass'.

'So that links in to Megan's case. And then, of course,' contin-ued the detective chief inspector, 'there's the killer's usual USP.'

Only Desmond ever used marketing jargon to describe a detail of a murder investigation. Unique Selling Point. That's what he called it. The killer's calling card. That tiny 'SORRY' written in blue biro on the right leg, just under the sock, which handwriting experts had concluded was done left-handed by someone who usually wrote with the other hand.

'And you're still working on the theory that he films the girls in some way?'

Leanne asked the question more out of an awareness that she hadn't contributed yet to the discussion than any real curiosity. She knew that Desmond would have said something by now if there were any new theories being bandied around. He loved to be the first with the news.

'Going by what our profilers have told us, that still remains our number-one avenue of enquiry, yes. No footage has shown up as yet but we do have several sources on the case.'

'Sir?' Pete again. 'Have you had a call from Helen Purvis yet? I bet Megan's Angels will be waiting to welcome the Glovers with open arms.'

'That's a bit uncalled for,' Jo remonstrated in her squeaky little voice. 'That group has provided strong support for the families. I don't know how any of them would have coped without it.'

'I agree with Jo,' Leanne said. 'No one else can understand what those poor sods are going through. Just them.'

'Yeah, well, not sure whether Fiona and Mark Botsford are getting much out of it,' Pete said.

'They still go though, don't they? Presumably no one is making them.'

Ten minutes in each other's company and they were already winding each other up.

'Much as I'd love to listen to you two squabbling, I really do have important things to do.' Desmond was making his Sucking on a Lemon Face, and leafing through some papers on the desk, and Leanne knew they were being dismissed.

Outside the building, the three of them blinked myopically in the white sun. Until a week ago it had felt like the disappointing spring would never end, but maybe now summer had finally arrived.

'Wish we could all stop meeting like this,' said Leanne, trying to lighten the atmosphere.

Jo smiled sadly. 'I know what you mean. Nothing personal, but I'd love it if we three never had to meet again.'

After Jo had gone to find her car, Leanne and Pete stood together in awkward silence. Leanne had forgotten Pete's habit of kicking the toe of one foot repeatedly against the ground when agitated. Bugger if that wasn't annoying.

'Well,' she said. 'I suppose I should get going. Dreading the rest of the day, to be honest with you.'

Pete nodded. He knew how tricky that initial time with the Reids had been in Leanne's life. He bloody well ought to. He'd been the one making a difficult situation unbearable.

'Never mind. I'm sure your boyfriend will be on hand to run you a hot bath when you get home,' Pete said.

It was nearly a year since she and Will had got together and the bitterness Pete felt was still there, bubbling away under the surface.

'Yeah, well. I'm off then.'

She'd gone about five paces before he shouted after her.

'Sorry!' he said. Or at least that's what she thought he said. But by the time she turned, he was heading in the opposite direction, shoulders back, same cocky walk as ever.

Standing up on the tube, clutching on to the railing during the long trip up to Highbury and Islington, where she'd get on the overground to Hampstead Heath, the nearest station to the Reids, Leanne replayed their conversation, and that word Pete had yelled out. The more she thought about it, the less convinced she was she'd heard right. When had Peter Delagio ever said sorry to anyone? Sorry wasn't in his DNA. She tried to think of other words that sounded like sorry. Lorry? Now that would be too random, even for Pete. Eventually she gave up. The thing was, Will probably *would* run her a bath when she got home. He knew how hard today was going to be for her. It didn't make him any less of a man, just because he wanted to make her life easier. Pete was an idiot. A Neanderthal. That's why their marriage hadn't worked. That and the small fact he'd cheated on her with a woman nearly ten years younger.

Still, she wished she knew what it was he'd said.

7

Having a murdered sister was like wearing a badge you couldn't take off. A loud, attention-grabbing badge. With flashing lights. And bells.

People didn't look at him and say, 'There's Rory Purvis, he's doing ten GCSEs,' or 'He's fit,' or 'He's five foot eleven and a Scorpio and has seven metal pins in his leg from breaking it snowboarding.' No, they said, 'There's Rory Purvis, his sister was murdered.'

Sometimes it made him fucking sick.

And now they'd found another body, things were going to get worse. All the same stupid people coming round insisting he must want to talk about it. Counsellors sitting expectantly on the edges of their chairs with their boxes of tissues. *You must be feeling this, Rory. You must be feeling that. Blah blah blah.* What he must be feeling is fed up with having to sit with people who just wanted to put a tick in the box saying, 'Victim's family has been offered support.' TICK.

Even worse, they would use that horrible photo again. Just thinking about it made Rory cringe – the school photo of him and Megan taken the year before she died when he was in the last year of primary. He looked like a geek. His hair was doing this thing where it sprang up, bouffant, like some kind of mushroom-head. And he was smiling a horrible fake smile so you could see where his adult teeth had come through insanely big. At least he didn't have braces back then. Metal-mouth as well as mushroom-head – now that would have been a seriously bad look.

He hated that photo.

Walking home from school with his mates, they passed the newsagent's with a board outside with a headline about the new murder.

'Kenwood Killer? Isn't that your sister's one?'

Jack W. was a twat sometimes. *Your sister's one* – like he was talking about her fucking phone provider. Dickhead.

Jake H. shot him a sideways look like you do when you want to see the expression on someone's face but don't want to freak them out by staring straight at them.

'Sorry, mate.' Jake H. mumbled at the best of times, but now his voice was all but inaudible. 'You OK?'

'Yeah, sound.'

'Hey, does that mean you get to see your *girlfriend* again?'

Jack W. again, of course.

Rory gave him a thumbs-up, but inside he was raging because Jack W. was right. Another murder meant Mum would insist on organizing another of her get-togethers, which meant another afternoon being stared at by Jemima Reid. Enough was enough.

Trudging up the road towards home, his steps became slower than normal. Last summer he'd been stopped and searched by police who accused him of 'walking slowly next to cars'. They'd thought he was casing them out or something. Those were exactly the words they'd used – 'walking slowly next to cars'. Like that was a crime. He smiled remembering how his mum had rung while they were searching him, and had insisted on being put through to the policemen and giving them a hard time. 'But that's how he always walks,' she'd snapped at them.

Now he was walking so slowly he wasn't sure it even counted as walking. The thing was, he really didn't want to reach the corner because he knew he'd see them, the usual little knot of photographers standing outside the gate leading to his house, smoking their fags and talking their usual bollocks.

As they saw him approaching, the photographers and reporters went quiet. Rory always thought it was rather funny how they didn't know quite how to treat him. He knew they were desperate to ask him all sorts of questions, but it was a bit dodgy as he'd only just turned sixteen, so they kind of hopped from foot to foot murmuring, 'All right, Rory?' as he pushed past.

All right, Rory? That was a joke in itself. It really fucking was.

He got out his key, praying it wouldn't be one of those days when it inexplicably decided not to work. His mum said it was because he'd lost his key so many times they were always having to make copies from copies. She'd tried to make him wear his key around his neck once. Like that was going to happen. As the door opened there was a chorus of frenzied snapping from the photographers behind trying to get a shot into the hallway. Of what, he wondered? The grief-stricken coat-stand? The sorrow-struck shoe-rack? Stepping inside, he heard Mum's worried voice calling from the kitchen.

'Rory? Is that you?'

Rory had read books where people said 'my heart sank' and he recognized the symptoms all too well. One minute his heart was sitting happily in its proper place behind his ribcage, and the next it was squelching around somewhere in his stomach along with the remains of the chicken tikka sandwich he had for lunch. His mum always did that.

He did his 'walking but not really moving' motion down the black-and-white-tiled hall. By the time he reached the five stairs at the back that led down to the kitchen-diner, he was practically going backwards.

'Oh darling, has it been awful for you?'

She flung her arms around his waist and pressed her head into his shoulder. Looking down, he was pleased to note her head stopped lower down his body than the last time they'd stood in this awkward position. He was still growing then.

Holding him at arm's length, she peered up into his eyes. He noticed she looked paler than usual but she had those red spots on her cheeks and on her neck that she got whenever she was agitated or excited (or drunk).

'I'm fine,' he said, crossing to the back of the room to toss his bag down on the kitchen table.

'It is all right, you know, to say how you're really feeling.'

Rory turned his back to her and pretended to be looking through the French windows into the garden, but really he was wondering how to get up to his room without having to go through another hug.

It wasn't that he didn't feel sorry for his mum. Obviously it was crap, having your daughter murdered and then having to relive it every time the freak did it again. But the thing was, life went on.

'That poor, poor woman,' Mum was saying.

Rory didn't need to ask who she was talking about. She said that about them all. All the mothers. All of them poor, poor women.

'I saw her on the news earlier,' she said. 'Just a glimpse. Just to think of what that poor woman is going through. No doubt the police will ask me to talk to her soon enough.'

'You can always say no,' he pointed out.

Mum looked over at him, frowning.

'It's not something you choose, Rory,' she said, and he noticed with panic that her eyes were starting to well up. 'No one *chooses* to be a bereaved parent. Choice doesn't come into it. You can't just say, "No, not today, thank you." Like it was a pint of milk.'

He stared down at the floor so as not to see her cry. The laces of her brown brogue-type shoes were undone and he almost pointed it out, but stopped himself at the last minute.

'People will start bringing it all up again, Rory. I want you to promise me not to let it get to you. Your exams are coming up soon and you must focus on those. What happened to Megan wasn't your fault. You mustn't let anyone upset you.'

Rather than having to meet her eyes, Rory followed the course of the tear snaking down her left cheek. Now he was feeling really awkward because he wanted to go to his room, but knew he shouldn't leave his mother crying on her own in the kitchen. He knew she wanted him to say something. It was what she was waiting for.

'It's all right, Mum,' he said finally, his voice coming out all croaky, like it did when he was really embarrassed. 'I know it wasn't my fault.'

For a moment her hand stayed resting on his arm, just where it emerged from the sleeve of his white school shirt. Her blue eyes, blurred by the tears, continued looking right at him and a strange expression passed over her face. Then her hand dropped and he was free to go. Briefly he considered stopping on the way out to grab a packet of biscuits from the cupboard because he was starving, but he didn't want to risk getting drawn into another conversation, so he went straight past.

Sometimes he really hated having to climb up the three sets of stairs to his room at the top of the house, past all those photos (though not the school photo used over and over again by the media, thank God), past Simon's stupid certificates in their stupid frames, but today he practically jogged up there without noticing. When he finally pushed the door open and flopped down on his bed, his whole body sagged with relief.

*

Much later on, Rory had a gatecrasher in his sanctuary at the top of the stairs. As soon as he heard the tell-tale slap-slap on the staircase, he knew it was his stepfather on his way to talk him into going to the next Megan's Angels meeting. As far as Rory was concerned, it was bang out of order for Simon to start telling him what to do. None of his business, Rory reckoned. Rory wouldn't dream of telling his stepfather how to live his life. If Simon wanted to sit around all weekend on his fat arse stuffing himself with junk food and playing online poker, that was up to him.

But this thing of meeting up with the fucking Botsfords and the fucking Reids, well, Rory just didn't see the point. If it would help find the killer, he'd do it, but just sitting around with a load of miserable people so they could all be miserable together, what was that all about?

So now Simon was standing in the doorway of Rory's room (out of breath from going up those few stairs – he really needed to get fit) and giving him that reproachful look.

'You know what this means to your mother,' he said in that voice that made every single one of Rory's muscles tighten up.

Rory fixed his eyes on his electric guitar propped against the wardrobe, and imagined playing the opening chords of 'Get Lucky', seeing where all his fingers would go on the fretboard.

But still Simon droned on and on. 'We've all got to pull together now and stop being so bloody petty. Your mother needs you. I know it's difficult when it all gets dredged up again, but you know what? Them's the breaks.'

Them's the breaks? Why did his stepfather have to be such a dick?

As Simon talked, he picked up Rory's phone from his desk where he was leaning, and started playing around with it, passing it from hand to hand. Rory's phone was a piece of shit, but still it was annoying. Rory would like to see what would happen if he went into Simon's office and started tossing his stuff around. He noticed, with distaste, how the skin around Simon's wedding ring was all puffy. Simon wasn't obese or anything but he needed to lose a few pounds. No joke.

'I think you need to think very seriously about your priorities.'

He fixed Rory intensely with his pale eyes and it was that same look he gave Rory's mum when he was telling her to do something but trying to disguise it as a request. Rory looked down to avoid his gaze and found himself staring at Simon's blue-white toes, emerging from the straps of his sandals. The toes had thick black hairs sprouting all over them.

Previous experience had taught Rory that Simon wouldn't leave without 'the bonding bit'. Maybe that's something you got taught at stepfather school: 'the bonding manoeuvre' to follow up the tough-love bit. Sure enough, the older man leaned in and put a hand on Rory's biceps which he instinctively tightened up.

'We're family, yeah?' Simon asked in his best fake young-person's voice. 'And families stick together.'

Listening to his stepfather lumbering back down the stairs, his sandals slapping on the carpet on each tread, Rory wondered whether there might actually be, right in the back of Simon's mind, a tiny millionth of a chance that he actually believed the stuff that came out of his mouth. He'd have to be pretty thick though, wouldn't he?

8

Emma could make out Leanne's shadow through the opaque-glass panels in the front door. When they'd bought the house, she'd wanted to replace the panes with stained glass that she'd specially commission from a local expert craftsman, to bring the entrance back into keeping with the period of the house, but Guy had baulked at the thousand-plus cost. Ten years on, she still felt a pang every time she went into the hallway. Now, seeing the dark shape through the glass, she hesitated with her hand on the brass latch. It wasn't that she disliked Leanne. You couldn't dislike Leanne. She was warm and straight-talking and she knew when to step back and give you space, reappearing discreetly some time later with a freshly made cup of tea, and a squeeze of the elbow or shoulder so fleeting you almost thought you might have imagined it.

It was just the baggage Leanne brought with her – trailing it through the house like mud – that Emma couldn't stomach: the memory of the first time they met, when Emma was still The Woman She'd Been Before, still believing Guy when he said that Tilly would turn up somewhere, and this would become one of those family legends that gets repeated at weddings and Christmas dinners. 'Remember the time . . .' And then those other memories that Emma tried to block out – Leanne's face when she came in from the back garden where she'd been talking on her phone in a low murmur, and how even before she'd sat them down and leaned forward to put a hand on Emma's knee, she'd known what she was going to say and buried her head in Guy's shoulder, closing her eyes as if that could shut out the truth. Leanne sitting two rows behind at the funeral, wearing a pink cardigan in compliance with the family's no-black request, mascara snaking down her cheek, while Emma's own dry eyes burned with unshed tears. Then a gap of more than a year before Leila Botsford's death brought Leanne once again to her door, just as she was now, causing all Emma's muscles to tighten and her head to ache with the effort of keeping the memories at bay.

Leanne had put on weight. That was Emma's first thought when she opened the door, and immediately she felt ashamed of herself for noticing. Another child dead, and she was thinking about how much someone weighed. Anyway, the extra pounds suited her. Leanne was one of those curvy women whose skin was better for being stretched smooth like the cover of a well-stuffed cushion, not sagging and puckered over pockets of air.

If only she dressed a little better, Emma couldn't help thinking, Leanne could be quite attractive. That black skirt was clearly from her thinner days and creased over her hips where the unlined material was pulled too tight. And the peculiar white wrap-around shirt had come loose, revealing a flash of flesh-coloured bra. Her thick, wavy hair was held back from her face by a brown hair elastic (she had a spare one around her left wrist) but some of it had come loose at the back and was curling damply in the heat of the day.

The longer Emma focused on Leanne's clothes and hair, the longer she could put off having to meet her eyes, and see that familiar look of pity and apprehension, and hear the new facts about this new child who'd got up one morning and pulled on socks and pants and brushed her hair and gone out into the world without looking back as if it was a normal morning. The longer Emma kept her mind trained on why Leanne was wearing tights on the hottest day of the year so far, the longer it would be before she had to hear about this new mother spending her first day in a world that was completely altered, unable yet to believe that every day now would be like this, that things would never go back to how they were.

'Can I come in?'

Leanne was smiling, which caused a dimple to form in her left cheek. She was pretty, the detached, objective side of Emma decided, and even that felt like an affront. Far better that the lost girls should have a spokesperson who was plain and unremarkable rather than a woman whose sparkling blue eyes reminded you that other people's lives were still going on, that when they went home they would still be laughing and loving, still getting pleasure from the sun on their skin or a glass of decent wine.

Inside the house, neither seemed to know how to start.

'You've changed the cupboards,' Leanne observed, looking around at the industrial-style kitchen. Immediately Emma felt reproached. How must it look to an outsider? Her daughter was dead, but still she found the energy to care about whether her doors were white or the ubiquitous downpipe grey? She could explain, she supposed, about those endless hours when Guy was at work and the girls at school and the only thing that stopped her going quite, quite mad was to go online and shop indiscriminately. New clothes for the girls, new cushions to replace the ones not even a year old, a £700 bike she'd ridden only once, a kitsch tablecloth in a designer print that she'd never even removed from the packaging. The cupboards had been an extravagance, but there had been other large purchases, most notably a beach hut in Whitstable.

'Sixty miles away, that's convenient,' Guy had mocked when she showed him the photograph. The first summer they'd used it exactly twice. In September, Guy had listed it for sale without consulting her on a website devoted entirely to beach huts, telling her only after an offer had been made. Amazingly they'd even made a profit. That's when Guy had started suggesting she go back to work, maybe set up another high-end recruitment agency, as she'd done before the children were born. 'You need to have another focus in your life,' he had said clumsily. 'You think a job will take my mind off my dead daughter?' Emma had demanded. But really she was scared. Scared because a job would reveal to everyone that her brain had crumbled inside her head, leaving nothing there but a pile of dust. Scared in case filling her thoughts with something apart from Tilly would mean she started to lose what little she had left of her daughter, the snapshots of memory driven out by deadlines and figures and profit and loss.

'The old ones were falling apart,' she lied, furious with herself for feeling she had to.

The two women sat down at the blond-wood table – two cups of tea in pewter-coloured mugs between them.

'How are the girls?'

Emma shrugged. 'Oh, you know. They were upset this morning when they heard the news. But on the whole they don't talk about it much. You know what kids are like.'

Too late she remembered Leanne didn't know what kids were like. 'Oh, I'm sorry.'

Leanne gave a dismissive wave of her hand. 'Don't be silly.'

Both awkward, they blew on their still-steaming tea.

Finally, Leanne took a deep breath. 'You know why I'm here, Emma.'

Ah, here it was. The conversation Emma had been dreading since the newsreader on the radio said Tilly's name that morning and everything in the world stopped.

She nodded.

'I know it's awful for you to have all this dredged up again,'

Leanne went on, and Emma almost snorted out loud at the phrase 'dredged up', as if Tilly's death was something she had successfully buried, something that needed to be dragged out from wherever it had been hidden, rather than something that was a constant presence in her brain.

'But, you know, we very much believe whoever killed Poppy Glover was also responsible for killing Tilly, so I need to ask you some questions to find out if there is any link between yourselves and the Glovers, or even just the two girls.'

'There wasn't a link last time, with Leila Botsford. Or with Megan Purvis.'

'No. Or if there is one we haven't found it yet.'

Leanne glanced towards the kitchen door.

'Is Guy here, Emma? I think it would be easier to talk to you both together.'

Emma was almost surprised to remember that he was indeed there – shut away inside his study. Since that moment this morning where he'd surprised her at his desk, they'd kept out of each other's way. She felt bad about how she'd pushed past him, knowing she was in the wrong, and had called up the stairs a couple of hours later to ask if he wanted any lunch. 'I'm not hungry,' he'd called back. 'I'll get my own later.'

Emma didn't like to think of how many meals they'd consumed separately under the same roof since Tilly died – she eating with the girls, or else skipping meals altogether, Guy standing at the kitchen counter spooning cold baked beans into his mouth straight from the tin. They'd always made such a big thing of sitting down as a family. Eating good food, like laughing and having sex, was one of the things she'd found most impossible after it happened. For a while she'd lost all sense of taste, so a fine steak in her mouth was the same as a plain baked potato or a lump of congealed macaroni cheese. Then, when taste returned, her own head prevented her from taking pleasure in what was on her plate. Sometimes she'd forget and catch herself mid-mouthful, savouring the flavours and textures of whatever she was eating, and a wave of self-disgust would sweep over her, turning the food to cardboard in her mouth.

When Guy appeared, he looked bewildered, as if he'd just woken up. As he approached the table, Emma put her hand out on impulse and gave his arm a squeeze. He paused, looking down at her, startled, and she dropped her arm quickly.

'Good to see you again, Guy,' said Leanne. 'Wish it didn't always have to be in such crappy circumstances.'

Guy nodded. 'Poor you. You always catch us at our worst.'

As if the rest of the time they were having a sing-song around the piano and playing amusing family games.

'So, how are things?' Guy wanted to know. 'With your husband? Pete, wasn't it?'

Emma's head shot up and she stared at her husband in astonishment. Since when did he ask personal questions? And surely he must remember how Leanne had appeared suddenly hollow and over-thin the last time they'd seen her, her eyes sunken into violet shadows. It was soon clear that the marriage, which had been under such strain when they'd first met her, had finally unravelled.

'Oh, you know,' said Leanne, her cheeks flushed pink. 'Suffice to say he's my ex-husband now. Still lives with that . . . woman he left me for. Where's karma when you need it, hey?'

Leanne had hesitated before the word 'woman' and Emma knew she'd wanted to say something quite different.

'Anyway,' Leanne continued, 'I'm over it now.'

By the way Leanne smiled then, Emma could tell she was seeing someone else and for a split second, a flare of jealousy shot through her at this reminder that for other people, life carried on. Other people were meeting, falling in love, fucking, arguing, making up, while she and Guy alone were like this, suspended in aspic.

'I know you've both heard the terrible news about Poppy Glover.'

Leanne's eyes, in some lights blue, in others green, flicked from

Emma to Guy and then back again. One thing you could always say for Leanne – she told it to you straight. Since Tilly died, Emma had spoken to a lot of police officers. So many she didn't ever want to speak to another one in her life. So she knew they didn't always look you in the eye when they gave you bad news.

'I can't reveal too much about the circumstances of Poppy's death at this point. I know you of all people understand that. But I need to find out if there are any overlaps at all between yourselves and the Glovers. Did the girls go to the same nursery? Might you have mutual friends?'

Though they pored over the sketchy biographical details of the Glover family Leanne was able to provide, they could find no obvious common ground.

The doorbell went and Guy and Emma exchanged a brief querying look. The shape through the opaque glass as Emma moved down the hallway gave away few clues.

The woman standing on the doorstep was slim and blonde and wearing a pale-blue well-cut dress that revealed just a hint of lightly tanned cleavage. The dress ended at the knee and her toned bare legs were set off by a pair of high-heeled nude court shoes. She had one of those faces that made you look twice, because at first glance you'd have placed her in her early thirties, but then something – a straining of the skin around the eyes, a hardness around the mouth – made you reconsider. Mid-forties, Emma decided now. And familiar somehow.

'Mrs Reid? I don't know if you remember me?'

There was a pause then, before she carried on.

'I can see you don't. I'm Sally Freeland. We've met before. I'm a features writer with the *Daily* . . .'

Now she remembered her. Pushy. Steely. One of those black-mailing journalists who told you that publicizing your story might help prevent other parents having to go through the same night-mare. *Don't you think it's what Tilly might have wanted?*

'I'm not interested in talking to—'

'How does it feel, Mrs Reid, to know it's happened again? What message would you like to send to the Glovers?'

The woman was waving one of those small, rectangular digital recording devices in her face, and Emma felt absurdly threatened.

'Mrs Reid has no comment at this stage, I'm afraid, Sally.'

Emma was relieved to find Leanne had come up behind her and was now positioning herself between Emma and Sally Freeland, so that the journalist's body was all but obscured from view and only her face appeared, poking over Leanne's shoulder like it was on a spring. The face didn't appear too pleased.

'Perhaps I could leave my card. You know, the other mothers have talked to me and found it very therapeutic. And, obviously, we could make a sizeable contribution to whatever charity you—'

'Thank you, Sally. Mrs Reid would appreciate a bit of privacy right now, but I'm sure she'll be in touch if she decides to talk to the press.'

The last thing Emma saw before the door closed was Sally Freeland's finely plucked eyebrows arched into two mountain peaks.

'Didn't take them long,' said Leanne, leading the way back to the kitchen.

Emma didn't answer. Now that Sally Freeland had gone, she was feeling weak all of a sudden. It was the déjà vu, she supposed, the sense that it was happening all over again: Leanne in the kitchen, the press at the door. All day, since the second she'd heard her daughter's name on the radio, the feelings had been building inside her and now they threatened to overwhelm her entirely. Each time another girl died, it was like experiencing Tilly's death all over again.

'Leanne, I have to ask. Was it the same? The writing on the leg? Is it definitely him?'

Leanne's expression visibly softened, as if someone was smudging it like a charcoal drawing.

'I'm sorry, Emma. You know I'd tell you if I could.'

Emma nodded, not trusting herself to speak.

Leanne carried on giving them details about Poppy Glover, reading from the notes the police had made last night while she'd still been missing, while there was still hope – where she went to school, the address of the ballet class she'd attended last year, her favourite playground ride, her friends, how she spent her time online looking at websites about puppies and had worn down her parents so much that they'd decided to get her one for her next birthday, the birthday she would no longer have.

Watching Leanne's face gradually slacken, the animation draining slowly away as time and time again they drew a blank, Emma was seized by a ridiculous notion to tell her about the photograph of Tilly she'd found in Guy's desk drawer. It would be an offering, a form of compensation for them failing to make a connection between the two girls. She opened her mouth, rolling the words around on her tongue. Then closed it again. What would she say, after all? That the picture had triggered a memory, but she didn't know exactly what it meant? That Tilly had loved matching things? She could just imagine how Guy would roll his eyes, and Leanne would smile her dimpled smile, but she wouldn't understand what Emma was trying to say. And why on earth should she, when Emma herself didn't understand what she was trying to say?

A woman's voice came blaring out of the blue, belting out an up-tempo song about never getting back together and making them all jump, and Emma lunged for her phone on the table.

She glanced at the caller display.

'Oh. It's Helen. Helen Purvis.'

'Call her back later,' said Guy.

But Emma stood up and walked towards the window, her back to the other two in case her expression gave away the excitement that was flaring up. All day she'd been lugging around the familiar dead weight of her own isolation. It was like when Tilly died, that awful loneliness that no one, not even Guy, had been able to lift from her – until Helen got in touch, and there was finally that relief of being understood.

'Emma? It's shit, isn't it? Are you OK?'

Emma felt something inside her, which she hadn't even been aware she was clenching, slowly relaxing and unfurling.

'Not really. And yes, it is shit.'

'How many have you got outside?'

'I don't know. Haven't really checked. That Sally woman just rang the doorbell . . .'

Too late she remembered about that business with Simon Purvis. No, that wasn't his name, was it? He was the stepdad. He had a different surname. Howard? Was that it? No, *Hewitt*. That was the one. Simon Hewitt. Hadn't there been some kind of relationship going on between him and that blonde journalist?

'Oh, she's back, is she? Might have known. Vulture.'

Helen's voice was clipped and Emma was sorry she'd brought it up.

'Leanne is here now,' she said, changing the subject. 'We haven't been much help, though. It's so awful, isn't it? That poor mother. I don't know if I can bear it.'

That last sentence was said very quietly, almost under her breath. Guy and Leanne were talking in the background, but Emma couldn't help feeling that they were listening to everything she said.

'I know. It doesn't bear thinking about, does it? What she's going through right now?'

For a few moments they both fell silent, Emma swaying by the window, the phone pressed to her ear.

'I think we should have a Megan's Angels meeting, don't you? Not now, obviously, but soon. It might be too soon for the Glovers, but I think the rest of us need a bit of support. How are the girls handling it?'

Emma shrugged. 'They don't show much. You know how it is.'

Again the relief that Helen, of all people, did know how it was.

'Yes, Rory is the same. Bottling it all up. He's even making a fuss about coming to the meetings now, even though I know once he's there he gets so much out of it. He still struggles with the guilt, of course.'

'Poor Rory.'

'Yeah, well, the rest of the time "Poor Rory" is a right pain in the bum, so I wouldn't get too sympathetic.'

Helen was only trying to lighten things up but part of Emma resented it. Surely they shouldn't feel the need to do that in front of each other?

'Is Jo with you?'

'I'm expecting her any minute. I'm even making an apple tray bake. Can you believe it? I pulled the recipe off the internet and it turns out to be from a kids' cookery site and it actually says, "Ask your grown-up to turn the oven on." You'd think after all this time, I'd have got past the cake-baking stage, wouldn't you? It's Jo, it's not the bloody Queen!'

When Emma came off the phone and rejoined the others, Leanne and Guy were talking stiltedly about his company and how they'd been affected by the financial crisis. 'I suppose the best you could say is that we weathered the downturn,' Guy said.

'How's Helen?' asked Leanne as Emma slid back into her seat, in front of her long-cold tea.

'Upset. As you'd expect. She's being hounded by the press, she says.'

'That's because she invites it.' Guy had always been critical of the way Helen made herself available to the newspapers and TV cameras.

It infuriated Emma. 'She just wants to see this guy caught – and if publicity is what it takes to catch him, then that's the price she's willing to pay. She's not exactly attention-seeking for the sake of it, you know, Guy.'

'All right, all right. I know.' Guy was looking away, and Emma knew he was probably wishing he hadn't brought it up. The issue of publicity had always been a bone of contention between them. Emma had been willing to talk to the press just to keep Tilly's memory alive in people's minds, even though the thought of that kind of exposure of their private grief made her feel sick. But Guy flatly refused. He thought it was ghoulish, he said it was turning their daughter's death into a freak show. And Emma was relieved they'd said no after Fiona Botsford's awful experience of being interviewed. Hadn't that been by Sally thingy as well? But sometimes she felt guilty, that she'd betrayed Tilly by not shouting louder and sharing her photo album with the world so that everyone knew who she'd been, and what the world had lost.

'She'll be organizing another meeting, then?'

The way Leanne said it was hardly a question, more like a statement of fact.

Emma nodded. 'It helps, you know?'

She was appealing directly to Leanne, and trying not to look at Guy. She knew what he felt about the meetings and about the whole 'Megan's Angels' label.

Leanne reached out a hand and placed her fingers gently on Emma's arm.

'Of course the meetings help now, but there might come a time when you don't need them any more, Emma,' she said softly. 'Just bear that in mind.'

Emma knew what she was saying. She was saying there might come a time when they'd moved on.

But what Leanne didn't know was how little Emma wanted her life to move on. Moving on would mean leaving Tilly behind. What Leanne didn't know was that Emma wanted time to go backwards, not forwards. And if that wasn't possible, she would stop it dead in its tracks.

9

What the hell was the use of nicotine gum if one ended up with lockjaw? In the back of the black cab, passing through the sun-splashed streets of North London, Sally Freeland dug around in her bag for a packet of tissues and discreetly spat the grey gum into one and folded it up inside her palm. Her mouth muscles ached and her tongue tasted furry. She still craved a cigarette.

Nothing, not a single damn thing was going to plan. Sally was fed up with it. She was doing this new routine where you stood in front of the mirror in the mornings and spoke out loud five things you were grateful for. It was supposed to make you very calm and Zen. That morning she'd told her reflection that she was grateful for:

1) Her modernist house set just back from the seafront in Hove with its white floorboards and (oblique) sea view and Japanese herb garden (sans functioning water feature).
2) Her size 10, well all right, 12, figure (although she bloody well ought to be grateful to herself for that, because it didn't come without massive sacrifice. The 5:2 diet, the Atkins, the bloody Dukan. All that protein – it'd played havoc with her bowel

habits. Not to mention the endless trekking to the gym, rain or shine, sleet or snow).

3) Not being with Noel any more. Although technically speaking, that was more of a negative than a positive, but really, what an escape she'd had, thinking about it. The final straw had been when they'd talked about sharing their fantasies, and Sally, who'd read that *Fifty Shades* for her book group (so they could know what they were dismissing, everyone said, although that didn't stop most of them reading all three volumes), had got in a pair of furry handcuffs and a very soft bristled brush that cost nearly a hundred quid from a specialist chemist, and prepared to submit to Noel's will, only for him to drop his trousers and reveal he was wearing her knickers. That was his fantasy! Not only that, but they were the brand-new ones from Agent Provocateur. Now, she was as broad-minded as the next woman, but everyone has a line, don't they? A tipping point?

4) Her family – her nieces and nephews and her beloved mother, ensconced now in a nursing home, and a few cards short of a full deck. The last time Sally visited, she'd called out a hello from the doorway of the residents' lounge, and a hush had fallen as her mother peered at her over the top of her glasses before asking her neighbour, sotto voce, 'Who, or should I say *what*, is that?'

5) Her Burmese cat Binky who treated everyone apart from Sally herself with utter and not displeasing disdain.

So she'd been suitably grateful, she'd tossed her good karma out into the universe and given thanks for all her blessings. And what had she got in return? Just a whole heap of problems. Sally thought she might ditch the blessings business. It was starting to feel just too much like when she'd taken up Buddhism on the advice of a friend who swore that she could chant for a parking space in Portobello Road and lo, one would open right up. Sally had chanted for loads of things – not just selfish things either, she'd made sure to ask for peace in Syria on a regular basis – but none of them had come to pass. Well, apart from the red-wine stain coming out of the living-room rug.

The taxi pulled up at the entrance to the private mews running behind the railway line in Holloway, where the Botsfords lived. It had cost thirteen pounds to go two miles down the road. Sally would claim it on expenses, but still she resented paying it. She had a pang of regret for her champagne-coloured VW Beetle, shut away in a garage in Hove that she rented at vast cost. Such a drag she couldn't drive it. Not couldn't, wasn't allowed to. Not with all those points on her licence. She'd assumed she could simply pay to go on another one of those speed-awareness courses, but the bastards had told her the limit was one every three years. It wouldn't be so bad if she had a man who could drive her around, but when you were on your own . . . well, it was just so unfair.

Sally wasn't looking forward to becoming reacquainted with Fiona Botsford. There are some people in life who are kindred spirits, she was a big believer in that. So it would stand to reason, she supposed, that there are other people who are the precise opposite of kindred spirits. Hostile spirits, maybe. Well, Fiona Botsford was one of those.

If only Emma Reid had been a bit more forthcoming. The problem was she'd pre-judged her. She didn't realize that Sally was on her side. If the situation had been reversed and something happened to her daughter, were she to have one, she wouldn't want to go sharing it with a national newspaper either, but the thing was, Emma had been around long enough now to know how the whole thing worked. You didn't get to be left alone. It was harsh, but there it was. Sally didn't invent the system, but given that it existed, it was her job to help people navigate it, and Emma didn't do herself any favours by being so stubborn. The

Reids' stand-offishness had counted against them. Sally had seen online forums where people had openly challenged their story, implying they might know more about their daughter's death than they were letting on. There would always be conspiracy theorists, Sally was well aware of that, and the fact was, Emma's refusal to talk to the press was fuelling ill feeling, even two years on.

Emma didn't seem to get that there were certain unwritten rules about how you behaved after a tragedy. Firstly, you had to be seen to cry. Sally could not over-emphasize the need for tears. You had to look on it as a kind of transaction. You want to find out what's happened to your kid, so as the grieving parent there are certain things you're expected to give – and one of those is grief. But Emma Reid hadn't cried even at the funeral. Sally hadn't been there, but she'd had reports. And, of course, it hadn't gone unnoticed. Emma had been 'stoic' in the face of tragedy, the *Mail* said, which everyone knew meant 'hard'.

And, secondly, you had to maintain a presence. Just be in evidence from time to time – drop in on the school your child used to go to, lay a few flowers at the spot where the body was found, open the odd charity auction. It didn't take much, but people needed *something* in return for their investment of time or money or empathy. But Emma Reid had never seemed to grasp that it was a two-way street.

Helen Purvis. Now, she was different. She had an innate understanding of what was expected of her. Sally tried to ignore the pang of guilt that flared up at the thought of Helen Purvis. Mina, her life coach, had told her guilt was a wasted emotion. And she was absolutely right, but on the topic of Helen Purvis, Sally's no-guilt resolve wavered.

She hadn't wanted anything to happen with Simon Hewitt. He wasn't at all her type. But she had been going through a particularly fallow period romantically. Plus she'd just had a rather big horrible birthday. So she was vulnerable. And Simon Hewitt took advantage of that. She'd first met him at the time of Megan's murder, and he'd been in a terrible state. She'd got a couple of comments from him but that was about it. She didn't even think he'd registered her existence, to be quite frank. But when she went back to do her in-depth catch-up interview with Helen nine months after Megan's death, he'd known exactly who she was, and by the time of the next murder, the Reid girl . . . well . . .

She still couldn't say what she'd found attractive about him. He'd been a good deal thinner back then than he was now. In fact she'd been quite shocked the last time she'd seen him. One read about chickens being pumped full of water so they weighed more – Simon Hewitt looked like it'd been done to him. You could almost see liquid moving under the skin at his wrists like the mattress of a water bed.

She'd been shocked when he made a pass. She knew she hadn't exactly been blameless, but then she wasn't the one breaking her marriage vows. They'd only slept together twice, and the sex hadn't been much to write home about. And then there'd been that awkward scene that last time they went to bed. They'd been about to do it and he'd suddenly started convulsing on top of her and had rolled off her and curled up in a ball, sobbing. She hadn't known what to do. She'd comforted him as best she could, but there had been no coming back from that. The next time he'd got in touch she'd told him she could no longer cope with the moral ambiguity of the situation. She'd always considered herself a good person. And now she couldn't face herself in the mirror. That was one good thing about having affairs with married men, Sally found, there was always a ready-made get-out clause.

With men like Simon, though, you never knew if they were going to have an attack of conscience and confess everything. Several times since their short-lived affair, she'd had the definite suspicion that Helen knew something, though she'd always been, if not friendly, at least cordial. Sally had to admire her. She was a pro. She would do whatever it took to keep her daughter's death in the news – even if it meant being civil to her husband's ex-lover.

Sally wasn't proud of sleeping with Simon Hewitt. In fact she was cross with herself for muddying the waters, and she'd never have done it if she'd known there would be two more murders that would bring her back here to the scene of the crime, so to speak. Still, she didn't believe in self-flagellation. Learn by your mistakes and move on. And now she was once again feeling that fluttering in her belly she always got when she was on the scent of a story. A new victim meant a fresh opportunity to build a connection and win a family over. That's what Sally loved about her job. Each assignment was a new challenge, another chance for her to do what she did best.

She wasn't holding out much hope for this visit to the Botsfords, though. That Fiona Botsford was a cold fish. And her husband – well, there was something very abrasive about the man, Sally thought, and something almost creepy about the way they were together, always standing so close as if they were conjoined. Still, she had to call in to try to get a comment, more of a courtesy call than anything else, just so she could say she'd tried. Then she could move on to this new family, the Glovers, where there was no unfortunate history and she was starting with a clean slate. Maybe they'd gel straight away. It happened sometimes – people respond to someone who's seen it all before and isn't shockable, someone with a warm voice and a comforting manner. And it didn't hurt that the newspaper paid the best rates going. Not that bereaved parents were interested in money, of course, but they almost always came round to the idea of a charitable foundation set up in their dead child's name so they could feel something good might yet come out of all this pain.

And there was always that minuscule possibility, that journalist's holy grail, that she'd find herself in the right place at the right time to crack the case open. It sounded unlikely but it did happen.

People tell journalists things they don't tell the police. They let things slip and give themselves away in a thousand little ways. Or you might be interviewing them when the phone call comes to say a suspect's been arrested. You're right there where you always want to be as a journalist. On the inside.

The mews where the Botsfords lived was accessed from the road via an electronic gate hidden at the top of a discreet cobbled driveway. When Sally couldn't get any answer from their house, she tried a neighbour.

'Hello.' She used her best estuary accent. 'I'm a friend of Fiona Botsford at number five. I've a card for her. Can you buzz me in so I can pop it through the letterbox?'

The voice was apologetic but firm: 'I'm afraid the Botsfords are very protective of their privacy. They've asked everyone in the road not to let in people they don't know.'

'Yes, but—'

The intercom clicked off. Sally's annoyance was tempered by her relief that she'd told the taxi driver to wait. She could hear the engine thrumming reassuringly behind her. Just for the hell of it, she tried the Botsfords' bell again and walked to the far right-hand side of the gate from where she could see down the mews. It was one of those trendy places where every house was painted a different colour with contrasting metalwork around the roof terraces and first-floor balconies. The Botsfords' was pale blue with burgundy trim – she recognized it from the last time she'd been here. As Sally peered through the railings, something moved at a first-floor window. She pressed her nose to the metal bars to get a better look, just in time to catch the pale disc of a face. But it was gone before she had a chance to work out who it was.

Back in the taxi, Sally tried to dispel the disquieting image of that face by logging into her emails on her phone. Damn. Another one from the gas company reminding her of her unpaid bill. She slid her phone back into its sleeve and stared out of the window.

The stop–start traffic gave her plenty of time to absorb the view of the grimy Archway Road. Up ahead, local landmark Suicide Bridge arched high over the gridlocked cars, its wrought-iron railings topped with black spikes in an effort to deter jumpers. Sally fought off a momentary flashback to a hospital ward and a burning pain in the back of her throat where they'd rammed in the tube to pump her stomach. She was glad when the taxi turned off to the left, cutting the bridge off from view.

The Glovers lived in a ground-floor flat in an unassuming road full of modest terraced Victorian houses. By the time she'd paid the taxi driver, making sure to ask for a receipt, there was already a knot of reporters outside number 17, with its neglected front garden and the printed 'No junk mail' notice taped to the utilitarian front door. She clocked a few familiar faces. That young guy with the trousers halfway down his hips revealing electric-blue underpants with BENCH emblazoned across the waistband, who looked like he should still be at school, was from one of the local news agencies.

'What's a nice girl like you doing in a place like this?'

She started at the voice, which was close enough to her ear to send a spray of spittle across the lobe. But when she turned round and recognized the man behind her, she relaxed. Ken Forbes was a creep, but he'd been a fixture on the Sunday tabloids since long before Sally cut her journalistic teeth. She felt a kind of affection for him.

'Oh you know how it is, Ken. Thought I'd step over to the dark side for a bit.'

'Yeah, well, this is dark all right.'

'Awful,' said Sally distractedly, trying to peer in through the ground-floor windows from their vantage point on the pavement.

'No. I mean, this one is even worse than the others,' he clarified.

Now Ken Forbes had her attention. She turned her eyes to him, taking in his florid nose, threaded with broken capillaries, and the thinning sandy hair through which his scalp shone lobster pink.

'What do you mean, worse?'

Ken smiled. His teeth were custard yellow and his breath pungently over-ripe; Sally had to stop herself from stepping back from him.

'Now why would I tell you that? Come on, darling. I've got to leave you a bit of legwork to do. Can't have your lovely arse getting fat from sitting on it all day.'

Sally knew no one was supposed to put up with being spoken to like that any more, but she couldn't be bothered to make a fuss. There was something a bit pathetic about Ken Forbes. She was just old enough to feel nostalgic for the Fleet Street days of three-hour liquid lunches and news stories bashed out on desks littered with overflowing ashtrays. Ken still had the contacts, and he didn't lose any sleep over what was and wasn't ethical. None of that Leveson crap for him. He'd obviously found something out. But from whom? No one had been briefed beyond that farce of a press conference, as far as she knew. She made a mental list of the police officers on the case she knew – Leanne Miller, Jo Barber. Not those two. By-the-book worthy sorts, both of them. The Botsfords' FLO then. The good-looking one. What was his name now. Pat? No, Pete. Or someone from the Murder Squad, perhaps?

'What are they like?' she asked Ken, nodding towards the flat with the cheap white canvas blinds in the windows. 'The new family?'

'They're like people who've had a ruddy great bomb dropped on their lives. What do you expect?'

Sally resented the way Ken was looking at her as if she'd said something crass.

She was about to say something sensitive, just to put him right, but as she opened her mouth a scream pierced the air – shocking and animalistic, like a sound dragged up from a person's guts and ripped out through their throat. As one, the gathered reporters and photographers turned to look at the house from where the harrowing noise was emanating. On Sally's right a TV camera crew scrabbled for their equipment, wanting to be prepared. And still it went on, a raw howl of pain that set Sally's nerves jangling. The young news-agency guy with the low-slung trousers dropped his eyes to the ground and kicked at the pavement with the toe of his suede trainer. Throughout the knot of reporters, people would catch each other's eyes, shrug and then immediately look away as if caught doing something not quite nice. Sally shivered, though the temperature had to still be in the low twenties.

She watched Ken Forbes reach his yellow-tipped fingers into the pocket of his nylon backpack.

God, she could murder a fag.

10

The noise is horrible.

The noise is coming from me.

'Susan, stop,' Oliver implores me. His eyes are sunk into his head like black stones.

'Stop,' he says again. 'You're upsetting Mia.'

That stops me finally. The word 'Mia' like a tap turning me off.

This time two days ago she was right here on the sofa scrubbed and pink, fresh from the bath, in the white pyjamas with pale-blue dogs on them. 'This is my favourite,' she'd said, pressing a small, chubby finger on a random dog that was just the same as all the others. 'His name is Max. When we get a puppy can we call him Max, Mummy?'

Now I'd buy her a puppy. I'd buy her a litter of puppies. I'd fill the flat with puppies until we couldn't move for them.

Why didn't I say yes? Why didn't I say yes to it all – sleepovers, trips to Disneyland Paris, a doll that wees like a real baby, just one more chapter, rollerblades, night-vision goggles, Super Soakers, great slabs of chocolate big as breezeblocks? Why did I purse my lips and frown and shake my head and shake it again watching the spark of hope fade in her blue eyes? Why did I dole out pleasure so grudgingly, snapping shut wallet and sweetie jar and favourite picture book with such brutal firmness, enjoying my own sense of control?

If You let her come back I'll never deny her anything again. If You let her come back I'll be a better mother, a better person. If You let her come back I'll never ask for anything. I won't complain about Oliver taking me for granted or about my brain atrophying through overexposure to children's nursery rhymes and soft-play areas in primary colours or about how there's never enough money for a babysitter or even a nice bottle of wine now that the cost of childcare has made it impossible for me to go back to work.

This time two days ago I was a different person living in a different world and there were no reporters outside on the pavement and no policemen in my living room drinking tea from the mugs that came free with the girls' Easter eggs. And she was here with her newly washed hair and her dog-print pyjamas. And I want it back. I want her back.

I want.

11

In the end his mum had got around the potential embarrassment of having Rory fail to turn up for the Megan's Angels meeting by holding it in their own front room as opposed to the upstairs room at the Victoria Arms where they usually went. It was too annoying, he reflected as he grudgingly set out bowls of peanuts and crisps, pausing every now and then to scoop out a handful and pour them into his open mouth. He'd been all set to boycott it but she'd teared up and he'd found himself saying, 'All right then. If it's such a big deal.' And she'd pressed his hand between both of hers and said that, yes, it was a big deal to her, and how grateful she was to have such a considerate son, until he'd have said yes to anything just to get her off his case.

His mum and Simon had been bickering all morning – about whether it was appropriate to supply wine and beer at an afternoon event, about why she was asking him to clean the very top loo when no one in their right mind was going to trek all the way up there. There was a hissed exchange in which the phrase 'that woman' was used several times. Rory had never fully got to the bottom of what had happened, and he was glad to be spared the details. Oldies with sex lives. Could there be anything more gross? But from the snippets he'd overheard over the past months, he reckoned Simon had had some sort of fling. Must have been someone with serious mental health issues, was all Rory could think. Who else would want to shag podgy Simon with his permanently shiny forehead and sweat-rings under his arms? Rory felt bad for his mum though. Kind of humiliated on her behalf, although he had to admit she wasn't exactly making the best of herself. Sometimes when his mates came round he'd find himself wishing she made a bit more of an effort. He didn't want her to go too over the top, though, not like Chigsie's mum who always wore skintight jeans and low-cut Lycra vests and he had to concentrate so hard on not looking at her chest he always came away with a headache. But often his mum just looked so *old*. What he really meant was that she looked so defeated. Like she'd given up trying.

Sometimes he tried to remember what she'd been like before Megan, but it was like trying to remember what it was like to be cold when you were sweltering in 80-degree heat. Too alien to compare.

Now Simon came stropping into the living room where Rory was trying to decant the remaining peanuts from one bowl into another to disguise the fact he'd eaten most of them.

'I hope you're not going to have that face on the whole time they're here.'

Occasionally, Rory would find himself thinking Simon wasn't so bad as stepfathers went, then he'd say something like this and it'd remind him what a complete knob he was.

'It is my face,' said Rory. 'Whose face would you prefer me to have on? Gary Lineker's?'

Simon put on his long-suffering look. 'Listen, mate. Would it be too much to ask you to stop the wisecracks, just for today? For your mum's sake. You know how much these occasions take it out of her.'

The doorbell interrupted the stare-off that followed this

request. Immediately there came the sound of Helen's shoes slapping against the hall tiles.

Rory's spirits sagged. It wasn't just that there'd be all those same faces, talking about their dead children, and Jemima Reid following him with her eyes everywhere he went – although that was bad enough, if you asked him. It was also that his mum would try to get them all to cry. She had this idea that crying was a good thing and that they'd all feel a million times better once they'd done it. What she didn't appreciate was that some of them didn't want to cry. It wasn't that he thought he wasn't allowed to, or it was wimpy to, or people would think less of him, or any of the reasons she expected were going through his head. It just made him uncomfortable. And the only reason he ever felt better afterwards was because he was glad it was over.

Now voices were coming nearer.

'The last ones upped sticks yesterday afternoon,' his mum was saying as she came into the living room followed by Flo-Jo. It had just been a throwaway comment when Jo first came to them as their FLO. 'Can I call you Flo-Jo?' the young Rory had asked. But of course his mum had seized on this weak joke as evidence that Rory was doing OK, being 'normal', and she'd insisted on repeating it so many times it eventually stuck.

'I was just telling Jo that the last of the media left yesterday,' his mum repeated as if they were all deaf. 'Probably all gathered outside the poor Glovers', I expect.'

She glanced at Flo-Jo for corroboration, but she just smiled in that 'I'm giving nothing away' manner she had and came over to give Rory a hug. He liked Jo well enough, but he found it embarrassing to be pressed against her huge bosoms and was relieved when she eventually pulled away. Plus there was something about her that gave him a sour taste at the back of his mouth. Something about the memories she stirred up especially when, as now, he hadn't seen her for a little while.

'How's life?' she asked him.

'Oh you know.' He shrugged. 'Usual crap.'

The doorbell sounded a second time, causing his mother to jump up out of her seat like it had caught fire or something. She'd got him and Simon to carry chairs in from all over the house, so the living room resembled a junk shop, and she had to pick her way around bits of mismatched furniture on her way to the hall. As she opened the front door Rory heard her say the same thing about the press having left only yesterday, and it made him feel unaccountably embarrassed for her.

She was just showing Fiona and Mark Botsford into the room when the doorbell rang a third time and, not long after that, a fourth. In a few minutes the living room was bursting with people, and more seats had to be brought, even the moth-eaten piano stool from the room next door. In the mêlée, Rory was conscious of Jemima Reid's eyes following him from where she sat with the rest of her family squashed up on the sofa in front of the window. He knew she was younger than him and everything, but did she really have to stare like that?

His mum stood up and flicked the side of her wine glass with her nail, then called out, 'Ting, ting.' Rory briefly closed his eyes so as not to see her. She was wearing a long shapeless pink cotton dress with thin straps that failed to cover her beige bra and she kept smoothing down her frizzy hair with her free hand, which was what she did when she was nervous. There was a tightness in his chest when he looked at her so instead he glanced around the room. All the FLOs seemed to be there, which was unusual, and there was even an extra one, a man who'd been introduced as having been assigned to the new family. Even though he was old, thirties at least, he still had raised red bumps all over his chin and neck like teenage acne.

Rory concentrated on the man's skin so he wouldn't have to think about the new family and what they were going through, which might remind him of what his own family had gone through.

'Thank you all so much for coming.'

His mum's cheeks were flushed pink like her dress. She wasn't used to drinking during the day. Rory hoped she wouldn't get pissed.

'I only wish we didn't always have to meet in such unhappy circumstances,' said his mum.

This was met with a low murmur as people resolutely avoided each other's eyes.

'We all know now that another little girl, another family's daughter, has . . . gone to join ours. Our hearts go out to the parents. Their grief is still too raw for them to be here today but Kieren, their FLO, is here on their behalf. Where are you, Kieren?'

The spotty policeman half raised his hand while his cheeks flushed to match the inflammation around the lower part of his face.

'I'm sure in time the Glovers will come to find solace in this group, just as the rest of us do. Sometimes I really don't know what I'd do without you all. When the news broke the day before yesterday, the only people I wanted to speak to are in this room. The only ones who can possibly understand.

'In a few moments, Pete Delagio would like to say a few words on behalf of the police. But first, as ever, shall we just have a minute's silence while we think about our girls. *All* our girls.'

Rory fidgeted on his uncomfortable kitchen chair. This was precisely why he didn't want to come to these things any more. As if they didn't think about the girls all the time anyway! Why would they want to come all the way here to sit in his living room and think about them some more?

Over the sea of bent heads, he caught Jemima Reid's eye. He was about to raise his eyebrows in a complicit 'what are they like' gesture, but she'd already looked away, frowning in that intense way she had.

After the uncomfortable silence, his mum chatted a bit about how she'd felt when she'd heard the news about the Glover girl. Tears spilled from her eyes but she didn't seem to notice them. Then Guy Reid said something, then Simon. Yawn. Yawn. Now they were talking about coping mechanisms. As far as Rory could see there was one really obvious coping mechanism: think about something else. Whenever he found himself dwelling on Megan and what happened to her, and his own part in it, he quickly substituted some other line of thought. Georgia Reynolds, for instance, and why she'd drawn a heart in the back of his maths book and whether that meant she'd finally finished with Connor Bateman and whether in that case she might do with Rory the things she and Connor were rumoured to have done upstairs in Maddie Jameson's parents' bed. Or he'd think about Arsenal and whether next season would top the last.

But not this lot. They were talking about ring-fencing their personal space and allowing themselves to grieve, and breathing exercises and standard responses to blundering questions, and now Fiona Botsford, who rarely contributed much to these occasions as far as Rory could tell, suddenly said, 'Of course we're adopting the most extreme coping mechanism of them all – emigrating to the other side of the world!'

Well. That shut them all up.

Flo-Jo was the first one to speak. 'You're moving to Australia?'

She made it sound like the moon. Rory knew it was a long way, but really, had they never heard of long-distance flights?

'There's nothing to keep us here,' Fiona Botsford was explaining. She was half smiling, but had one of those faces where it looked like smiling hurt. 'Unlike the rest of you, we haven't got other children already settled in schools. Leila was all we had. We just want a fresh start.'

That made sense to Rory. If you didn't *have* to stay here where every few months, every time there was an anniversary or a birthday, the whole thing was dredged up again, if you didn't *have* to be forever Tragic Girl's Mum or Brother, then really why would you? But now something else was occurring to him. How was his mother going to deal with this piece of news? She set such store by this little group. For the two years after Megan died she'd been a shadow of a person, but meeting the Reids and then the Botsfords had brought her back to life. How was she going to cope with the break-up of Megan's Angels? He didn't have long to wait for an answer.

'Oh Helen, I'm sorry. I shouldn't have just blurted it out like that. I wasn't thinking.'

Fiona Botsford was crouching down by his mother's chair, holding on to her hand, and Rory wasn't surprised to see more tears snaking down his mum's cheeks.

'No. Please ignore me. It's just a shock, that's all.'

His mother had on that face she sometimes pulled over her real face when she was trying to keep her feelings under control.

'Of course you should go,' said Guy Reid, whom Rory had always secretly found intimidating with his brooding misery. One of those intense types who rarely looked you in the eye. 'Sometimes I wish we could just pack up too and go somewhere – anywhere – where no one knows us and we can be a normal family again.'

Rory sneaked another glance at his mum. Her eyes were fixed on Guy Reid's face and the skin was tight around her mouth.

'Not that that's in any way a possibility,' quickly added Guy's wife, Emma. She was looking at Jemima as if trying to reassure her daughter they weren't going to be on the next plane out of there. 'We're very much rooted here. As much as anything else, London was Tilly's home. It's where I feel a connection to her.'

'And what about the investigation?' His mum's voice was unsteady and higher than normal. 'What if the police need you?'

'We'll keep in regular contact with Fiona and Mark,' the Botsfords' FLO piped up. His name was Pete, Rory remembered suddenly. The last time they'd met they'd had a long, involved conversation about England's chances in the World Cup, now just a few weeks away. 'And of course we'll keep them up to date with any developments. The wonders of Skype.'

After that the conversation limped on for a little while, but never recovered its rhythm.

'More drinks, anyone?' asked Simon as if this was a fun social event. No one took Simon up on his offer, but he still disappeared into the kitchen to fetch himself a beer. Rory wished he could have one. Might make this whole excruciating afternoon more bearable.

'Is this a good time for me to say a few words?' It was Pete again, looking at Rory's mum with his eyebrows raised expectantly. She nodded slightly, hardly moving her head.

Still Pete held back. 'I'm not sure if this is really suitable for the younger ones.'

His eyes were on Jemima Reid and her little sister, but Rory felt his face burning. That was all he needed to really round off today perfectly – to be lumped in with the kids.

'Come on, you lot.' Flo-Jo had her jolliest face on as she stood up and moved towards the door. 'Let's go and raid the kitchen and see what we can find.'

Jemima and Caitlin Reid had already got reluctantly to their feet but Jo was looking pointedly at him. 'Jump to it, Rory. You can show us where your mum stashes the goodies.'

Like he was five years old or something. He heaved himself upright.

'Good man,' muttered Simon as he walked past.

Could life actually get any worse?

12

Leanne's eyes followed Rory Purvis from the room. Poor kid was at that age where every emotion was displayed on his skin. Even his Adam's apple was blushing. After he'd left, her eyes remained glued to the door, trying to put off the moment when she would have to look at Pete. It was so weird, after all these months of hardly seeing him, to find herself yet again in close proximity to her ex-husband. She glanced at his left hand, and immediately felt angry with herself for minding about that blank space on his fourth finger where even now if you looked carefully, you could spot a band of skin slightly whiter than the rest.

As penance she forced her thoughts back to Will. Her tensed muscles relaxed thinking about his gentle brown eyes, and the way, while having dinner, he'd pause mid-sentence and reach out one of his slender fingers to stroke her cheek as if she was some lovely thing he couldn't help touching.

'Detective Chief Inspector Desmond asked me to have a quiet word with you all.' Pete looked ill at ease. Leanne didn't blame him. She was glad not to have been burdened with this particular task. They were in a room of parents who'd lost children. There were so many things that could not, should not, be said.

'The thing is, there seems to have been a leak from somewhere, which obviously we are taking very seriously, leaving no stone unturned, and if it's established that it's come from the police end, rest assured there will be serious consequences.'

Leanne stared at Pete. *Leaving no stone unturned.* When had he started talking like Desmond?

'Anyway, we were hoping to keep this information under wraps for a little longer, but now it's out there it's only fair that you should all be told so that it doesn't come as a shock. The latest victim – and please remember that at this stage there's no proof that the cases are connected – but the latest victim, Poppy Glover, was found in slightly different circumstances to the last two, Leila and Tilly.'

Pete took a deep breath that Leanne only noticed because she knew what was coming next and how little he wanted to say it. 'I'm sorry to say that in this instance the body was partially unclothed and there seems to be some indication of a sexual motive, just as with Megan. I can't tell you any more than that.'

The silence that greeted Pete's announcement had that loaded quality where the lack of noise seems to be covering up the din of things unsaid.

Emma Reid was the first to break it, removing the hand that had been clasped to her mouth since Pete first spoke.

'Oh, that poor girl. Those poor parents. That's too much. Really too much.'

Tears were filling her black-lashed eyes, but Leanne noticed that Emma's husband, Guy, sitting just inches to her right, made no attempt to comfort her. Things were not right between those two. Leanne ought to be able to recognize the signs by now.

'Was she raped?'

A gasp followed Mark Botsford's question. Leanne stiffened. Sometimes that man was too direct. Not for the first time she wondered if he might be somewhere on the autistic spectrum.

'I'm afraid I can't give you details.' Pete shrugged helplessly and Leanne remembered that he and Mark had become friends, despite them appearing to have so little in common. Sometimes it could be hard in those situations to draw a line, despite what they were taught in training. Pete would miss them, she supposed, when they moved away.

'But it doesn't make any sense.' Now Guy Reid was talking over the top of everyone else. 'Surely it doesn't fit with his pattern. After Megan none of them were interfered with, were they?'

He was looking straight at Leanne now, and she realized he was looking for reassurance that they hadn't been lied to all this time, that Tilly had really been untouched. Obviously they knew the police were working on the theory that the girls had been filmed or photographed, but it wasn't something they ever talked about directly.

'We are convinced that's the case with Tilly and with Leila. We haven't kept anything from you.'

'Then why would he suddenly revert to his old pattern? Are you sure it's definitely him?'

The families all knew about the 'SORRY', in the latest case smudged to a biro bruise on Poppy Glover's skin, but had been sworn to secrecy so effectively that they never mentioned it out loud.

Pete nodded. 'All signs so far indicate this is the same—'

The cry was so sudden and so reed-thin that at first Leanne didn't even register what it was and looked towards the window, expecting to hear a car alarm on the road outside. It was only when there was a kerfuffle by the door that she grasped the noise was coming from inside the room, and specifically from Helen Purvis. When Leanne leapt up she could see that the older woman was deathly white. Her hand, resting on her husband's arm, was shaking.

'I don't understand,' she was saying. 'I just don't understand.'

'It's brought it all back,' Simon said to the rest of the room. 'It's very distressing.'

Leanne hadn't much taken to Simon Hewitt over the years, but now she felt sorry for him. How awful it must be to keep having to rake over the worst thing that had ever happened to them, again and again, every time there was a new victim. How impossible to move on with your life when you were trapped in this endless agonizing *Groundhog Day* scenario.

The afternoon limped on after that, but never quite recovered the cosy camaraderie of the first half-hour. Leanne felt uncomfortable, unsure of whether or not they should really be there, but when she suggested to Jo, Pete and Kieren they leave the families to it, Emma and Fiona turned to her with such fervent entreaties to stay that she had found herself sitting back down again. She couldn't help comparing her relationship with Emma to Pete's with the Botsfords and again she felt she'd let the Reids down. Not that she necessarily wanted to be their friend, but she'd have liked there to be more of a connection. She'd have liked to know she did them some good. It had just been such poor timing for her. When they'd first met she'd been dealing with the aftermath of the infertility blow and her imploding marriage, and the next time, the following year, she'd still been reeling from the split. Sometimes, she thought, life was all about timing. It was a miracle, really, that any of them ever managed to connect.

When Leanne finally extricated herself from the meeting, Pete insisted on leaving too. Together they made their way down the wide tree-lined road, flanked on both sides by huge, red-brick Victorian houses with neat front gardens. At the nineteenth-century clocktower, which stood on its own on an island amidst the traffic, they stopped, trying to remember which way to go.

'If I was going to pay millions of pounds to live somewhere, I'd make damn sure it had a tube station,' Pete grumbled.

'If you were going to pay millions of pounds to live somewhere, I'd make damn sure I pressed for alimony.'

They half smiled at each other, but the comment was too near the bone and Leanne immediately wished it unsaid. Why, after all this time, did Pete still make her feel so wound up? He was still living with *her*, wasn't he? Leanne still could rarely bring herself to use the name of the twenty-seven-year-old who'd wrecked her marriage. Kelly, that was it. She'd once asked Pete what she did and instantly forgot. Corporate sponsorship, blah blah blah, the kind of nothing job where you put on heels to go to work and have brain-storming meetings and go to the gym at lunchtime.

'You know they're going to think it's you, don't you?' asked Pete as they waited at the bus stop. They'd already agreed that if a taxi came past they'd flag it down, but it didn't look likely.

'What's me?'

'The leak. Who else has connections to the press?'

'Don't be ridiculous.'

'What? Your live-in boyfriend is a journo and you don't suppose they're going to put two and two together and think he could make a nice little extra in his back pocket?'

'For one thing, he's not "living in", and for another, you're being a dick.'

But Leanne could feel her face burning. Could that really be what people were thinking? And why did Pete have to use that tone to say 'boyfriend', like it was something nasty on the bottom of his shoe?

A taxi came along on the other side of the road and Leanne instinctively waved her arm.

'Doesn't make any sense for us to share, with you living south and me east,' she said, not looking at his face. Not looking at his eyes. Especially his eyes. 'So I'm going to love you and leave you.'

Climbing into the cab her cheeks were still stinging with heat.

As she leaned forward to close the door, Pete put his foot in the way.

'Are you?'

She screwed up her eyes questioningly. 'Am I what?'

'What you just said? Going to love me and leave me?'

'Oh, give over.' She pulled the door to and his foot slid out of the way. 'See ya,' she trilled out of the open window, avoiding his face.

All the way home to Stoke Newington she heaped loathing upon herself. Why had she said that thing about loving and leaving? Since when did she use the phrase 'see ya'? And was Pete right that people would suspect her of being the source of the leak? The thought that others might be looking at her and doubting her commitment and loyalty gave her an uncomfortable tugging sensation in the pit of her stomach.

She closed the window and leaned her forehead against the glass, hoping to cool her still-burning skin. She thought about the awkward afternoon at the Purvises' house, remembering how anxiously Helen had offered around the drinks and the bowls of crisps and peanuts, and she felt a rush of sympathy for the grieving mother. It had clearly been a huge blow to find out the group was to lose the Botsfords. And then the news about the circumstances in which the Glover girl had been found, which must have brought back such terrible memories of Megan's own death.

Every now and then Leanne was thankful she hadn't been able to have children, so she'd never risk knowing the pain of losing one.

13

For the two days since the Megan's Angels meeting, Emma had been in the grip of despondency.

'For God's sake, Mum, can't you at least *pretend* to be interested?' Jemima had yelled the night before after she'd broken off from a long story about her maths teacher to ask Emma what she thought, and her mother had just blinked at her, her face and mind completely blank.

It was the bombshell from the Botsfords that had thrown her, Emma thought. The idea that this option existed for them, to choose to exit their lives. It had never crossed her mind that this might be possible, that she might simply leave this life that had become impossible to her and start another one somewhere else where Grieving Mother wasn't the first thing people saw. The thought of it – of being, just for an hour, a minute even, someone other than who she was – made her giddy.

She mentioned it to Guy only once. It was on the Saturday evening, when they'd been home from the Purvises' for a few hours, and Caitlin was at a sleepover and Jemima in her room playing angry music loudly and doing whatever she did on her computer.

They were sitting side by side on the sofa and the television was on, although she couldn't have said what show was playing. She doubted Guy knew either. She used to choose carefully which programmes to watch, arguing her case with Guy if he had other ideas (which he so often did). But now, unwilling to risk any unnecessary interaction, they both gravitated, without speaking, to whatever they felt the other would dislike least, so their television watching was a question of the lowest common denominator – featureless programmes that bled seamlessly from one to the other arousing neither interest nor passion. But on this evening Emma's mind wasn't on the screen where a harried nurse was leaning against a hospital wall, sobbing. Instead all she could think of was the Botsfords, and their seemingly miraculous escape.

'What do you think about Fiona and Mark?' she asked Guy, turning to face him for the first time in weeks. 'What's to stop us doing that? Starting again somewhere new?'

Guy looked at her, shocked, although whether at what she'd said or just the fact that she'd addressed him so directly, she couldn't have said.

'Their situation is completely different. They're self-employed. They run their own business. They have no other children. They have the luxury of simply leaving everything behind. We don't. What about my job? What about our parents? What about Jemima and Caitlin? They need continuity in their lives after everything that's happened.'

Emma persevered. 'But can you imagine it, Guy? The freedom?'

He turned back towards the television, shaking his head as if unable to believe what he'd just heard.

'Tilly is dead, Emma. Even if we went to the fucking moon we'd still take that knowledge with us. At least here we're surrounded by things she knew. Her bedroom is here. Her friends are here. We can keep a connection to her through the things and the places and the people she knew and loved. How can you even think of leaving her behind?'

That wasn't what she'd meant, but when she tried to formulate the words to explain herself, she wasn't sure they'd ever existed. Still, two days later, she couldn't stop thinking about the Botsfords' new bid for freedom. And she wasn't the only one dwelling on it. Helen had been in touch yesterday, still upset about the break-up of the group.

'Of course they must do what they think is best for them,' she kept saying. 'But I think they're making a mistake. We need each other, all of us. We need each other's support. Out there they'll be completely alone.'

Now it was Monday, mid-afternoon, and Emma was still thinking about the whole thing as she attempted to tidy the kitchen in advance of the girls' return from school. There was a time she'd have baked cakes or biscuits for them, so that they'd arrive back to the delicious smell of fresh-from-the-oven Victoria Sponge or trays of cookies oozing melted chocolate. But now it was as much as she could do to remember they were due and have a superficial clear-up, quickly stacking breakfast bowls in the dishwasher and wiping milk from the worktops.

She was just folding an empty cereal carton ready for the recycling when the landline rang. Emma hesitated. Usually the landline meant one of their parents, hers or Guy's, all four of whom still clung to the notion of mobiles being for emergency use only. Either that or a cold-caller. PPI, double-glazing or someone asking if she'd had an accident at work. Still, it might be the school. Something to do with one of the girls. Maybe Ceci's mum, Nancy, had forgotten it was her turn to do the school run. But when she finally located the phone – why was the cordless never where it was supposed to be – it was Denise, Guy's Australian PA.

'I've been trying his mobile,' she apologized, 'but it's switched off. And the broker he was supposed to be seeing tomorrow morning has just pitched up. Apparently they changed the time. Only Guy's obviously forgotten. He said he had to go home to sort out some stuff. Is he there?'

Emma found herself looking around the empty hallway, as if Guy might after all turn out to be at home.

'No, sorry. Did he say what he needed to sort out?'

'No, I don't think so, but he left forty minutes ago, so he ought to be there by now.'

'Sorry,' Emma said again. It sounded so inadequate.

Still Denise stayed on the line, and Emma got the distinct impression there was something else she wanted to say.

'Is everything OK?' Emma asked eventually, unable to stand the silence.

'Yes, fine, absolutely. It's just . . .'

'Just?'

'Well, Guy's been going early a lot recently, and I simply wanted to make sure everything was all right. With Caitlin and Jemima, I mean.'

'Well, of course it is.'

Emma hadn't meant for her voice to come out quite so sharp. She found it so hard these days to moderate herself.

'Thanks, Denise. Guy's just been finding it easier to work in his study at home at the moment. You know how it is.'

After Denise had hung up, Emma remained with the phone cradled in her hand, staring into space. Since Tilly's death, Guy had often left the office early, getting home at around five so he could spend time with the girls before catching up on work in the evening. It was one of the perks of being a partner, she supposed. But according to Denise he had now started leaving even earlier – at quarter to three. Yet he wasn't coming home. So where was he?

For a few seconds, her husband's lost hours shimmered softly in Emma's mind like a heat haze. Then reality kicked in. An affair.

At first she couldn't tell how she felt about this new revelation.

She had to turn the thing over and over in her head, searching for a reaction until finally one suggested itself.

She was jealous. But not in the way wives were supposed to be jealous.

Guy had something in his life he felt about strongly enough to lie. He had something outside of all this. Outside of the house with its memories and its oppressive silences that cushioned the airless rooms, outside of this little world where they would always remain The Parents Who'd Lost a Child. He had a separate life that didn't revolve solely around grief and guilt. For a moment, she was immobilized with longing, just imagining how such a thing might feel.

And then came the crushing despair. Was there to be no one to share with her the burden of living without Tilly? Then she remembered that she and Guy weren't really sharing it, and that they were each quite alone, despite the other. And now she was enraged rather than despairing. So he had found someone to off-load on. No wonder he had been so dismissive when she talked about escaping their lives as the Botsfords were about to do. He had already found his escape right here.

Yet even through her anger she had to acknowledge her own culpability. She had closed herself off from him long before he followed suit. She remembered how he used to beg her to talk to him, to hold him, and how she tried to explain that she couldn't, that Tilly's death had opened up a hole inside her through which her feelings had drained out until all she had left was the trickle she kept for Jemima and Caitlin. After that he'd given up trying.

So maybe she shouldn't blame him, and yet she did. How could he leave her to suffer alone?

Still torn between rage and despondency, she found herself moving towards her handbag.

Reaching into the zipped-up inside pocket, her fingers closed around the photograph. She'd promised herself she'd put it away for good after spending chunks of time lost in a trance, gazing at it with unseeing eyes. But something about it kept pulling her back. The picture of Tilly in her painting overall, her lips rounded into a perfect 'O' as if in the act of relating something important, if only Emma could hear it, her hair held in two perfectly symmetrical bunches by the thick yellow, red and orange bands, at exactly the same level.

'They have to match, Mummy. If things don't match I feel funny all day . . .'

Emma put the photograph down on the very same blond-wood table where Tilly had been pictured. Then she leaned forward until her forehead was resting on it and closed her eyes until the world went away.

14

The thing Sally hated about staying in hotels – well, one of the things – was that one got so bored with one's clothes. She'd packed expecting the weather to break. Well, whoever heard of a whole week of sustained heat in this country? But she'd already been at the hotel five nights and still it was sweltering, with the result that she'd worn to death both the blue shift dress and the lemon-yellow spaghetti-strap one that she usually teamed with a cream jacket to give it a bit of gravitas. And so here she was in the garden of a historic pub by Hampstead Heath, wearing a long-sleeved, oyster-coloured top and feeling like she was being broiled alive.

Daniel Purvis was late and it was becoming harder and harder to keep his seat from the beady-eyed drinkers circling the tables, waiting to pounce the minute one became free. Though it was a Tuesday evening, the place was packed with the after-work crowd, drawn by the large beer garden. She'd already turned two people away, their eyebrows dipped in disapproval when she announced, 'I'm saving it for a friend.'

She wasn't sure she'd recognize him. After all, it was four years since she'd watched him and his ex-wife, Helen, hosting that emotional press conference that had kick-started this whole thing. Who could have foreseen then that Megan's disappearance would be only the first act in what was turning out to be a prolific serial-killing spree?

She'd tried to interview Daniel at the time, but he'd refused to have anything to do with the press. As far as she knew the relationship between the exes was as amicable as these things get. Simon Hewitt had been dismissive the couple of times the subject had come up between them but that was only to be expected. So she'd been greatly surprised when she'd picked up her phone the previous day to find a call from the office to say that Daniel Purvis was trying to get hold of her.

Finally she spotted him, lurking by the gate from the car park, scanning the crowds with a helpless, lost air. She jumped up but didn't dare wave for fear she might have damp patches under her arms. Instead she shouted his name. As he approached she came up with a quick mental description, as she always did automatically now, filing the details away in case she should need to slot him into a piece at some future time. Tallish, skinny, older than Helen and Simon, early fifties? Crumpled linen shirt, khaki chinos, pink face that really ought to be kept out of the sun. Rimless glasses that lent his face a hard, bureaucratic look, longish greying hair, receding and hanging in sweat-slicked strands, nylon man-bag slung over one shoulder.

'Daniel? How lovely to meet you. Yes, it is warm, isn't it? Inside? Well, of course, if it's too hot for you out here.'

As she gathered up her things to head into the pub, the first tier of loitering drinkers jostled for position behind her like runners at a starting line.

Once seated in the cool, near-empty interior, nursing half a lager, Daniel Purvis seemed strangely disinclined to speak. He kept glancing around as if he'd never been inside a pub before.

'What's on your mind, Daniel?' she prompted him eventually

after they'd discussed the unusual weather until there was nothing further to say on the matter.

His face, already pink from the sun, flushed dusky rose.

'I wanted to know,' he began, staring furiously at the coaster he'd just picked up and was holding lightly between his surprisingly elegant fingers. 'I want to know what you think about Simon Hewitt.'

Oh. She hadn't been expecting that.

'Why is that important?' she asked, playing for time.

'Look. I know you had a thing with him, but I don't give a shit about that – although, frankly, I question your taste. I just need to know what you think about him. I need to know if you think he could be . . .'

Daniel's voice dried up and he seemed to be struggling to finish his sentence.

'Could be what, Daniel?'

'Dangerous.'

'What?'

'To children. Do you think he could be dangerous to children.'

Sally very nearly spat out her mouthful of gin and tonic. *Dangerous to children.* It was absurd.

'Look, I know you'll think this is just sour grapes because he's married to my ex, but, really, they're welcome to each other. I've a good life now, thank you very much. Peaceful.'

'So what's brought this on then?'

'I found a letter. From him to Megan. Hidden in one of Megan's magazines at my place. She used to collect these comics. I'd give her one every time she came to stay. You know the kind of thing, with free gifts on the front – plastic bracelets and so on. It was our thing that we did together. Anyway, the other day I decided it was time I started clearing out her room. I picked up the stack of comics and noticed there was one where she'd filled in a wordsearch on the back. So that made me stop and start leafing through it to see if she'd written anything else. You can't imagine what it feels like to find a new connection with your child, even if it's only some words they scribbled in felt pen.

'That's when I found the letter, tucked inside one of the comics.'

'But the police must have searched your house.'

'Flat. Helen took the house after the divorce. I had to accept a slight drop in living standards.'

Aha, so there was bitterness under the supposedly peaceful, civilized surface.

'Of course they searched the place, but they can't have done it that thoroughly.'

'So what did the letter say?'

Daniel began turning the cardboard coaster over and over between his fingers. Sally saw his eyes dart towards his nylon bag.

'It's in there, isn't it? Can I see?'

Excitement fizzed in the bottom of her stomach, as it always did when a story threatened to catch light.

Her companion looked uncomfortable and placed a protective hand on the bag.

'I don't think that would be . . . appropriate. It's private and you're, well, you're a journalist. I don't want to get the police involved because chances are it's all completely innocent, and much as Simon Hewitt isn't exactly my best mate, he is my son's stepfather and it's taken us a long time to get to some sort of *entente*.'

Entente? And he'd used a proper French accent as well. Daniel Purvis was like a parody of a middle-aged academic, she decided, with his too-long hair and his crumpled shirt, tossing foreign words into the conversation so casually. And he was clearly cautious by nature.

'So what exactly were you hoping for from me, Daniel?'

She leaned forward so he had no option but to meet her eyes and see how frank and open and positively pulsating with intelligence she was. The sort of person you could trust with family secrets. Also it gave him a good view of her cleavage, which couldn't hurt.

He looked away, finding something suddenly fascinating in his drink.

'I thought someone outside the family, a third party so to speak, might be able to give an impartial opinion as to whether he might be capable of . . .'

Daniel's voice tailed off wretchedly, and Sally found herself losing patience. Still, she had to play this game carefully.

She ran a finger absently around the rim of her gin and tonic, as if lost in thought.

'Are you asking whether in my opinion Simon Hewitt is a normal, red-blooded male?'

Daniel nodded eagerly, relieved not to have to spell out what he was implying.

Sally pretended to consider this carefully.

'I'm more than happy to tell you whatever I know, obviously. I'll do anything that might shed some light on this terrible case and bring us closer to finding the killer. However, I would need to have a quick glimpse of the letter afterwards, just to reassure myself there's nothing that ought to be shown to the police. I could never forgive myself if I made their job even harder.'

Sally was quite pleased with herself for how this sounded, but one look at Daniel Purvis's sceptical face left her in no doubt as to his interpretation of what she'd just said.

'Fine. I'll show it to you. To satisfy your *conscience*.'

Now she had promised to talk, Sally struggled to think of what she to say. Had Simon Hewitt shown any signs of deviant behaviour? Had he suggested she might dress up as a schoolgirl or call him Daddy? Her memory wasn't perfect, but as far as she could remember Simon had been very much a 'meat and two veg' kind of lover. Nothing unexpected, nothing out of the ordinary. Both occasions had taken place in the hotel where she'd stayed while she was covering the Tilly Reid murder. Naturally one didn't catalogue these things, but she was fairly sure it had just been the usual ten minutes of hot and heavy foreplay followed by the same length of anti-climax. Twenty minutes in bed and then suddenly you're standing side by side in the bathroom unable to meet each other's eyes in the mirror. It was the depressing reality of most of her romantic encounters.

For a few seconds, she thought about telling Daniel Purvis a slightly different story. Not lying, but just leaving some things open to misinterpretation. There always was that temptation, wasn't there, to big up one's own part in a news story. She came across it all the time. But she wanted to win this man's trust. Who knew what other information he could be holding? Plus after her seriously misjudged *thing* with Simon Hewitt, she didn't want to give Helen Purvis any more reason to hate her, as she would if it should come out that Sally had slandered her husband as well as bedded him. And there was that nagging shred of loyalty. One didn't sleep with a man and then feel absolutely nothing for him afterwards. One had standards, even if sometimes it was hard to remember what they were.

So, after extracting from him a promise of secrecy, she explained to a clearly uncomfortable Daniel more or less how things had been between her and Simon, without getting either graphic or emotional. In fact, if anyone had been eavesdropping they might have imagined a different subject of conversation entirely, so obliquely did she describe what had taken place – some kind of sporting activity perhaps, a hobby that, luckily, hadn't taken too extreme a turn.

The man in the creased linen shirt listened with his head to one side, as if half hoping the sound of her voice would travel clear over his shoulder without ever properly entering his ears. Finally he sighed deeply.

'In that case,' he said, 'I think it best not to make waves by contacting the police. My situation vis-à-vis my ex-wife is still rather delicate. I wouldn't like to jeopardize it by starting scurrilous rumours.'

'Very sensible.' If Sally nodded any more fervently her head was in danger of coming loose. 'However, I'd feel much better if I could just reassure myself by having a quick peek at the letter.'

Daniel reached for his bag, spending what Sally considered to be an unnecessarily long time struggling with the zip. She stifled her impatience watching him rifle through the papers in his manbag. What did he have in there anyway? Finally he withdrew a piece of paper – A4, unlined. But even now he was reluctant to hand it over.

'Do I have your word that this is absolutely one hundred per cent off the record?'

'Of course. If that's what you want.'

If there was one phrase in the English language that Sally would ban it would be 'off the record'. People imagined it gave them all sorts of power, whereas in reality it was as meaningless as the right to make a citizen's arrest. Fine in theory, but just try putting it to the test.

The letter was written in a fine blue felt-tipped pen, in cramped, messy writing that struggled to stay in straight lines. There was a date at the top: 10 March 2010. Sally did a brief mental calculation before working out this would have been two months before Megan was killed. She started reading:

Dear Megan,
I know we had a rocky start, but I like to think that we've become mates, and mates look out for each other, don't they? Which is why I'm asking you to keep our secret, just like I'd keep a secret of yours. You know how unhappy your mum was before I came along and I know you wouldn't want her to be sad again, would you? Not for something that was a mistake. Sometimes people do silly things when

they're drunk. Let's put it behind us and focus on good things – like that pony you're desperate for! Something tells me that particular dream might come true sooner than you think!

   Lots of love,
   Your mate Simon

Foreboding prickled at the back of Sally's neck as she finished the letter. She read it through a second time, hoping she might see an innocent explanation, but she felt even grubbier than before. Not that it proved anything about Simon and Megan, but he'd obviously done something seriously awful to warrant the blatant bribe at the end. She shuddered. She'd been a pretty lamentable judge of character when it came to men, but this could take the biscuit.

'Well?' Daniel wanted to know. 'Do you think there's anything sinister in it? Do I risk involving the police?'

Sally shook her head. Once the police knew about this letter, word would get out and she'd lose her head start. Obviously if there'd been the slightest bit of concrete evidence incriminating Simon Hewitt, she'd absolutely have told Daniel Purvis to hand over the letter. No one wanted to put any more little girls at risk. But this was so nebulous. It could mean anything. And she wanted to protect the Purvis family after all they'd been through. Far better for her to do some private digging and find out what had been going on.

'You're right to hold back,' she told Daniel. 'Whatever this secret was, I'm sure it was harmless – maybe he owed someone money and she found out, or he kissed someone at a party and Megan saw. You know how little girls can blow things out of proportion. Holding on to the letter is the right thing to do. Helen and Rory have been through enough.'

15

Desmond had on his Solemn Face today. It was one of Leanne's least favourites.

'Sir. If there's been a leak, it hasn't come from me.'

'I wasn't implying that it had, Leanne. I was merely pointing out that someone has been tipping off the press about aspects of this case that need to be kept confidential. Today's *Chronicle* mentions a DNA sample taken from the spot where Poppy Glover's body was found. How did they know that? The entire investigation could be compromised if this continues. I'm just asking you to be extra guarded in what you say, and to check that other people are being guarded too.'

Leanne could feel her cheeks flushing pink as if she really was guilty, and cursed her Irish heritage which had bequeathed her both the pale skin, which worked like litmus paper to broadcast her emotions, and her enhanced sense of Catholic guilt, which meant she felt responsible even for actions she'd had no part in.

'Anyway, that wasn't what I called you in here to talk about.' Desmond leaned back in his chair and made a steeple out of his fingers before resting them on his mouth in a reflective pose. 'I wanted to have this little catch-up to give you a heads-up before I tell the rest of the team. We've got a new lead.'

Now he had Leanne's full attention. They'd had leads enough over the years – sex offenders who'd made dramatic confessions only for it to be revealed they were nowhere near North London when the murders took place, a convincing woman who swore it was her husband before retracting the accusation when he finally agreed to sign the divorce papers. But those had been nearer the beginning of the investigation. In recent months, there'd been very little credible new information.

'Reliable intelligence has reached us of a paedophile ring with a particular fascination with the case.'

'With all respect, sir, I imagine there are quite a few paedophile rings who are getting off on the details of this case.' Leanne didn't even try to disguise her disgust.

'No. This ring's interest is obsessive – to the extent of knowing things that haven't yet been made public.'

Leanne raised her eyebrows.

'We think there's a chance these bastards might be directly involved in the crimes somehow, but so far it's all second-hand information. This gang is like the Bilderberg Group – so clandestine none of our sources have managed to infiltrate it.'

Desmond smiled when he referred to the Bilderberg Group – the world's most powerful secret society – and Leanne got the feeling this wasn't the first time he'd used the analogy.

'What kind of things do they know?'

'How long the most recent body was there before the police arrived, what she had on. That sort of thing.'

Leanne closed her eyes. If this was the work of a group of men, not just a lone nutter, it was far worse than any of them had imagined. One loose cannon was bound to slip up sooner or later, but a sophisticated gang? Even if they caught one of them, there were still God knows how many more of them out there. Leanne had been to psychologists' talks about paedophilia and the profile of a paedophile. She knew there were no monsters in real life, just people who'd been dealt shitty cards and had grown up believing that's how life was. She knew that if you grew up feeling powerless sooner or later you'd seek out someone even more powerless than you to repeat the cycle. She knew all that and yet when she saw the damage adults did to children in the name of self-gratification, when she heard the testimony from young girls, their shoulders already hunched with self-loathing, or toddlers, still struggling with vocabulary for everyday objects, having to learn the words for things they shouldn't even know existed, all this washed the logic and the teaching and the understanding clear from her mind so all that was left was hatred and revulsion and a primal desire for retribution.

Back at her desk, she glanced around before calling Will. Listening to the ringtone, she pictured him in his cramped central London office, his desk piled high with books and papers and invites to product launches and PR parties.

'Hello you.'

'Hello you too.'

Instantly she felt the knots in her stomach loosening. It was something about his voice, the way it softened when he spoke to her as if she were some kind of honey it was coating itself in.

'They think I'm telling you stuff.'

'Well, sweetheart, it'd be a bit odd if you weren't. We do virtually live together.'

'About the investigation. There's been a leak and they think it's me.'

'Ach. That's tough. You're an easy target, Lee. They've got to find someone to blame.'

'Yes, but why me?'

She was aware she was whining now, but it felt good. Sometimes it really got to her, dealing with the kind of things she dealt with day in, day out. Women with bruises bigger than their faces and cigarette burns on their chests and wide scared eyes, swearing blind they'd walked into cupboards or seared their own skin. Old men mugged for their pensions, skin mottled from fear and humiliation. Leanne coped with it. That's what she was trained for. She interviewed and processed and took statements and recorded and filed, and most of the time she wasn't even aware of it bothering her. But then she'd get home and talk to Will and out it would come – all the horror and anger and disgust and revulsion – and just for once it would be about how *she* felt and about how it affected *her*. And she'd revel in the luxury of being allowed to have feelings and be human.

'You're good at your job, sweetheart. It's not surprising some of the others get jealous and want to dig the knife in.'

Leanne exhaled the long breath she hadn't even been aware of holding in, relaxed so that her shoulders were halfway down the chair back, and let Will's voice roll over her like a gentle wave. From the corner of her eye she noticed a small knot of colleagues had gathered around a desk on the far side of the room. They were making quite a lot of noise, then all of a sudden a great bark of laughter went up. She frowned and straightened up trying to get a glimpse of what was so amusing. A phone rang and someone stepped away to answer it, leaving a gap in the circle through which she could just make out a familiar figure.

Pete. Well of course it would be. Centre of attention. As always.

Will was talking to her about the holiday they had booked for September. Two weeks in Majorca. She couldn't wait. They'd spent a whole Sunday on the internet poring over photos of hotels with vast turquoise infinity pools and empty sandy coves before finally picking a place in the north-west of the island that had a

126

path from the hotel garden leading directly to the beach. As he talked, Leanne avoided looking over to the other side of the room. Finally she glanced that way, to see Pete looking directly at her. He raised an arm in greeting.

Leanne immediately turned her head away as if she hadn't seen.

16

The first text came when Rory was at lunch, which was a charitable name for a selection of soggy bread-based products with a smattering of wilted lettuce. At least in the old pre-Jamie Oliver days there used to be chips and pizza and stuff. Not exactly healthy, Rory knew that, but at least you knew they were unhealthy. He was biting into a panini with the exact texture of wet cardboard when his phone beeped with an incoming text.

'You got a new girlfriend, Pervy?'

Rory gave a mock smile to Jack M. sitting to his right, and inwardly cursed his stupid surname and the nickname it had gifted. Thanks, Dad.

Thinking about his dad made him feel anxious as always. He didn't understand how it was possible for kids to feel responsible for their parents, yet somehow he did. He got that his dad had been a dick and had left his mum to live with someone he worked with and it had all been a huge horrible crying mess. He got that. And then the thing with the other woman hadn't worked out, but by then his mum had met Simon and so his dad had ended up with no one, living in a crappy rented flat where you couldn't even put posters on the walls in case the Blu-Tack left marks. His dad was like a weight he carried around with him. And since Megan wasn't there any more there was no one to share it with.

He slipped his phone out of his pocket and pretended to study it until his irritation passed, then finally he clicked on the flashing envelope icon. He hated his phone. All his friends had iPhones but his mum insisted it was too risky for him to walk around with £400-worth of kit on him.

In his inbox, he saw a 'withheld number' message. He got a lot of texts from withheld or unknown numbers. People asking if he needed help repaying a loan, or if he'd had an accident at work, or taken out payment-protection insurance. As soon as he clicked on the message, he realized it wasn't one of those.

How does it feel to know you killed your sister?

His heart froze inside his chest.

'Come on, Pervy. Who's texting ya? You got a new girlfriend?'

'Nah, man, just some bell-end trying to sell me something.'

Jack M. seemed satisfied with that and the conversation quickly moved on to Jessie Campbell's party this coming weekend and whether Archie's fake ID would work at the local Londis. But even while he was joining in with the others, the inside of Rory's chest was tightening and tightening until he felt his words were being squeezed out through a straw. What did it mean, that text? How did he kill Megan? Why would anyone say that? IT WASN'T HIS FAULT! Everyone said that. The fucking therapist had said it so many times Rory thought he probably heard it in his sleep. He'd only looked away for a minute. And he shouldn't even have been in charge of a seven-year-old. He was only twelve at the time. That's what oldies did. They put you in charge of things when it suited them even though you said you didn't want to, telling you that's how you learned responsibility, and then when something went wrong they blamed you even though you never wanted to do it in the first place.

But it hadn't been his fault. He'd turned away for a minute, well, maybe a couple of minutes. At most. And when he looked back she'd gone. And afterwards he'd gone crazy trying to find her.

How does it feel to know you killed your sister?

The thing was, it wasn't the first text he'd received. They'd started a year or so ago, always from a withheld number. *Murderer*, the first one had said. He ignored it, half imagining it was meant for someone else. Then a couple of months later there'd been another one: *You killed your sister.* This time there was no doubting it was meant for him. He thought about showing it to his mum, but he knew it would cause such a fuss and he found he didn't have the energy. She'd want to get the police involved. She might even start going through the rest of the messages on his phone and that would be a disaster beyond all measure. So he'd kept quiet. And when more messages had dribbled into his inbox every few weeks, he'd kept quiet about those too, because by then it would have been too difficult to explain. But every time he opened one, he experienced that same split-second feeling of vertigo and vomit-inducing plummeting of the stomach.

The one time he'd cracked and tried to bring them up with his mum – not being specific but just saying he'd had a nasty comment – she'd been sympathetic but distracted and had suggested he just switch his phone off. *Switch your phone off.* Like that was going to happen.

All through double maths, he kept playing with his phone in his pocket, and when Mr Whitman tossed the whiteboard rubber at Sam P. and hit Maisie instead and she said, 'Fuck sake, sir,' Rory didn't even smile.

Walking home with the usual crowd, he was distracted to the point where someone asked him if he was ill. By the time he turned into his road, he'd come to a momentous decision. He was going to tell his mother about the text. Bearing in mind he'd rather eat his own arm than willingly confide in her, this was an indication of the fucked-upness of his state of mind.

But as he let himself into the house, he felt instantly that familiar heaviness in the air he remembered from the time after Megan's death. His steps slowed as if his trainers were suddenly made of lead. His mum hadn't been herself for days, since that stupid meeting on Saturday. He didn't know why she put herself through it. Put them all through it. Still, at least now that the Botsfords were leaving the whole Megan's Angels thing might simply fizzle out.

After checking that his mum wasn't in the kitchen, Rory crept up the stairs, feeling a prickling sense of déjà vu. After Megan died there had been months and months where he'd come home from school and walked straight into a wall of unhappiness, just like this.

As soon as he reached the first-floor landing, he could tell his mum was in the bedroom she shared with Simon. The *master* bedroom. That phrase still made him snort inside. When he'd first heard it, he'd still been in his *Doctor Who*-fanatic phase and had been convinced the Doctor's arch-rival had a room in his house. If it was empty, the door was always wide open as his mum insisted on letting the daylight from the bedroom windows flood into their windowless landing, but now it was pulled almost shut. Rory stood at the top of the stairs and took his phone out of his pocket, ready to show his mum the text. He was determined to talk to her about it this time. He was about to call out to let her know he was there when the most awful sound went up inside the room. A horrible wailing sound like foxes make in the night. He stopped still, rigid from shock and embarrassment.

'I'm sorry,' came his mum's voice, only it wasn't his mum's voice, it was a wrung-out, twisted version of his mum's voice. 'I'm so sorry.'

He froze. She mustn't know he was there. Rory remembered

all too vividly that period where she'd spend whole days up in her room like this, curled around a photograph of Megan, apologizing again and again and again, for not being there to pick her up, for not finding her in time, for allowing it all to happen. It used to drive him crazy.

He returned his phone silently to his pocket, intent now on leaving without being heard. The last thing he wanted was a sob-fest with his mother. He retraced his steps down the stairs and went silently into the living room where he exhaled loudly.

Throwing himself down on to the sofa, he retrieved his phone. Even though he'd seen it so many times now, when he called up the text he tensed as if anticipating a punch. He read it through again, and then a second time.

His finger hovered over the trash-can icon.

'Rory,' came his mother's misery-soaked voice from the floor above. 'Are you home?'

He pressed delete.

17

'I want to see her. You can't stop me seeing her. I'm her father! I have rights.'

'Don't you think you lost them when you did what you did? Don't you think you lost all your rights when you did that, you sick fuck? You agreed. You agreed to stay gone.'

Jason took a deep breath and counted to ten. He'd been doing a lot of work on himself recently. Everyone needed to take a good hard look at themselves from time to time, that's what he thought. See what could be improved. Sometimes when he walked around the city centre and saw the state people allowed themselves to get into – rolls of fat squeezed into leggings and tight tops. Or late at night when he saw the slags on Oxford Street, staggering around drunk with their false eyelashes hanging off and their hair extensions all matted, or when he walked past a burger place and saw the rows of lardy, spotty blokes in the windows stuffing their faces with handfuls of those limp stringy chips. Didn't they know they sprayed those things with chemical crap before frying them? Didn't they know what they were doing to their insides? Sometimes when he saw all this, for a moment or two he thought he understood those people in America who pick up a gun and walk around shooting indiscriminately, full of despair and rage against these pathetic creatures with their cellulite and their bad teeth and their total lack of will-power. It was practically mercy-killing.

But him, he worked on himself. He knew his own weak points and he put in a lot of effort to improve them. His temper had got him into trouble all his life, so he'd been working on that. Anger-management classes. Not the courses the courts made you go on to avoid a prison sentence if you'd done a number on someone. He knew people who'd been on those and come home and punched through walls with frustration at having to go back. He'd done it properly. Proper shrink, £75 an hour. Control. That's what he was after. That's how come he was able to not rise to it when she called him a sick fuck.

'Look, Donna, this isn't about you. It's about Keira and what's right for her. And it's right for her to see her dad. Kids need their fathers.'

That was the way. Calm, reasonable. Even though he could feel that ball of hot rage building in his gut, he wasn't going to let it get to him. He was in control of the situation, just like he'd been taught.

'You are fucking kidding me, ain'tcha? Are you really going to use the "what's best for Keira" card on me? After everything you did?'

And then suddenly the ball was expanding and growing hotter and hotter until there was nothing he could do but let it burst out of him.

'Look, bitch, Keira is my daughter, right? Mine. Got that? My blood runs in her. She is part of me. You cannot keep her away from me.'

And now he could hear her voice rising to match the shrillness of his own.

'You come anywhere near her and you know what's going to

134

happen. I'm warning you, Jason. I'll go to the police. I'll tell 'em what you did, what you are.'

'With what evidence? And don't forget I'm your cash cow, you dozy bitch. How will you carry on living like a fucking queen if I'm locked away and your money dries up?'

Her breath was coming in sharp rasps that vibrated down the phone, and he could picture how she'd look with her blonde hair all stringy and hanging out of that hideous claw-type clip she always put it in, and her bony fake-tanned chest rising and falling like a set of dried-up leather bellows. She'd have that look in her eyes that used to drive him crazy – scared but defiant. If she'd left it at scared perhaps he wouldn't have got so riled up, but she knew the other look pressed his buttons. That's why she did it. She'd be biting her nails as well, he bet, chewing on the bits of skin around the cuticles until they bled. When her voice finally came, it was screwed up with spite.

'Don't forget there's a restraining order out on you that I know for a fact you've been breaking. Think I haven't seen you out there in your car? You come anywhere near us again and I'll have you banged up, I swear to God. Just leave us alone.'

Afterwards he paced around his flat, unable to settle. He was angry with himself for losing control. After all the exercises he'd been doing, all the practice. But who could blame him? Keira was his daughter, his flesh and blood. Donna had no right. Thinking about his ex brought bile to his mouth. The way when she opened her mouth she smelled of old ashtrays even though she swore she'd given up the fags. He knew she didn't have the will-power. The way she used to undress at night with a sly look as she took off her bra as if she thought she was making him hot, as if she thought she had some kind of control over him. Her controlling *him*! The way she'd tried to please him in those early years, the little presents – a bottle of aftershave here, a bracelet there (engraved with both their names, of course).

When did those gifts dry up? Somewhere around their second year together? Third?

He'd tried. Jason had always hated to admit he'd made a mistake. He knew that about himself. It was one of the other things he was working on. So he'd tried long after it became obvious he was flogging a dead horse, long after he realized she'd tricked him at the start of their relationship by putting forward a version of herself that wasn't real – and by the time he cottoned on, Keira was on her way and it was too late. That was the thing about women. They weren't ever who they pretended to be. They were like cheap gold jewellery: scratch the surface and underneath the shiny stuff it was ugly old tin. And the older they got, the more tarnished. Donna hadn't been like that when they first got together. She'd had something about her, a sparkle. But now she was all twisted up like a dirty old dishcloth, just like his mother.

He fired up his laptop looking for some kind of displacement activity like he'd been taught, somewhere to channel all the emotions that bitch had churned up inside him like heartburn.

He was so wound up about Donna that he forgot to be on the alert for news items and when the Yahoo homepage came up, his eye was immediately drawn to the headlines: KENWOOD KILLER MOTHER'S ANGUISH. His heart thudded to a stop. He shouldn't read it. He should shut that page down straight away. Yet somehow he couldn't. As he read on, he could feel the sweat prickling on his back and neck, his breath coming out in shallow pants. He wouldn't think about it, shouldn't think about it. He'd made a pact with himself to seal those memories off, to think of that man as someone else, so he'd never give himself away. Only when lying in bed late at night did he allow himself to relive what had happened. But now here they were let loose and flying at him too fast to stop them. The smell of apple shampoo on clean, shiny hair that had never been wrecked by chemical dyes. The softness of skin that had never been allowed to shrivel up in the sun. The salty taste of another person's fear. The power pumping through his body, the dizzying knowledge that he could do whatever he wanted to someone else.

And now the blood was pumping everywhere, engorging him until it felt like he was going to explode. But along with the excitement of the forbidden memories, the headlines also brought the usual anger. As he read through this most recent story, Jason was assailed by a sense of helpless rage that he knew from bitter experience would linger for hours. Between that and the conversation with Donna, he'd have to spend twice as long in the gym today trying to work off some of the frustration he felt, before heading off to the City and the club where he worked. People fucked you over. That was the truth of it. They fucked you over, and the only way to survive was to fuck them over first. That's why you had to get them young, before they had a chance to turn cynical and hard, and start looking for ways to take advantage. When there was still a chance to make your mark.

His stomach was still churning when his phone dinged, advising him of an incoming text. Seeing Suzy's name flash up soothed him, reminding him that he was still in control. The last date had been amazing!! said her message (winking face). She couldn't WAIT for the next one!! She knew Bethany would JUMP at the chance of going bowling after school tomorrow. Normally she wouldn't introduce her daughter to a new bloke so early on, but she felt she'd known him for AGES. His sister was SOOOOO NICE to give them her booking, and wish her better very soon!! Smiley face, smiley face, face with tongue flopping out of the side of its mouth.

He was proud of himself for the work he'd been putting in with Suzy over the last few days – two dates and endless calls and texts. And now it was paying off. He was going to meet Bethany at last. That story about his non-existent sister who'd paid for a bowling session she now couldn't use had done the trick. Once again he called up the picture of the girl and tried to push those other memories to the back of his head. He wouldn't think about blood matted in shiny hair, or clear blue eyes turning filmy like old milk. It was just a question of will-power. He could do that. He was the better man.

18

The pills are all that keep me going. I love the popping noise they make as they burst through their foil containers. I love the feel of them between my fingers, the promise of oblivion. Oliver has started hiding them from me. He doesn't like the way I reach for them before I'm even fully awake, wanting only to be sent straight back to sleep again. He doesn't like how Mia stands by the side of the bed, shaking my arm. 'Wake up, Mummy. Wake up.' She wants to know where her sister is. 'In a fridge,' I tell her, and Oliver snatches her away.

This time last week I complained of being tired, but I had no idea of what tired meant. I thought tired was sleeping five hours instead of eight or being woken up at one by a seven-year-old's nightmare and then again at five by a teething toddler. I had no idea about the kind of tiredness you feel in your very bones. The tiredness that makes words die unsaid in your mouth and everything impossible – standing, sitting. Breathing.

This time last week I met a friend for coffee after school drop-off time. Mia was sitting at the table of the café with a plastic beaker full of crayons, the tip of her tongue protruding as she filled sheet after sheet with wild, single-colour drawings, and I was talking, whining, complaining. 'It's not enough, all this. The girls. I need to exercise my mind. I don't feel fulfilled.' As if fulfilment were a right. As if Poppy and Mia were holding me back.

This time last week I got up in the morning and cared about my reflection in the mirror, got out the tweezers to pluck stray hairs from my eyebrows, put on mascara even just to take Poppy to school. When I pulled on my jeans, I minded that they had toothpaste drips on the leg and I got out a clean T-shirt because it mattered enough to make the trip from bed to chest of drawers and then to open a drawer and select.

This time last week I thought pills were for people who gave up too easily, who looked for an external fix to internal problems. When I had a headache I held out against paracetamol until my whole brain was throbbing. When Poppy was ill antibiotics were a very last resort. I slid the foil sheet out with mistrust as if the box contained a dangerous wild animal not a mild pharmaceutical aid. Now I stack the pill packets high on the bedside table, so they're the first thing I see when I claw my way groggily out of sleep. And if the stack is low, I feel a clanging anxiety building in my chest, my heart bouncing in my ribcage like a rubber ball in a box. Because if the stack gets too low, and the foil wraps are all empty, their contents popped, then there is nowhere to go but inside my own head, and that's the place I cannot bear to be. The pills keep me outside of myself. They keep me in this bed. They keep me away from the door that leads to the hall that leads to the empty room with the ceramic 'P' on the door and the piece of paper where the words 'Mia Keep Out!' are scrawled in thick red capitals.

I pop another one out from its blister pack, loving the purity of the white capsule, and then I pop one more for luck. Oliver will count them when he comes back and his mouth will tighten into a thin line as it does when he is annoyed.

A week ago he woke me in the morning to have groggy,

half-conscious sex and I was half resentful of the precious lost sleep and he kissed my stale-breathed mouth and said, 'You shouldn't be so damn gorgeous then.'

I clutch the extra pill in the palm of my hand like a good-luck charm as I slip gratefully back into the void.

19

The woman had that particular hard-faced, red-raw look that comes from a combination of self-abuse and disappointment. Her bleached hair was pulled tightly back from her face, stretching the skin thin over her cheekbones and exposing a good half-inch of dark roots at the temples. When she'd first walked in, Leanne had put her at around forty, but now she could see she was much younger than that. Early thirties, maybe even less. Some people's lives were ironed directly on to their skin, Leanne often thought. Growing up on a rough estate in Kent, she'd met a lot of women who looked like Donna Shields. Funny how when she told people where she was from they always said how lovely it must have been to grow up on the coast, whereas the truth was the nearest beach was four miles away and without a car it might as well have been four hundred. If you were lucky you got out, like Leanne. If you weren't, you ended up looking like Donna Shields.

'I still don't understand, Mrs Shields, why you believe your ex-husband is linked to these murders.'

Ever since the first murder, there'd been a steady stream of women just like this one presenting themselves at police-station receptions to accuse husbands, stepfathers, brothers, even sons.

They fitted the bill. They'd never been 'normal'. They were perverted, ill, dangerous, evil. They needed to be locked up. It was
only a week since the discovery of Poppy Glover's body, so Leanne
fully expected there'd be another flurry of denunciations. Each
time she dealt with one, Leanne felt another layer of skin grow
over her existing one, until she worried she'd end up with a hide
as thick as some of the older police guys who liked to boast that
nothing could shock them. The day brutality came to seem like
the norm was the day Leanne would hand in her badge and join a
hippie commune somewhere to meditate for world peace.

'He was obsessed with that first murder when we was still
together. Spent hours every day on the computer going through all
them newspapers. Even the ones he never read like the *Guardian*,
which he said was a socialist rag.'

'Didn't you ask him why?'

'Course I did. At least I did at the beginning, when we was
still talking. He just used it as an excuse to have a go at me. Our
daughter Keira was four then and he said he was just doing what
any concerned parent would do and I was showing myself up as
a bad mum because I didn't care enough. That's what Jason's
like. He twists everything. Except if there's anyone who's twisted
around here, it's him. Do you know what he did, he—'

Leanne held up a hand to stop her and tried to stifle a sigh. It
was always the female officers who got allocated these kinds of
interviews, and it was always like this. Some of these women had
spent months, years, lifetimes tiptoeing around violent, abusive
men, and then the same amount of time gearing themselves
up to reporting them, so when they finally got here, it was like
a dam bursting. Every grievance – some heavy-duty, many petty
– every misdemeanour, every harsh word, every beating, every
mistress, every sexual perversion. Every single disappointment
and heartbreak and put-down and slap, every bruise and black
eye and 'walked into a cupboard'. Every lie, every dashed dream,

every time you locked yourself in the bathroom and ran the taps to disguise your sobs, watching the door frame shake with his kicks. All of those things came pouring out while Leanne or whoever else was on duty sat on the other side of the table and tried to corral the flood of words into some kind of structure, a neat box to tick.

'Lots of people read the papers, Mrs Shields. And some people do take a ghoulish interest in the most horrendous crimes. But we can't prosecute anyone for rubbernecking. You must understand that.'

'He touched her. He would have done more if I hadn't caught 'im at it. And after he left, I found there was stuff on our computer. Kids' stuff. Absolutely disgusting. Filthy!'

Leanne held up her hand again. 'Hold on a minute, Mrs Shields. He touched who? Your daughter?'

'No. Her friend. She was on a sleepover. He was in their room. If I hadn't come in—'

'Did the girl make a complaint?'

The woman looked at her through narrowed eyes as if she wasn't quite all there. 'No, she was asleep, wasn't she?'

'Then how—'

'I told you. I woke up and he wasn't there, and I knew. I just knew. I went into Keira's room and there he was with his hands under the covers.'

'And what did you do?'

'I put the light on, didn't I? Bastard jumped up like someone had shot him. Insisted he'd heard her crying out in her sleep and had come in to check on her and she'd thrown her duvet off so he was putting it back. The girls was both crying their eyes out because we'd woken them up shouting.'

'But you never reported it.'

The woman pressed her thin lips together and shook her head.

'And what about the porn. Child porn, did you say it was? I'm assuming you've kept that.'

144

The woman widened her eyes as if Leanne had just made the most ludicrous suggestion.

'You're kidding, right? As if I'm going to leave that perverted stuff on the computer. My daughter uses that! Anyway, we don't even have that computer no more. Had to sell it when we split up. I wasn't exactly left well provided for. In fact, he said he'd stop paying altogether if I came to see you lot.'

'So, just to get this straight, you've got no evidence against your ex-husband, Mrs Shields. Just that he showed a particular interest in the case when you were together.'

Donna Shields leaned back in her chair rubbing together her thumbs and fingers with their glued-on nails as if rolling an invisible cigarette. She still looked scornful, but at the same time the slump of her shoulders indicated defeat.

'I knew you lot wouldn't take me seriously. Don't know why I bothered.'

'I'm sorry. We will run a check and make sure there are no other reports against him. And obviously if he breaches his restraining order, you call us immediately.'

The woman looked infuriated now. 'He's always doing that, but by the time you lot turn up, he's long gone.'

'Well, like I say, contact us with any further breaches, but otherwise I'm afraid there's really not a lot else we can do.'

Leanne was already filing away the form she'd been filling in and putting her pen back in the holder on the desk. But still the woman opposite didn't get up. When she finally looked at Leanne, all trace of the earlier bravado was gone.

'I'm scared of him. I'm scared of what he'll do to me and Keira. You don't know what he's like. There's something missing inside him where other people have feelings. He never had no dad and his mum was a bitch, and nothing grew in him, d'you get what I'm saying? He never developed that thing most people have that makes you care how other people feel. I just wanted you to know that. So if another little girl is found with a rope around her neck or her pants around her ankles, or if I wash up with my throat cut, you'll know who it is. Right?'

Afterwards Leanne made her way back to her own desk only to find the normally buzzing open-plan office hushed and everyone facing the front where Desmond stood checking something on his phone.

'What's going on?' Leanne whispered to Ruby Adjaye who occupied the seat to her right.

The other woman rolled her eyes. 'We're awaiting another papal address – one-week review of the Glover investigation, I think. Rumour has it—'

'OK, could I have everyone's attention please.' Desmond held up a hand for quiet. 'Thank you. For the benefit of DC Scott O'Brian and the other two new members of the team, I just wanted to grab five minutes to go over where we are with the Poppy Glover case. Just to recap, the facts of the case are these: Poppy was seven, the same age as Megan Purvis. She and her parents, Susan and Oliver Glover, were picnicking with their younger daughter Mia by the pond on the Heath.'

''Scuse me, sir.'

Leanne bit her lip. She'd worked with Scott O'Brian before and he was a lovely guy, but he had this terrible pedantic streak that meant he was constantly asking pointless questions.

'There are quite a few ponds on Hampstead Heath, aren't there? Which one are we talking about here?'

Desmond consulted with his slight, perpetually nervous deputy, Andy Curtis, who stepped forward to explain.

'Strictly speaking, it's one of the Highgate ponds. The one nearest the Highgate entrance to the Heath. You come down Merton Lane and where it meets Millfield Lane there's an entrance where there's always an ice-cream van parked, and some toilets, and then the pond is just down to your left with

146

a big grassy bank around it where people picnic.'

Now Curtis withdrew, and Desmond resumed, the two changing places with a seamlessness born out of nearly a decade of working together. 'Which is exactly what the Glover family was doing late afternoon last Wednesday. If you remember, it was the day the weather turned fine, the first proper warm day of the year. They'd been there an hour or so when Poppy asked if she could get an ice cream. She wanted to go by herself, to show she was a "big girl", is how her mum put it.'

Desmond made quote marks in the air when he said 'big girl', as if he were translating from a foreign language.

'From the blanket where they were sitting on the slope, the Glovers could see the exit and the ice-cream van perfectly.'

Here Desmond held up his hand.

'It's not our place to judge the rights and wrongs of letting a seven-year-old go off on her own. We'll leave it to the great British public to do that.' They were all aware how hard-lined people could be when it came to other people's parenting. 'Anyway. Mr Glover gave Poppy the money and she went up the slope to join the queue. They could see her the whole time. Mrs Glover swears she never took her eyes off her – until there was some sort of disturbance. A woman standing just ahead of Poppy in the queue found her purse had been snatched and she started yelling and then a crowd gathered around her, and when it parted, Poppy had vanished. That's the last anyone saw of her until her body turned up the next morning.'

'And just to clarify, sir, she'd been sexually assaulted?'

Desmond closed his eyes briefly before responding to Scott O'Brian's question.

'As you all know, we were hoping to keep the details of how the body was found quiet, but somehow they seem to have got out. We all know the body was found on the Heath Extension. For those not familiar with the area, that's a completely separate green area to the north of the main Heath. We're still examining CCTV footage from the road that runs directly around the extension, but the body was found in woodland in the quietest section, which is between cameras. Nonetheless we're hopeful some footage of the car used will turn up and we have people on that as we speak. The body was partially unclothed but according to the pathologist there is no evidence of sexual assault, although traces of semen were found on a dock leaf just a few feet away. And yes, Scott, before you helpfully point it out, it is a departure from the last two victims.'

'But not from the first one.' Leanne stifled a smile when she saw Scott lick his finger and start busily flicking through his notebook. 'Megan Purvis was also found partially unclothed and in that case there was clear evidence of sexual motivation, and semen and other DNA were recovered – if I can just find the place where I wrote down all the details . . .'

'No need, Scott. I think we're all quite familiar with the facts. And I can tell you the lab has now finished comparing the samples of DNA from the Poppy Glover and the Megan Purvis crime scenes, and they are unequivocally not from the same person.'

Leanne's head shot up and something bitter and acidic coursed through her gut. So there was more than one of the bastards. It had always been a possibility, but hearing it spelled out made her feel sick in that part of her she tried not to show at work.

As if he were reading her mind, Desmond carried on: 'This means we're looking for at least two men. Maybe a gang. As some of you might be aware, we've had some intelligence about the existence of an online paedophile forum that has taken a particularly strong interest in this case. That's one of the leads we're following up.

'I don't need to tell you all that it's vital that none of this information goes further than this room. Now, Scott, since you're the one with the answers, perhaps you might suggest what other lines of inquiry we might follow.'

Put on the spot, Scott blushed and looked down at his notebook as if the answer might be written down there.

'Leanne? How about you?'

She might have known he'd pick on her next. One of Desmond's fondest claims was that he liked to 'keep his staff on their toes'. Sometimes, back in the good days, Pete used to pirouette around their flat like a ballerina, shouting, 'Come on, Leanne. On your toes!'

'Well, if the DNA samples don't match, sir, couldn't there be the possibility of a copycat murder?'

'Exactamundo, Leanne. It's pretty rare, thank God, and it would mean that the detail of the "SORRY" written on the leg had somehow got out, either from the families or from the killer himself, but it does happen and we have to cover all the bases.'

After Desmond had gone, Ruby Adjaye leaned across Leanne's desk and whispered, 'Exactamundo, Leanne,' in her ear, which made them both giggle.

'Who was the woman you were interviewing before?' Ruby wanted to know, and Leanne was startled at how completely Donna Shields had slipped from her mind.

'Oh, just another woman wanting to nail her ex for the Kenwood Killings – and probably the Jack the Ripper murders as well while she's at it. Though he does sound like a wrong 'un. I could see she was scared stiff of him, but she had no evidence at all. Only that he was particularly interested in the case, which would make half the bloody country suspects.'

'Worth checking the records, making sure he's not on any registers?'

'Unlikely. She said he'd never been in trouble with the police. He did keep a stash of child porn on the family computer, she claimed, but she deleted it and then sold the computer as well.'

Ruby shrugged. 'Not much you can do then. And like you said, she's hardly the first bitter ex we've had in here, is she? That's why I'm never going to allow Carl to divorce me, in case he starts coming down here pointing the finger at me for every atrocity going.'

'Don't say that,' said Leanne, making a mock scared face. 'Now I know what Pete was up to when he disappeared into Desmond's office with a photo of me and a list of unsolved crimes.'

They both smiled, but for a long time afterwards Leanne couldn't rid herself of the image of Donna Shields with her scraped-back hair and her disappointed face. *You don't know what he's like*, she'd said.

That was the problem, Leanne thought. No one ever really knew what anyone else was like – until it was too late.

20

All week the knowledge of Guy's affair had been a barbed wire around her heart. To all intents and purposes, Emma inhabited the world in the same way she had done for the last two years, but now every time she moved or swallowed or ate or spoke the wire tightened, reminding her of all she didn't have. Whenever she thought about Guy preparing to leave work early to meet whoever he was meeting, having that butterflies feeling inside him, standing in front of the mirror in the toilets at work making sure his hair looked just right, feeling that pulse-racing, heat-building excitement as he drove nearer, feeling *alive*, she wanted to tear him into little pieces. Her rage frightened her. It was as if all the anger that she carried around inside towards Tilly's killer had been transferred suddenly to her husband. And yet, when it came down to it, who could blame him? She'd rebuffed every overture of intimacy from him until he'd given up making them. They hadn't had sex in nearly a year. When they watched television, side by side on the sofa but inches apart like strictly arranged cushions, she tensed at any portrayal of physical affection on screen, a lingering kiss or, God forbid, a bedroom scene. At those moments the silence between them thrummed and she felt her cheeks burn, staring rigidly ahead while her nails dug into the soft palm of her hand.

So why shouldn't he look for love somewhere else?

Because if she was suffering, so should he.

Emma knew her feelings were inconsistent, but still she couldn't help it. She tried to remember what kind of wife she'd been Before. Had there been a time when she'd have put Guy's happiness ahead of everything, even her own, given anything to save him from suffering? She suspected so, but as always when she delved back into the past, it was as if she was another person and when she tried to ascribe to her other self motivations and emotions, she was doing so from the outside, as an observer, not a participant. It was all guesswork in the end. Occasionally a memory would be triggered – she and Guy on honeymoon in Italy, dragging a mattress up on to the sun-baked roof of their borrowed apartment and making love to the sound of a million revving scooters and car horns; the two of them slumped exhausted on the sofa the time all three girls had chickenpox at once, surrounded by DVD boxes and crisp packets and broken crayons and endless sheets of paper with pictures of rainbows and houses and aliens and ponies and those folded-paper things you put over your fingers. 'Pick a number!' Tilly had commanded, her beautiful face studded with livid red spots. 'Now pick a colour. No, pick *orange*, Mummy. Orange is better.' Unfolding it with barely suppressed laughter to reveal the words 'You're a poo'. And she and Guy, limp with exhaustion, still managing to look at each other over the heads of their giggling daughters and smile. But now, though Emma could see those memories in her mind, she couldn't feel them. That other Emma, that other Guy, they were just people she used to know whom she'd lost touch with a long time ago.

It was one forty-five in the afternoon. Too soon to be thinking about the school run. Too late to begin preparing a lunch which she anyway would only pick at.

She recited her daily litany in her head. *Maybe home-made chips? Must buy potatoes. But didn't they have potatoes last night and the night before? Rice? Caitlin would object, but perhaps with pesto . . . Jemima's maths tutor tonight. Remember to call in at the cashpoint. And make sure I have a fiver this time. He never has any change and I'm always too embarrassed to remind him the following week. Caitlin MUST practise the violin tonight. Be firm, don't accept any excuses.*

She sank down on the sofa and drew her legs in their plain-black capri pants up underneath her. So many things she needed to get done, but instead she thought about Guy and whether he was at work or had left early again and who he might be with and what they might be doing.

For the first time Emma considered what had driven her and Guy apart. Was it the thing that had happened itself, or was it the fact that they couldn't bear to be around each other and see their own suffering reflected back at them?

Her chest tightened, as it always did when she thought about the past. In a panic, she tried to switch her mind on to something else.

Her hands were on the strap of her handbag before her brain had even had a chance to catch on to what she was doing. What harm could it do, anyway? Why shouldn't she look?

She knew the harm and she knew why she shouldn't, but she did it anyway.

The photo of Tilly in her painting overall was looking frayed around the edges, yet still there she was, gazing at the camera with her clear blue eyes. Again that tugging feeling in the back of Emma's mind as she looked at the opened mouth, those two perfectly symmetrical bunches on either side of her head, secured with the bands of red and orange flowers.

Hair accessories had once been a currency in this house. With three little girls so close in age, all nurturing dreams of waist-long, swishy princess hair, how could they not? Tilly used to have a little box in which she kept her 'special' ones – the pair of silver-sequinned scrunchies she'd got as part of a birthday present, a different pair with tiny pink diamanté kittens.

Emma smiled remembering the ceremony with which her middle daughter had opened the box, retrieving each precious item from the box as carefully as if they were priceless jewels and laying them out on the table in front of her.

And yet again that flash of memory, that prickling sensation as if little fingers were drumming on the inside of her head. *Think, silly Mummy. Think.*

And then suddenly her hand flew to her mouth and her stomach lurched and her heart threatened to gallop clear out of her chest.

She ran to the kitchen where her mobile was charging on the work surface and quickly called up a number, cursing when it went straight through to answerphone.

'Leanne? This is Emma. Can you call me back. It's urgent!'

21

The thing about knowing something no one else did was that it wasn't worth a bean unless other people knew that you knew something they didn't. Even after only two days, Sally was struggling to keep her knowledge of the letter Daniel Purvis had found to herself. Not that it necessarily meant anything, one must always avoid jumping to conclusions. Still, it added another element to the case. And to be frank, new elements were hard to come by on this investigation.

Out for a lunchtime drink with Ken Forbes in one of those child-friendly pubs where you couldn't get to the bar without tripping over a stray toddler, she came close to blurting out something that would alert him to the fact that she was in possession of some knowledge he would be very interested in. Only self-interest stopped her. And a faint but surprising sense of allegiance to Simon Hewitt. True, he hadn't been the most dynamic of lovers, and naturally you had to have reservations about a man who'd cheat on his wife, particularly his recently bereaved wife (although Sally was inclined in these matters to see the institution of marriage itself as faulty rather than the act of infidelity). And yet there had been an appealing sense of quiet satisfaction about him, as if he acknowledged his ambitions were modest, yet was still grateful to have fulfilled them. Since reading Simon's letter to Megan she'd gone over and over her limited encounters with him, looking for hints of a darker personality lurking beneath his bland surface, but had found none.

Could she really have slept, not once but twice, with a man capable of harming a child, either emotionally or physically? Could she have had relations with a paedophile and not have had the slightest inkling? These were the thoughts that were helping her keep the contents of Daniel Purvis's letter to herself. Sally knew herself to be a piss-poor judge of men but this would be a personal low.

Despite it being not yet one, Ken was drinking a pint of bitter with a whisky chaser. When she'd taken their order the girl behind the bar, who was wearing a tight *Game of Thrones* T-shirt and whose hair was so shiny you could practically see your own reflection in it, had looked shocked.

'Don't worry, darling,' he'd said, winking. 'Booze is a performance-booster. It's a well-known fact.'

Afterwards Sally had reprimanded him. 'You're not allowed to sexually harass the bar staff any more, Ken. Don't you think it's time you joined the twenty-first century?'

'No, thanks,' said Ken, showing her his yellow teeth. 'I'm quite happy back here in the 1980s, thank you very much.'

Sally refrained from asking whether the clothes he was wearing also hailed from that halcyon decade. Really, what was the point? She had a grudging affection for men like Ken, deliberately stuck in their time warp.

'So how are you getting on?' she asked him, though she was well aware he knew she hadn't asked him out for a drink just to make small talk.

'Not so bad,' came the infuriating reply. Ken was a freelancer. He made his living out of getting stuff the staffers on the nationals hadn't. He wasn't about to share it with her just from the goodness of his heart.

'Made any inroads with the Glovers?'

He shook his head. 'No one in that family is talking. The mother's a total mess, apparently. One of the coppers let slip she's heavily sedated. I reckon we can write them off for now.'

'And what about the cops? Haven't they got anywhere yet?'

Everyone knew Ken had close links with the Met going back yonks. Of course, lots of his original contacts had either retired or been 'relieved of their duties', but a few remained. Sally would have loved a chance to go through his contacts book, but she knew those old-style coppers wouldn't trust her. In her experience, sad old gits tended to confide only in other sad old gits.

'Oh you know,' said Ken, winking in an obligingly sad-old-git way. 'They don't like to give too much away.'

Even without the wink Sally could tell that he knew something. It was in the expectant way he looked at her as if waiting for her to name a price. She would have to offer something in return. But then she'd guessed that. That's the whole reason they were both here. She played for time by looking around the pub. If you asked her, it couldn't really be called a pub. 'Crèche with alcohol' was more like it. At the next table sat four women with small children. The women were drinking coffee and the children were building things out of brightly coloured Play-Doh. Sally had much preferred the days when a pub was a pub, full of adults drinking and talking about adult things amid the blessed cigarette smoke. Not that she had anything against children, but weren't there other places where they'd feel more at home?

'Tell you what, Ken. You give me an idea what it is you've got on Poppy Glover, and I'll let you in on a lead I have in the Megan Purvis case. How does that sound?'

Ken leaned right back in his chair and stared at her. He was wearing a pale-blue shirt that was now straining across the middle, and there were discoloured patches of dried sweat under his arms that Sally tried not to see.

'All right,' Ken said, sitting forwards abruptly. 'Let's hear what you've got.'

Sally described her meeting with Daniel Purvis and the contents of the letter, omitting only the small detail of who the letter was from. Let Simon keep his anonymity for now. Instead she told Ken the letter was unsigned.

Ken looked thoughtful. At least that's how Sally interpreted the way he furrowed his brows at her while drumming his yellow-nailed fingers on the table. 'OK,' he said eventually.

'OK?'

It came out tetchier than she'd intended.

'What I mean is, that might very well tie in with the tip-off I've had,' Ken added.

Now she was interested. All she needed was for that child to her right to stop screeching long enough for her to hear what Ken was saying.

'Apparently the cops are now looking into the idea that the Kenwood Killings are down to a paedophile ring, not just some lone nutter.' Ken sat back in his chair with an undisguised air of satisfaction. 'So what do you think about that, then?' was written all over his face.

Sally didn't much know what to think of it. Ken clearly thought the two things were connected – the letter and the possible existence of this paedophile ring. But if he was right, the natural conclusion was that the person who'd written the letter was part of the ring – perhaps had even been grooming Megan, or worse.

On the way back to her hotel, Sally felt herself sliding into gloom. She tried half-heartedly to combat it using some of the techniques her life coach Mina had taught her. She listed her many achievements and reframed her negatives into positives. In place of 'I've been an idiot' she thought 'This is another opportunity to learn and grow'. But nothing seemed to shift the knot of dread in the pit of her stomach.

She came to a decision. If she was going to find out she'd had sexual relations with a man linked to paedophilia and child murder, she'd rather get it over with, instead of hearing it from someone else. And what better way to do that than to ask him directly?

Stopping outside an artisan bakery, she was momentarily distracted by the price tag on the large round sourdough loaf in the window. £5.50? For a loaf of bread? Then she unbuckled her leather bag and dug around for her smartphone. When, finally, she managed to access her contacts list, the nail of her second finger, which had been so perfectly lacquered when she left Hove but was now looking a little chipped around the edges (she couldn't help but notice), hovered over the screen as she scrolled down her 'H's.

She popped a piece of nicotine gum in her mouth and pressed call.

22

It was the perpetual existential riddle about undercover cops – did UCs come to resemble their roles, just as dogs are said to resemble their owners, or were they chosen for those roles precisely because of that resemblance? Looking at Howard Walsh, Leanne could understand how he'd been able to pass himself off as a paedophile so successfully for the last three years. It wasn't that he was sitting there on the bench in a long, dirty mac – his black polo shirt and dark-blue jeans drew no second glances, nor did his pale, thin face and round wire-framed glasses – but there was a diffidence in his manner that was off-putting, a hesitancy that seemed to be born not from shyness but from some gap between the surface of him and whatever was going on inside.

'I do appreciate you agreeing to meet me,' she said again, trying to quell her own misgivings. She'd had little choice in the matter. It had been one of the tasks Desmond had allocated her after the earlier briefing. She tried to sound encouraging: 'I know it's not—'

'Look, can we just get on with it? I'm doing this as a favour to my guv'nor, but it needs to be quick. The cover story won't last for ever.'

The cover story to which he referred was currently sniffing around by Leanne's feet and she instinctively put out a hand to stroke it behind the ears. The chocolate-brown labrador sat down and gazed up at her contentedly, leaning into her caress. The Heath – or at least the north section where they were sitting – seemed to be teeming with chocolate-brown labradors. As cover stories go, it was perfect.

'Of course. Sorry. I just wanted to ask you about this Nemo ring. What exactly do you know about it? And how might it be linked to our investigation? You know I'm the FLO to the Reid family. It would be so nice to be able to give them a few answers.'

'*Nice?*' Her new acquaintance wasn't looking at her, but she could hear the mockery in his voice. 'I don't think you could call any of this "nice".'

Leanne was annoyed with herself for getting flustered, and annoyed with Howard Walsh – although of course his name wasn't really Howard Walsh – for making her feel so uncomfortable. She knew he was simply a police officer playing a role, but still there was a part of her that was finding it very difficult to disassociate the man next to her from the daily reality of the life he was leading.

'I have to tell you again that I haven't managed to crack that ring. I don't pretend to have any in-depth insider information about who they are or how they work.'

'No. I appreciate that.'

'All I know is that the ring, or network as it is, exists. And it seems to be dedicated entirely to the Kenwood Killings. At first I thought it was just another fetish group. There are loads of them, they attach themselves to a child celebrity or a particular child abuse case and then they swap information about it or gossip or fan fic.'

'Fan fic?'

Again that creepy hesitation.

'Fan fiction. They write fantasies about the people involved and pass them around, you know, in the same way teenage girls do about boy bands. Except these aren't exactly love stories.'

Leanne was overtaken by a wave of nausea. What must it do to a person to see day in, day out the kind of things Howard had to see? How did it affect your view of the world, your relationships with other people? No one was allowed to know quite how far and how deep UCs had to go to gain acceptance. Just as well.

'Anyway, at first I thought it was just that. Fantasy. But then I started hearing things on the grapevine – that these guys knew more than they should about the case, that they might actually be involved.'

'Involved how?'

Howard was still facing away from her, gazing out across the grassy slope, peppered with green spreading trees, as befitted a stranger she'd just struck up a conversation with on a public bench, but still Leanne could sense his quiet tension. The meeting, which had been set up through channels far above her, was as safe as it could be. She had no idea of Howard's real name, and so there was no risk of her calling him anything other than the alias he'd been living under for the past three years. She knew he worked for CEOP, the Child Exploitation and Online Protection agency, and was masquerading as a self-employed web designer living in a one-bedroom ex-council flat in one of the sprawling estates that lurked behind the Victorian pastel-painted prettiness of Kentish Town. Of course it was natural for him to walk his dog up on the Heath, and of course he was likely to chat to random strangers while he was out, in that way dog walkers do. Nevertheless, his discomfort was tangible, and Leanne knew she didn't have long.

'I don't know exactly how they're involved. It's one of the most secretive groups I've ever come across. Gaining admission is next to impossible.'

Leanne shuddered. She'd once had a friend on the force who'd gone out with a guy who'd worked undercover for five years investigating paedophiles. Her friend had told her that to pass the 'test' to be accepted, her boyfriend had to provide an original photo or video of a child being abused, not one they'd seen before, and as most of these creeps spent all their spare time combing through libraries of images, they knew pretty much everything already out there. Leanne hadn't asked how he'd got hold of what they required, but she had found out that to get to the next level of acceptance, the inner sanctum, he'd have had to provide photographic or video evidence of him actually taking part in that abuse. She didn't look at Howard Walsh. She didn't want to know what he'd had to do or pretend to do to get where he was.

'Any idea why it's called Nemo?'

Her companion shrugged. 'I'm guessing it's to do with the kids' film, *Finding Nemo*. Maybe they're looking for something, or someone. All I know is that it's a very small network, only four or five members, I think. They bonded over a fascination with the Kenwood Killings case, the fantasies growing more and more lurid. What the girls were wearing, what had been done to them. All the usual shit. They're all local to North London and swapped snippets of information about where police had been searching, who they'd been talking to, where exactly on the Heath the bodies had been found. They knew a lot, but nothing that couldn't have been got legally, if you see what I mean. And then all of a sudden they took it to a private chatroom, and no one knew any more about it until last week when one of my contacts told me that he'd heard Nemo was actively involved in the killings. You should have heard his excitement – it was like he'd found out someone he knew was actually royalty.'

Something occurred to Leanne. 'But couldn't you approach them with some bit of information from the police investigation

they can't possibly already know – as a sort of sweetener, to help you infiltrate that way?'

The labrador was getting restless and Howard leaned forward to give it a treat he'd retrieved from his jeans pocket.

'And how exactly do I do that without them questioning exactly how I got hold of it?'

Leanne had no idea. Her handbag – a scruffy black leather thing whose zip was starting to go – was in her lap, and she could feel the tell-tale vibration of an incoming call. Surreptitiously she reached her hand in and tilted the screen so she could read the caller ID. Emma Reid. Now that was unusual. Emma almost never called her. Probably because Leanne triggered such unwelcome memories.

'Look, if you haven't got any more questions, I really do have to go.'

Howard hadn't moved, yet still Leanne could sense his restlessness. When she glanced at his profile she saw a muscle in his jaw was twitching.

'Will you let me know if you hear anything more? Anything at all?'

'If there's anything that helps the case I'm sure you'll be told.'

He was so closed up, it was as if there was no way into him at all. Leanne could never do undercover work. She'd always known that. The idea of having to wear someone else's life like armour, never allowing it to slip for a second, was anathema to her. She'd known one or two over the years who'd tried to slip back into normal police life after working as a UC for a few years but had really struggled. It did something to a person. All those lies.

Leanne watched Howard Walsh head down the hill, labrador in tow, a solitary figure in dark clothes holding himself rigidly in the buttery sunshine of an early summer afternoon. Then she checked herself, remembering she was just some random stranger he'd got talking to on a bench. It didn't do to stare. Instead she got her phone out from her bag intending to check her emails or compose a pretend text, but then she saw the missed call message from Emma Reid.

'Emma? It's—'

Before she'd even had time to finish her sentence, the other woman launched into a speech in a voice so uncharacteristically animated that for a few seconds Leanne doubted it could actually be Emma at all, something about photographs and hair elastics.

'Sorry, Emma, I missed that. Can you repeat it?'

An impatient sigh, then she started again, and this time the words were slower, with space to breathe between the sentences.

'I found a photograph of Tilly in Guy's desk that reminded me of something, but I couldn't for the life of me work out what. She had her hair in bunches as she always did and in my head I kept hearing her saying how both sides had to be the same and the elastic bands had to match. I kept staring at it for hours like a bloody lunatic trying to dislodge whatever it was that was floating around my brain, and then a few hours ago it just came to me.'

Emma's voice had been speeding up as she spoke, the pitch growing higher, and Leanne was shocked at the barely suppressed excitement in her voice. Was this what Emma Reid had been like before what happened to Tilly? This woman whose voice pulsated with energy? Leanne felt herself being swept along by it. She tried to stay calm, but a part of her couldn't help feeling she was on the verge of a discovery.

'Slow down, Emma. What came to you?'

'The thing that had been nagging at me. And then I went to look at the box in the wardrobe where I keep it.'

'What? Keep what?'

'The Ziploc bag that the police gave me with all Tilly's things that she was wearing – the things they didn't keep as evidence.

165

And there they were. And they'd been there all that time and I simply hadn't noticed.'

'Emma. What was in the bag? What hadn't you noticed?'

'The bands Tilly was wearing in her hair when she was . . . when they found her. They didn't match!'

In the expectant silence that followed, Leanne hoped Emma couldn't hear the sound of her heart plummeting. 'They didn't match,' she managed to repeat.

'Tilly was kind of OCD about things like that,' Emma explained. 'If things didn't match perfectly, she couldn't relax. We were always trying to reason with her about it, but she was so stubborn. So many times we were late because she'd thrown a tantrum about something not exactly matching something else. And it wasn't just hair stuff. Her socks had to be pulled up to exactly the same height, the loops on her shoelaces had to be tied the same size, with military precision. She would never, ever have gone out with hair bobbles that didn't match.'

'So what exactly are you saying, Emma?'

'Don't you see?' She sounded frustrated as if Leanne were being deliberately obtuse. '*He* must have switched them. The killer. One of them looks like Tilly's but the other isn't. I'm sure of it. It's a clue, isn't it? We know he sometimes brushed their hair. But this is a step further, isn't it? What kind of man buys girls' hair elastics? One of your profilers would get a lot out of a detail like that.'

Leanne tried to stifle the sigh that had built up inside her. 'Emma, I know you're desperate to uncover something we've overlooked. It's only natural. You want to know who did this to Tilly. We all want to know. But surely you must see that this is grasping at straws. There might be any reason Tilly had mismatched bands in her hair. Maybe she lost one at school and a friend lent her a different one.'

'But that's just it. She would never have allowed that. She would rather have had her hair loose or in one single ponytail down the centre of her back. She just wouldn't!'

Leanne heard the crack of emotion in Emma's voice.

'Look, I'll bring it to the attention of the team. Maybe it will ring a bell with someone else.'

'But don't you need to take them back? The hair bands she was wearing?'

'If they had any DNA on them, Emma, they'd have kept them.'

'But maybe they didn't check for the right thing. Maybe he got the other band from some other girl. Her DNA might be on there, mightn't it?'

Leanne closed her eyes. She didn't need this right now. Not after the tense meeting with Howard Walsh. Opening them again she looked around, her gaze sliding over the grassy slope which was beginning to go brown in places after the recent heat, over the solid oak trees in the shade of which people were either stretched out napping or picnicking on blankets.

'I'll talk to my boss, Emma. If he thinks there's something there, we'll come round to pick up the hair bands. After all this time, it's not going to make any difference if you hang on to them a little while longer.'

There was a pause then, and Leanne could almost feel the energy draining from the conversation as if someone had taken a pin to a balloon and let all the air out.

'You think I'm mad, don't you?' Emma's voice was once again flat.

'No. Not at all. I'm really glad you're still trying to think of details we might have missed.'

'Please don't patronize me, Leanne.'

And then she was gone. Leanne remained sitting with the phone pressed to her ear, long after the gentle click that told her Emma was no longer on the line. She should have handled things differently. She could see that now. She should have called round to see

167

Emma rather than trying to deal with it over the phone. She had a pressing urge suddenly to call Pete to get his advice, or at least his sympathy.

Then she tossed the phone into her bag and set off down the hill in a different direction to the one Howard Walsh had walked just moments before.

Back at the station, she found a Post-it note on her desk from Ruby Adjaye saying 'Call Desmond!!' After the double exclamation mark, she'd drawn a heart in red biro. Leanne glanced over at Desmond's office where the clear-glass door revealed an equally clear desk and empty chair. Plunging her hand into her bag, she pulled out her phone along with a couple of old, furry-edged receipts and a packet of Polos, the wrapper shredded with age.

'Hello, sir? It's Leanne here. I had a message to call you.'

Wherever Desmond was, it sounded lively. There was a lot of low-level talking in the background punctuated by the odd roar of laughter, and Leanne could clearly hear a glass clinking nearby.

'Ah, Leanne. Let me just go somewhere a little quieter.'

In the distance, Leanne heard someone shout, 'And it wasn't even switched on!' to the accompaniment of braying laughter.

'That's better.' Desmond's voice was clearer now, the background noise all but gone. 'I'm at City Hall. One of Boris's civic functions. You know how it is.'

Alone at her desk, Leanne rolled her eyes. No. She didn't know how it was.

'I wanted to let you know of a development that has arisen in the Tilly Reid case. It goes without saying that this is utterly confidential, but as FLO to the Reids it seemed imperative to keep you up to speed.'

This time Leanne's eye-rolling was so automatic, she wasn't even aware of having done it. 'Of course, sir.'

'It's about Mr Reid. Guy Reid. Apparently his car has been

spotted several times loitering outside a girls' prep school in St John's Wood around the end of the school day. A teacher first noticed it a couple of weeks ago and got suspicious when he didn't pick anybody up. Since then she's seen him five or six times.'

Leanne's mouth went dry and she closed her eyes momentarily.

'Guy Reid has two other daughters, sir. Couldn't this be one of their schools?'

'No. We've already checked that out. It's definitely not a school his daughters attend.'

There was painful throbbing at Leanne's temple and she hoped she didn't have a migraine building.

'And what does he do while he's there? Did the teacher say?'

'Just sits there, apparently. And watches. We've made some enquiries and it doesn't seem like he's ever talked to any of the girls or approached them, but a couple of the older ones did say he made them feel uncomfortable.'

Leanne tried to picture Guy Reid in the black executive saloon she'd seen parked outside the house the last time she was there. She was hopeless at remembering makes and models of cars but she knew this was a different one to the car he'd had when Tilly was killed. That one had been a silver convertible. She assumed men like Guy Reid got a new company car every year. She had a momentary image of Will's car, a twelve-year-old Honda hatchback with a dent in the driver's side and a clutch that had been on the way out for almost as long as she'd known him.

'I want you to sound out Emma Reid,' Desmond was saying. 'Don't tell her what we've found out, but try to get some info on her husband's routines and about what's going on between the two of them.'

'But, sir, he was investigated at the time of Tilly's death. Nothing came up then.'

'No, but we were fairly sure from early on that we were dealing with the same perpetrator as in the Purvis case, so maybe we just weren't looking for the right things. Maybe we missed something.'

Long after Desmond had gone back to his function, Leanne remained at her desk with her phone in her hand, staring into space.

23

'I did it! I did it! Oh yeah. Get in!'

Bethany was leaping around excitedly as the electronic voice shrieked, 'Strike! Strike! Strike!' Dancing over to the table, she demanded a high five from her friend Emily who held up a hand so small and fragile-looking it was a wonder it didn't snap when Bethany smacked it with her own.

Sitting opposite her, Jason took the opportunity to assess Emily. Slight and small for her age, certainly compared with Bethany who really could do with laying off the chips and chocolate, Emily had straight dark hair which she wore in a fringe that was far too long, as if she was trying to hide behind it. Her skin was that kind of pale that didn't look completely healthy. She needed to get outside more, Jason decided. Maybe then she'd grow a bit. Still, there was something appealing about her. Jason liked the way she shrank into herself when he looked over at her, and then gave the faintest ghost of a smile like she was smiling just for him.

'Ah, look at them. They're having such a great time. They can't believe their luck, going bowling on a school night.'

Suzy put her hand on his thigh and squeezed. Glancing down, he caught sight of her nails which were long and painted with some sort of rainbow motif. Happy Hands, she'd called them earlier when she held them up to show him. She'd had them done especially for today, even though it meant she touched the bowling balls as gingerly as if they were unexploded bombs. Jason couldn't believe she was allowed to go to work like that. He couldn't stand nail varnish. He hated the way women painted layers on themselves to try to fool men into not seeing who they really were. The older they got, the more layers they needed – foundation so thick it cracked when they smiled, hair that had been dyed so many times they couldn't remember its original colour. It was like they thought men were idiots.

'They're great kids,' he said to her. 'I just wish . . .' He tailed off, as if too choked to continue and she squeezed his leg tighter.

'I know,' she cooed, nuzzling his neck so that her perfume shot straight up his nostrils, bringing on a sudden surge of nausea. 'You're missing your baby, aren't you?'

He nodded as if unable to speak, taking the opportunity to discreetly reposition his head so that his nose was turned away.

He'd given Suzy the whole sob story the first time they'd gone out together. How his ex-wife had cheated on him and then thrown him out so she could have a shag-fest with her toy boy, but still expected him to pay for everything for her and Keira, even though she'd stopped him seeing his daughter, making up all sorts of lies so that he couldn't get access.

'I don't like to bad-mouth anyone, and us single mums ought to stick together, but your ex sounds like she's being a complete bitch,' said Suzy now. 'If she'd only let you have her for just one day. She and Bethany would have such a laugh together, I know they would.'

'Your go, Jase.' Bethany was bouncing up and down in her seat and looking at him coquettishly with her head to one side. Next to Emily, she looked almost clownish with her blonde curls and plump pink cheeks. She'd grow up exactly like her mother, he could see that now. Steadily gaining weight as she got older, a few pounds every year, because she couldn't resist her little treats, stubbornly clinging to her 'little girl' mannerisms long after she'd outgrown them, putting her head to one side and looking up through her lashes as if she was still a cute child rather than an adult woman. Emily, on the other hand – she was different. Her body was still like a boy's. No curves or lumps and bumps. Though she wasn't pretty, with her parchment skin and her deep-set brown eyes and the wide mouth with the thin lips she kept pressed close together to cover the tombstone front teeth, there was something other-worldly about her that made his breath catch in his throat every time he looked at her.

'Go on, babe, show them how it's done.'

Suzy gave him a playful shove. Already she was acting in that proprietorial way women did, sending out silent 'he's taken' messages, like they were spraying their territory.

Jason got to his feet and perused the bowling balls stacked up on the rails, eventually selecting the black which was the heaviest. He picked it up with a casual gesture as if it weighed nothing and flexed his elbow, enjoying how the muscles of his arm strained against his white T-shirt. As he moved towards their bowling lane, he could feel the others' eyes on his back and he allowed himself a slight swagger before stopping and bringing his arm back, then lunging forward in a fluid, easy motion.

'Strike! Strike! Strike!' called the electronic voice.

'Yes!' shrieked Suzy, leaping up to plant a kiss right on his mouth with her own sticky glossed lips. As she pulled away, it was all he could do not to wipe a hand across his face. Over Suzy's bare shoulder, he could see Emily smiling her shy smile at him. He puffed out his chest.

An hour later, he was in his car sitting opposite a terraced house in a rundown street near Turnpike Lane. People were always going on about the place being up and coming, whatever that meant, but as far as Jason was concerned it was still as much of a shithole as when he'd lived here. He wanted better for Keira, but what could he do with his bitch of an ex refusing to let him near her?

The front door had a heavy, metal frame and grubby dimpled glass. He could picture the cramped communal hallway that lay behind it with its lino perpetually covered by a carpet of flyers and takeaway pizza menus, and the pushchair belonging to the selfish cow who lived upstairs always blocking the way. Through the narrow bay window to the left of the door, Jason could just make out the framed print of a beach scene Donna had insisted on putting up on the wall. Said it cheered her up. Not as if anyone would notice – with that sour expression she wore 24/7. Though he hadn't been inside the flat for months, he knew there was a black leather sofa under that print, far too big for the cramped room. Donna had insisted on it when they'd seen it in the furniture showroom, and like a mug he'd signed up for the monthly repayments. She'd always been grasping. Take, take, take. That's all Donna had ever done. And now she'd taken his daughter too.

When he'd first met her, her neediness hadn't been an issue. In fact it had been a bit of a turn-on. He'd liked doing things for her, giving things to her. She was just a scrawny, underdeveloped kid addicted to vodka and prescription pills. He'd helped her get clean, forced her to eat proper food, stared down the pushers when they came sniffing around. And in return she'd been grateful, eager to please. For the first time in his life someone relied on him and it made him feel good. For a while he'd thought this was it. The disturbing thoughts he'd had ever since he was thirteen, the urges, the images – all those would disappear now he had a proper girlfriend. Then they got married, and almost instantly the novelty wore off. Whereas before when she'd ask for things, it would make him feel powerful, now it just felt like she was constantly nagging. But even that wasn't as bad as the look

174

of disappointment he'd catch on her face sometimes. That junkie bitch? Disappointed in *him*?

After Keira was born there was a brief honeymoon period where things seemed to go back to how they were. For a while they'd almost been a team – he working all the overtime he could to support his family, she staying at home to look after the baby. For the first time in his life, he'd felt like he belonged somewhere. But after a couple of years it had fallen apart again. Donna didn't have the first clue about being a mum. She was inconsistent, veering wildly between over-indulging Keira one minute and yelling at her the next. And that made him lose his temper in turn. He was only protecting his daughter, like any father would. The atmosphere in the flat had gone from shit to poisonous. There'd been a few incidents. Nothing major, but it was before the anger-management stuff so he hadn't had the self-control he had now.

Donna grew hard and bitter, half scared of him, and half openly goading. She said things about him and how he was with Keira, just to wind him up. Now he realized she'd been waiting for the opportunity to shaft him. If the nosy bitch hadn't come in to Keira's room at that precise moment, none of this would have happened. He wouldn't be sitting in a car outside his own flat that was filled with stuff that he'd paid for, not even allowed to set foot through the door. He wouldn't be reduced to loitering around to get a glimpse of his own daughter, taking orders from social workers in shapeless cardigans, their briefcases bulging with files about so-called problem families.

Just in time, he glanced in his wing mirror and saw Donna and Keira approaching on the other side of the road, leaning close together, hunched over something. He slid down in his seat but the two of them were too engrossed in whatever they were carrying to notice him. Anyway he doubted they'd recognize the car. It was the second time he'd changed motors since he'd had to get rid of that Golf.

As they passed, Donna yelled, 'Oi, hands off, you little thief!' and then gave that awful smoker's laugh of hers that sounded more like a dog's bark. Jason saw now that she was carrying a cardboard box from a fast-food place and they were stuffing themselves with chips and he had to clench his fingers around the steering wheel to stop himself from flinging the car door open. This was the woman the courts had decided was more fit to be a parent than him? This slag who couldn't even be bothered to cook their daughter a decent meal?

No wonder Keira looked so pale and unhealthy. Keeping his head low, Jason observed his daughter carefully, frowning at the cropped T-shirt and skimpy shorts. Only eight years old and Donna had her dressing like a whore. The two made their way up the overgrown path, Donna's harsh, grating voice rabbiting on all the while, and Jason felt the red mist building in front of his eyes. He slammed his fist down on the steering wheel, enjoying how the sharp jolt of pain cut across the searing loneliness he felt watching his wife and daughter at the front door – *his* front door, *his* daughter – arm in arm. Briefly, as Donna pushed inside, he had a glimpse of the junk mail littering the hall and the bare bulb hanging from the ceiling. He watched Keira's narrow back following her mother into the building before the door slammed shut, leaving him in his car, poleaxed with anger and grief.

All through the drive to work, through the bumper-to-bumper traffic, he kept thinking about Keira in those shorts and getting himself worked up all over again. He tried to remember the anger-management techniques he'd been taught, but his mind wouldn't focus. What the fuck was Donna doing letting her go around looking like that? Didn't she realize what kind of sick perverts were out there?

Even when he arrived at the club in a part of Old Street where City traders still just about outnumbered the poncy hipsters with their stupid beards, and headed inside to take up his usual position guarding the cordoned-off VIP area, standing feet planted firmly apart, hands clasped in front of him, he couldn't stop thinking about it. Donna needed her head examining.

On the main stage straight ahead of him, the new girl launched into her routine, slowly gyrating in her skin-tight catsuit, edging the zip down as she did so. The smattering of early punters gazed on, largely impassive. A couple of them had their hands buried in their laps. Pigs, the lot of them. Filthy *pigs*. His thoughts swung back to Emily, the slight girl with her shy smile and curtain of dark hair. There was something about her that had reminded him of that other girl. He allowed himself a quick flashback – the silkiness of soft skin, a smell of apple shampoo, the rustling of the plastic bags he'd tied over his shoes as he carried his load through the still, dark trees . . .

'You gonna let us through or what?'

The man in front of him was wearing a suit and clasping the hand of one of the younger girls. Tanya. That was her name. Pretty. Soft. Not like some of the hard bitches around here. The man had been in a few times before, flashing his cash, making a show of ordering two bottles at a time of the £450 champagne or shots of whisky at £90 a pop. The punters weren't supposed to touch the girls but often they tried to cop a feel on the way to one of the small rooms at the back of the VIP area reserved for a private dance. As he wordlessly unhooked the gold-braid cordon, he watched the man's hand carefully, as it came to rest on the small of Tanya's back before working its way lower.

Pigs. All of them.

24

'I mean, when are we ever going to need this stuff? Like, how often in your daily life do you think, oh thank God I learned quadratic equations when I was thirteen?'

Jemima was glaring at her as if Emma were solely to blame for the national curriculum. Normally Emma might have attempted to explain how the principles of maths impact on daily life or the importance of getting as wide an education as possible at an age where one was still open enough to absorb it, but today she had no energy for appeasement. She kept glancing at the retro Bakelite clock on the wall. Quarter to five. An hour and a quarter since she'd realized she could use Guy's FindMyPhone app synced with the family computer to track the whereabouts of his phone, and therefore of Guy himself.

St John's Wood.

Nowhere near his office in the City. Not on the way home.

So that's where she lived. This woman who'd given her husband something to get up for, to live for, to breathe for. It figured. St John's Wood was where all the serious money was. Guy had always been drawn to wealth. Well, let her have him. She was welcome to him. But for now Emma needed to find him. She needed him, just this once, to be *her* husband again. Emma was still reeling from the casual way with which Leanne had knocked back her revelation about the odd elastic bands the previous day. She'd been so sure she'd leap on it as a new clue, that it would unlock a whole unexplored avenue of investigation, but her own bubbling excitement had died in her throat at Leanne's flat reception of the news, and barely suppressed sighs. And now she found herself re-examining it, this detail that had seemed so crucial at the time. What did it mean, after all? A different band. So she swapped one with a friend. Would that be so strange?

Yes, said the voice in her head. Yes, yes, *yes*.

The night before, she'd kept it to herself, not wanting to risk her own husband looking at her as if she'd lost her mind, but all day it had been eating away at her until now she couldn't keep it in any longer. She needed to know she wasn't crazy.

'Mum!' Jemima's face was scrunched into that dangerous scowl Emma knew only too well.

'Sorry, sweetheart. You know, you're quite right. I can't recall one single occasion in my whole adult life where I've been called on to use my knowledge of quadratic equations.'

Sitting at the kitchen table, her school books spread out in front of her, Emma's oldest daughter gazed at her mother, momentarily nonplussed. Emma's heart hiccuped as she noticed how young Jemima suddenly looked when divested of the confrontational attitude she wore like armour.

'Yeah, well, it's just stupid,' said Jemima, recovering. 'School is stupid. It's a big stupid waste of time. They're making us do Shakespeare next year. He doesn't even write in proper English.'

Emma smiled but her attention was distracted by the sound coming down the hallway of a car pulling up in front of the house. Suddenly her mouth felt dry, her chest tight. She couldn't remember the last time she'd been so nervous about seeing her own husband.

Footsteps crunched on the gravel outside and she waited for the sound of his key in the door. It was a long wait and it occurred to her now that he might be deliberately dawdling, drawing out the seconds till he had to come in and face her. Is this what he did every day, she wondered. Loitering outside his own house to delay going in?

When Guy finally appeared in the doorway of the kitchen, Caitlin, who'd been quietly drawing in front of the television in the next room, came pelting out to hurl herself at him, arms clasped around his waist, face buried in his shirt.

'Hello, squirt,' he said, leaning down to plant a kiss on the top of her head. Emma noticed how he took a deep breath in as he did so, as if trying to inhale his daughter whole.

'Where have you been?'

She had planned to be casual, knowing it was silly to put him on the defensive from the outset. But the words were out almost before she was conscious of saying them, in that accusing voice. Standing at the sink, she wiped a tea towel over a wine glass too tall to fit in the dishwasher and kept her head bent so her expression didn't give her away.

'Work,' he said, as if the question was ridiculous. 'I go to work every day. In case you hadn't noticed.'

Emma wished she'd waited until they were alone before embarking on this conversation, but it was too late to turn back and anyway, his sarcasm inflamed her.

'Only Denise rang here earlier in the week looking for you. She said you'd left early. She said you leave early a lot.' Emma kept her back to him.

'Why are you giving him such a hard time?' Jemima, of course, had picked up on the tension in the room. Sometimes Emma could talk to her and it was as if she was wilfully deaf, her mother's words sliding off the surface of her as if off an invisible force shield, yet if there was ever anything she wasn't supposed to

180

hear – a piece of gossip whispered by an indiscreet friend, an aside hissed under someone's breath – she was suddenly all ears.

'I'm not giving him a hard time, Jem.' Emma tried to make her voice sound light. The fake jolliness jarred. 'I'm just asking—'

'Yes, but you're asking in *that voice*.'

'I'm going up for a shower.' Guy was already moving towards the hallway. 'I've had work stuff to do. Denise should have checked the diary before ringing up here bothering you. It was all down in there.'

It sounded so plausible.

'See?' Jemima hissed, vindicated.

But Emma was already halfway out of the room, following her husband, heart thumping in her ears like the drum 'n' bass that boomed nightly from Jemima's bedroom. Her thoughts were racing. On the one hand she longed to put Guy on the spot, to force him to tell her where he'd been going, to admit he'd been unfaithful. Not to her. Not that. But unfaithful to their grief, to Tilly herself. But more pressing even than this desire to make him admit to his transgressions was the need to tell him about the hair elastics. He was Tilly's father – *is* Tilly's father, she reminded herself. He alone would grasp the significance of what she'd remembered, maybe even tell her what it meant.

Guy was in the bedroom, sitting on the edge of the bed, his head in his hands.

'Oh,' she said, taken aback.

'For God's sake, Emma.' He sounded so tired. 'I already explained. Denise got it wrong. That's all.'

'It's not that. Well. Not just that.'

Emma explained as best she could. About the photograph, and how fastidious Tilly used to be. 'Remember?' she kept saying to him. 'Remember how she was?' Reaching into the top drawer of the low unit next to her side of the bed, she withdrew the Ziploc bag the police had given them. Guy physically flinched as he recognized it but she pressed on, sliding the black zipper across the top and withdrawing the two bands from inside.

'See?'

She thrust her hand in front of Guy's face, the two colourful elasticated rings resting on her palm. 'They're completely different. I know this one was Tilly's. I remember buying her a set of these in different colours.'

She'd picked up the thicker of the two – bright blue with a yellow-duck motif repeated all the way round.

'But this one' – she raised her hand so the band, a plain dark-red thing that suffered in comparison to its brasher, more colourful companion, was practically touching his face – 'I don't recognize this at all. It's not the sort of thing she'd ever wear, and definitely not paired with the other one.'

'What are you saying, Emma? We know the killer had a thing about hair. We know he brushed their hair. We've always known that.'

'Yes, but this is different, don't you see?' She was almost crying. 'He must have gone out to buy different bands. Why? Why would anyone do that? OK, supposing the other one came off somewhere. Why not just leave her hair down, or put it in a ponytail with one band? Why go to the trouble of buying another one?'

'I don't know!'

The vehemence of Guy's shout seemed to shock even him. For a moment in the silence that followed, he and Emma stared wordlessly at each other. Then his whole body seemed to slump.

'I don't know,' he repeated in a tired, flat voice. 'I don't know anything, Emma. I don't know why Tilly was killed. I don't know what I could have done to save her. I don't know what kind of a monster could do what he did. I don't know why he brushed her hair or wrote on her leg. I don't know and, d'you know what, I don't want to know. I don't want to understand, because evil can't be understood. Don't you get that?'

Emma did get it. She got that knowing what happened to Tilly wasn't going to bring her back and that understanding how and why it happened wasn't going to help her sleep at night. And yet she had to keep on trying to find out because that was all that was left to her.

'Where were you?' she asked Guy.

He raised his dark-shadowed eyes to her, the green eyes whose corners she'd once liked to probe with the tip of her tongue as he lay spent beneath her. Again they looked at each other, as if seeing one another for the first time in a very long while.

'It was work stuff,' he told her again. 'I told you.'

There was a buzzing in the front pocket of Emma's jeans, her phone vibrating against her hip bone. She tore her eyes from Guy's and walked out of their bedroom.

'Hello, Fiona,' she said, amazed at how her voice came out level and steady, betraying no hint of the scene that had been interrupted.

'Emma. Yes.'

Fiona Botsford had a very distinctive way of talking, her words coming out in staccato phrases like the clacking of an old-fashioned typewriter. Emma knew some people – Guy for instance – found her abrasive. 'Spiky' is how he'd described her when they first met. But Emma liked the way she didn't ever try to be anything she was not. She didn't pretend to like people or to be having a good time. She was unapologetically herself. And obviously they had never known her Before, just as none of the others had known Guy and her Before. They had no idea that once Emma and Guy had been so close he would call her from his car on the way to work in the morning. 'I just wanted to hear your voice,' he'd say as though it had been ten days, not ten minutes, since he'd left the house.

'How are you, Fiona? Have you been coping with it all?'

She didn't need to explain what she meant by 'it all'.

'Not really. I'm worried about Helen. She's taken it very badly, our move to Australia.'

'We'll all miss you. It won't be the same without you.'

Only now did Emma grasp the truth of this. Fiona and Mark weren't part of her day-to-day life, but their not being around would leave a huge gap. Who else was there who understood? Only Helen and Simon, and this new family when they finally emerged from the pit they were in right now. If they emerged.

'I know. And we'll miss you too. But we need to get away. Find a new way of living. Here we'll always feel like parents. Parents without a child. Maybe somewhere else we can just be people again. I hope Helen can understand that.'

'Fiona, was there anything weird about Leila's hair? After she was found, I mean. Was it tied back?'

If Fiona thought this an off-the-wall question, she didn't show it. 'No. It was loose. She always wore it loose. She used to say she liked the swishing noise it made when she turned her head from side to side. Why?'

For a moment Emma considered telling her about the hair bands, but the thought of explaining it all over again and being met once more with that blank, unspoken 'And?' stopped her.

'No reason. Just forget I mentioned it.'

25

The dog had its nose in the crotch of Sally's newly purchased crisp white linen trousers and was making a snuffling noise.

'Oh, he likes you,' said the woman at the next table, who was holding the end of the dog's lead but making not the slightest effort to rein it in. 'You should be honoured. Normally he growls at people he doesn't know.'

Sally nudged the dog away and turned to the side so that her back was now to the table with the dog-owning woman. So what if it was rude? Really, as far as she was concerned, allowing your pets to attempt oral sex with random strangers was the greater social transgression. She snatched up her phone from the wooden table and tried Simon's number. Again. Beep beep beep beep.

Crossly she looked around. It had been her idea to meet at the Kenwood House café on the northern edge of Hampstead Heath. She'd thought the setting – near where all the girls had been found – might make Simon more forthcoming. She'd imagined the two of them enjoying a quiet tête-à-tête in the sunshine, Simon unfurling like a flower under the blaze of her gentle but expert probing, revealing the secret that would unlock the case and reignite her flagging career. She hadn't reckoned on the

Active Retired cluttering up the place with their lightweight jackets and baseball caps and hiking sticks, nor the Scandinavian nannies giggling over cappuccinos while their charges munched their way through family-size bags of artisan crisps, nor all these bloody dogs, and of course, being Hampstead, they weren't any old dogs, they were designer crossbreeds with those ridiculous names like cockerpoos and cavapoos and labradoodles. The place was jam-packed. She'd only managed to get a table by standing next to a middle-aged man and staring pointedly at his empty tea cup and crumb-strewn plate until he finally got up and moved away. And now Simon wasn't even bloody well here. It was too much.

'Sorry, sorry.' He'd walked up from behind so she hadn't noticed him. 'There was nowhere to park. I've been driving round and round like a complete dick. Saturdays are a nightmare around here.'

Sally got to her feet to kiss him on each cheek. She got a whiff of cologne and couldn't help feeling flattered he'd made an effort for her. But then she remembered about the letter and what he might be capable of and she felt angry with herself for even noticing. When Simon sat himself down opposite her and she got a proper look at him, she felt a jolt of shock. He'd really let himself go. There were pillows of flesh where his neck emerged from his just-too-tight yellow T-shirt, and his face was puffy, the cheeks stained deep red from what she guessed was a combination of careless exposure to the sun plus a serious wine habit.

'It's wonderful to see you again, Sally. You look great. Really great.'

'How kind of you to say so. Even though I know I look like shit. Never could sleep well in a hotel.'

Why had she mentioned hotels? Now the memory of that hotel by Swiss Cottage with the white, clinical-looking lobby and the heating you couldn't turn down was looming large between the two of them.

'I have thought about you, you know?'

His pale eyes were sunken and Sally felt a wave of revulsion, re-membering again the letter and what it implied. She looked at his broad, meaty fingers resting on the table and had a sudden awful memory of him thrusting one of those fingers into her mouth. She jumped to her feet.

'Oh really? How nice. Now what shall I get you from the café? Tea? Coffee? There's a yummy-looking carrot cake I could tempt you with.'

'Yummy'. She hadn't used that word in years.

By the time she re-emerged, balancing two Earl Greys and a slab of orangey-brown cake topped with thick white icing, she'd given herself a strict talking-to. She'd made a mistake with Simon Hewitt. But people were allowed mistakes. It didn't make them bad people. She would get Mina to do some work with her on self-forgiveness. But in the meantime she needed to focus on getting Simon to talk – in whatever way possible.

'How have things been?' She reached out her hand and rested her fingertips briefly on his pudgy arm.

He glanced at her and then concentrated on adding two lumps of brown sugar to his tea, and stirring vigorously.

'It's not exactly a barrel of laughs at home. But what can you do? We make the best of it.'

'Of course. Of course.'

'I hope it goes without saying this meeting is completely off the record, Sally.'

Simon narrowed his already narrow eyes, and Sally could hear in his voice how much he enjoyed saying the phrase 'off the record'. She had noticed that about him before, that propensity towards the pompous.

'I don't think Helen would be jumping up and down with joy if she knew I was meeting you.'

'She knows about us then? How the fuck did she find out?'

Sally had guessed as much but it was uncomfortable having her suspicions confirmed.

'She found the hotel receipt.'

Now Sally remembered how he'd insisted on paying for the room in that swaggering manner some men adopt when they're trying to be macho, even though she'd told him she could put it on expenses.

'I told her I was helping you with an article. That we needed somewhere quiet to talk.'

'Ha! Bet she bought that one!'

'Not really. But I stuck to it, and she didn't push. Helen doesn't push on anything. It's not her style.'

No wonder Helen had seemed frosty at Fiona's interview. It was all so tawdry in hindsight.

Simon picked up his fork and shovelled a wodge of cake into his mouth. A large ginger crumb fixed itself to his lower cheek.

'Come on, Sally,' he said through his mouthful of cake. 'Don't look so pissed off. You weren't exactly an unwilling party as I remember rightly. It takes two to tango, wouldn't you say?'

'Whatever. Anyway, that's not why I wanted to see you. Actually, there's something I need to ask you. Something that's come to my attention.'

A loud Latin samba suddenly cut across the table and Sally cursed herself for not having turned her phone to silent before sitting down.

'Excuse me a moment,' she said, clocking the name that had popped up on the screen. Clutching her phone to her chest like a newborn baby, she threaded her way through the tables and out on to the main path. To the right, the magnificent cream façade of Kenwood House rose up stark against a cobalt sky, its regiment of vast windows gazing out on to manicured lawns sloping down to the glittering lake at the bottom. Finding an unoccupied bench, she sat with her back to the building.

'Sorry,' she said at last. 'I had to go somewhere a little more private. How are you? How have you been?'

The voice that came back was so soft she had to jab at the volume button on the side of her phone to hear it.

'Yes. Can't complain,' it said. 'Work takes up most of my time. Kids are growing up far too fast. What can you do?'

Despite the superficial chattiness, the underlying tone was one of suspicion. There was a hesitation there, a betraying tightness. Sally knew she had to get her questions in quickly, before he found an excuse to ring off.

'Thank you so much for calling back. I'm really just after a bit of information. All totally anonymous of course.' Silence. 'And obviously I'd be happy to reimburse you for your time, in the same way as before.'

The last time Sally had dealings with the man she knew only as 'Serge' there'd been a complicated arrangement of payment involving Western Union, and it had all been a great big faff. Actually, it had caused a bit of a hoo-ha with the features editor who'd commissioned the piece and who'd questioned the ethics of paying a self-confessed would-be paedophile, but then Sally had pointed out that he'd never, as far as they knew, committed an actual crime. His transgressions were all in his head. If they were all to be judged on their private fantasies, the world would come to an abrupt halt, she'd argued. So the feature had come out: INSIDE THE MIND OF A PAEDOPHILE. And as they'd all thought, it had generated a huge reaction, with thousands of people writing in to express their outrage at a national paper devoting column inches to perverts and deviants. It had been one of the high points of her career.

She'd never met Serge in real life – she'd been introduced to him via a network of contacts and their communications had remained purely via telephone – but she'd often thought about him, almost fondly. He'd seemed so genuinely ashamed of his impulses, so eloquent about the struggle of living a lie – on the surface a happy family man, but underneath tormented by urges he knew to be wrong. Afterwards people had accused her of making him up. There was that jealous git Jeremy who worked for the weekend paper, who'd told her a 'real paedophile' would never admit to being wrong, as they thought their feelings were perfectly natural. 'And you became the official Paedophile Spokesperson when exactly?' Sally had asked him.

'What kind of information?' Again that hesitancy, as if he suspected her of trying to catch him out. Sally had never discovered what 'Serge' did for a living, but she imagined him as some kind of middle manager – cautious and thorough. She knew he had a wife who suspected nothing and three children he adored.

'I'm digging around into the Hampstead Heath murders in North London. I've been told by a source that there might be a paedophile group involved. I just wondered if you'd heard anything. Not that I'm suggesting for a minute you yourself might be . . .'

'It's all right. I understand.'

'And? Is that something you've heard too?'

Sitting on her bench, Sally found herself stiffening with anticipation as she always did when she felt she might be on the verge of a breakthrough. Just in front of her, a little boy was running down the sloping lawn on chubby legs, the handle of a kite clutched in his hand, but without a breeze, the neon diamond just trailed disconsolately in the grass behind him. 'I told you,' his mother could be heard to say. 'I said it wouldn't work.'

'Before we get into anything, I'd just need to check about the, um, reimbursement. Would that be at the same rate as before?'

Sally opened her mouth to argue and then closed it again. She needed this information. If the paper baulked at the four-figure tip-off fee, she'd just pay it herself.

'I'll probably get into trouble, but yes, fine. So what have you got?'

Sally glanced over to her left, conscious of the man she'd left sitting at the café table. Might she be about to hear something that linked Simon Hewitt to this whole grisly business? The thought both horrified and excited her. That she might yet find herself once again at the very heart of an international news story.

'Well. I have heard rumours.' Pause.

Sally dug her fingernails into the skin of her arm to stop herself from crying out with frustration.

'There is this online group. It's called Nemo.'

'As in the cartoon fish?'

'One would presume so.'

'And?'

'The rumours are that they're involved somehow.'

'But who are they?'

'Come on, Sally. You know better than that. I haven't a clue who they are. We don't exactly sign in with all our personal information. Everything is scrambled through a series of relays so there's no chance of tracing IPs.'

'Yes, but you said there were rumours. Someone must know something.'

'Not really. The only things I've heard about it are that there are only four members and that a couple of them are very high-profile. A radio presenter of some sort, I heard.'

Sally sat up straighter, trying not to get over-excited. The case was already massive, but a celebrity would send it into the strato-sphere.

'Who? Any idea?'

'I need to go now, Sally, I'm afraid. I'll see what else I can find out.'

And then he was gone, just a soft click betraying that he was ever there at all.

Sally's heart was racing as she made her way back to the café.

Of course there was nothing to say there was any truth in any of this. But she had a gut feeling about 'Serge'. She'd felt it right from the start, and if there was one thing Sally had learned by now it was to trust her gut. At least when it came to a story. When it came to men, her gut should frankly be sent packing.

'Oh, you've come back, have you? Thought you might have done a runner.'

Simon was tapping his car keys on the table.

'Sorry!' Sally made an exaggeratedly apologetic face. 'The bloody office always manage to pick the worst possible moment.'

She smiled at him as she slid back into her chair. The conversation with 'Serge' had focused her mind. She needed to find out what Simon Hewitt was really all about without coming out and telling him about the letter. She wanted to hold that particular card back.

'I do sometimes think about it,' she said, casting her eyes down so that they fixed on the knotty grain of the table. 'Those afternoons at the hotel, I mean. I'm guessing it wasn't a one-off scenario for you. I got the impression you were a bit of an old pro.'

She knew she needed to feed his ego. Even so, she felt whatever muscle was linked to her internal moral compass contract in protest.

Predictably, he looked pleased, his fleshy cheeks, already deeply coloured, flushing claret. 'I wouldn't say that. But you're right, there have been others. Not many, mind. I wouldn't want you to think I was some kind of player.'

It occurred to Sally that that's exactly what Simon Hewitt would want her to think. But now he was looking at her again with suspicion.

'This is completely private, this chat, yeah? Don't forget, I'm not the only one who'd lose out if anything about what happened between us got into the public domain. I can't imagine your boss would look kindly at you fraternizing with your interviewees.'

Sally suspected her boss would probably sign her up for a three-part exclusive on the spot, but she kept quiet about that.

'I've told you. It's totally off the record. Go on, you were talking about your chequered past. So I wasn't the one who tempted you away from the straight and narrow. And there was I thinking I was special.'

'You were. Are. I just meant . . .'

'I'm teasing. Tell me a bit more about the others. Bet you have a type.'

Was she really expecting him to say, yes, underage?

'The type that would go for a fat old git like me?'

Simon was smiling and Sally suddenly remembered what it was she'd liked about him. They'd had fun. She'd forgotten that.

'Yes, but there must be a common factor. Blonde? Solvent? Young?'

She deliberately left the last word hanging, but Simon didn't pick up the bait.

'To be honest, Sally' – his shoulders slumped now and he looked defeated – 'there were only one or two. I'm not a complete shit, you know. I love Helen, in my way. In fact before you, there hadn't been anyone in ages.'

'I suppose having a murdered stepdaughter can play havoc with your love life.'

She hadn't meant to sound so arch. Simon made a face.

'Even before that I'd stopped. The thing was that Megan . . . God, this is pretty embarrassing.'

Sally felt a tingling at the base of her spine.

'Come on, Simon. As if I'm one to judge.'

'Well, Megan saw me. Us, rather. The woman was one of the mums at her school. Divorced. Kind of came on to me, if you know what I mean. Anyway. There was a Christmas party at her house, kids and parents, and much vino was drunk, and Megan walked in on us in the summerhouse. She didn't say anything to

Helen in the end. I wrote her a letter practically begging her not to. Even offered to buy her a bloody pony. But it was a massive reality check. That was the only time it happened, really. Apart from you. Blimey, there's no need to look so disappointed. What were you hoping for? Some kind of salacious history of serial womanizing?'

Sally didn't answer. What had she been hoping for? That Simon's letter to Megan would solve the case – even while at the same time exposing the huge void that lived at the heart of her where her sense of judgement should be?

'You've got a crumb stuck to your face,' she told him.

26

'How's Guy getting on? I mean, it can't be easy for him either, all these feelings surfacing again. How's he taking it?'

Leanne wished she didn't feel like there was a great big sign above her head reading 'insincere' as she spoke. Even as a child she'd had difficulty dissembling, and as for straight-out lying, forget it. Whenever there was any hint of trouble, her mother used to ignore her brother and sister and focus solely on Leanne because she knew she was incapable of not telling the truth. 'You got the honesty gene,' she'd told her more than once. 'It's either a blessing or a curse.' Sitting here at a café table in a newly gentrified paved square in an area of King's Cross that had once been a wasteland, populated only by prostitutes, pimps and lost tourists, Leanne felt sure that Emma Reid would be able to see through her right away. 'Question her gently about the husband,' Desmond had instructed her at the end of the previous week, 'but without alerting her to the fact that something's wrong. We need to know more about him – who he is, what he's into, what earthly reason he would have for hanging around primary schools his children don't even go to. Maybe we missed something when we checked him out at the time of the daughter's death.'

'He's much the same as ever, I suppose,' Emma snapped, her face closing up as she thought back to their latest row.

She leaned back in her chair and turned her head away from Leanne towards where small children with bare legs were dashing excitedly in and out of the jets of water that rose up in grids from the square. Around the fountain were deckchairs, many of them containing colourfully clad students from nearby St Martin's School of Art. Leanne had asked Emma to meet her here in a deliberate attempt to get Emma out of her house and on to neutral ground. Directly opposite them, through the columns of water, stood vans selling cocktails and street food. Everything had 'pop-up' in the title these days – pop-up restaurants, pop-up bars. Leanne wondered if she should call herself a pop-up police officer – here today, but who knew about tomorrow? Had she been a pop-up wife?

'Is everything OK between the two of you? A crisis like you've gone through can pull a couple together, but it can also leave each of you feeling very lonely and isolated.'

The clichés were just pouring out of her – no wonder Emma Reid was keeping her face averted, pretending she couldn't hear.

'I know the two of you weren't interested in counselling after Tilly died, but maybe now some time has passed . . .'

'You mean now that it's easier? More manageable? But you see, Leanne, it isn't either of those things. In fact it gets harder, not easier. The older I get, the older Jemima and Caitlin get, the further we get from her, like we're leaving her behind.'

'And Guy? Does he feel the same?'

Emma shrugged. She was wearing a shapeless black silk dress that hung, sacklike, to just below her knees. Leanne could tell it was expensive but couldn't help thinking it looked like something you'd put your rubbish out in.

'Guy doesn't really tell me what he thinks any more. We lead very separate lives. In fact I think . . .' Emma shot her a look as if weighing up whether to go further. 'Well, I think he might have found someone else. I wouldn't blame him. I'm not exactly fun to be around any more.'

Leanne didn't know what to say. It was the first time she'd felt a sense of kinship with Emma Reid.

'Well, obviously, I'm the go-to woman for cheated-on wives,' she joked. 'Ask me anything you want.'

Emma looked aghast. 'Oh, I'm sorry. I didn't know. I mean, I knew you'd separated, but not that there was another woman.'

Leanne held up her hand. 'It's fine. Don't worry. But seriously, Emma. What makes you suspect that?'

'Oh the usual. Secretary rings trying to get hold of him, says he's been leaving the office early, claiming to be coming home to work, but he never shows up.'

So Emma had no idea about him parking outside schools, watching little girls. It didn't seem fair to let her go on thinking that her husband was sneaking off to see another woman. And yet the reality might turn out to be so much worse.

'We hardly speak any more,' Emma continued, playing with the straw of her drink – a green concoction of juiced vegetables. You wouldn't catch Leanne drinking vegetables. 'Our relationship was pretty bad anyway, and since I tried to talk to him about the hair bobbles it's reached rock bottom. He thinks I'm crazy just like you do.'

Now it was Leanne's turn to look away. She'd almost forgotten all about Emma's strange obsession with the mismatched bands.

'It's not that I think you're crazy. It's just that we need something more to go on. You must see that.'

'You think I'm some grief-deranged mother. So does Guy. And maybe you're both right. All I know is I feel it right here.' She made a fist of her tiny hands and knocked it against her breast bone. Leanne heard the soft thud from across the table. 'I thought Guy might understand, but he doesn't. Too busy thinking about *her*, whoever she is. Well, good luck to her. Guy might look on the outside like he's healed, better than me anyway, but what nobody sees is that inside him there's a mass of scar tissue. Hard and lumpy and knotted up.'

Despite the sunshine, Leanne felt goosebumps rise up on her arms. Across the square a group of art students who'd been lounging in deckchairs drinking wine straight from a bottle started singing the theme tune from a children's programme from years before. 'Tinky Winky, Dipsy,' they yelled, 'Laa-Laa, Po.'

All the way back to the station, Leanne kept thinking about Emma's tired face and the sadness when she'd said that thing about Guy having another woman and her not blaming him, and then the bitterness when she talked about the knotted scar tissue inside him. She remembered how she'd felt when Pete had first admitted he'd been seeing someone else. At first it had been almost a relief, knowing that she wasn't going crazy after all. For weeks she'd been thinking something was wrong but whenever she'd asked him, he'd round on her, denying everything, making out it was her own paranoia. Then they'd been watching television side by side during a rare evening when they were both at home. *The Great British Bake Off*, it was. They watched it as a kind of food porn, each vowing to get the ingredients to make whatever it was the contestants were making that week, though they never did. For once she was relaxed, not thinking about anything apart from the show, and the cakes obviously.

And then he'd said it, out of the blue, without a preamble, without even looking at her. 'I've been seeing someone else. She's pregnant.'

Pete had cried later. She remembered that. He didn't want to leave her. He loved her. But they'd both known that he would go. A baby was a baby in the end. Anyway, she'd found Will a few months later, so everything had worked out for the best, she supposed.

Pete wasn't at the station when she arrived back, which was a relief. She couldn't wait for this case to be over, so he could go back permanently to his own station two miles away and they'd stop being thrown together like ingredients in one of Mary Berry's recipes. She went into Desmond's office to brief him on her meeting with Emma. 'She has no clue what he's up to. She thinks there's another woman.' Awful to think there was a reality where your husband having another woman might turn out to be the least-worst scenario.

Back at her desk, she was just logging on to her computer when a call came through from reception. 'There's a Donna Shields on the line. She says she needs to speak to you.'

At first Leanne had trouble placing the name, then she remembered the sharp-faced woman with the red-raw complexion. She sighed. Could she get away with pretending to be on another call? No, she'd just call back again. And again.

'Mrs Shields. What can I do for you?'

'I did it. I've got the bastard!' The woman's voice was raspy and breathless, as if she'd been running, and there was a manic edge to it.

Leanne took out her notebook and clicked her biro on. 'What do you mean? Who have you got?'

The tip of the pen hovered over the paper.

'Jason. That cunt. My ex-husband. Like I told you, he's not supposed to come within two hundred metres of me and Keira but he's been out there all the time, not that you lot give a fuck. Anyway, earlier on I came home from picking up Keira from school and there he was sat in his car opposite the flat and I just lost it. He hadn't seen me cos we came a different way on account of Keira needing to pick up her PE kit from her friend. It was boiling so he had his window down, and I just put my face right up to his and was yelling at him and then he put his hand out to

199

grab my throat and I fucking saw red. I grabbed on to his hair – all slimy with gel it was – but I managed to get a bit from the front where he keeps it a bit longer and I yanked it out, so now I've got it. I've got the bastard.'

Leanne wrote 'got the bastard' in looping writing.

'What exactly do you mean?' she asked, although she had a fairly good idea.

'What the fuck do you think I mean? I've got evidence, haven't I?'

Leanne remembered about Donna Shields' insistence that her husband was behind the Hampstead Heath murders.

'You want us to do a DNA test?'

'Yeah. You lot must have picked up something from all those poor kids. All you got to do is match it up to the hair and boof! Got him.'

'Boof,' wrote Leanne.

'OK, Mrs Shields. Why don't you pop the hair in an envelope, and hand it in to the duty sergeant on reception. If nothing else, it might help prove your husband was in breach of his RO.'

'But you'll test it for the other thing?'

'It's not quite as simple as that, Mrs Shields. If I submit a sample without following procedure, we wouldn't be able to use it in court.'

'Yeah, but you can get other evidence then, once you know it's him.'

If only policing were as simple as most of the population believed it to be.

'If Mr Shields was in breach of his restraining order, technically a crime was committed so I might have grounds to proceed with testing, though I'm not committing to anything. So fine. Yes, bring it in.'

'Is that it?'

'Pardon?'

'I basically hand you on a plate the guy who's been going around murdering kids and you tell me to pop into the station like it's no big deal?'

Leanne took a deep breath. 'As I say, Mrs Shields. If you drop in the sample, I'll do my best to put it through our database and we should know within a few days if there's any need to take things further.'

There was an explosion of air from the other end of the phone.

'A few days! *Are you kidding?* How many people does he have to kill for you lot to get off your arses and do something?'

'I do appreciate what you're saying, Mrs Shields, but you must understand you're far from the only person who's contacted us convinced they know who the perpetrator is.'

After Donna Shields had rung off, Leanne tried to lose herself in typing up notes but the other woman's voice kept sounding in her head, both accusatory and scared. She hadn't been prepared for it, when she first joined the force as an idealistic twenty-one-year-old, how it would make her see men differently. Marriage differently. There were so many terrified women out there, living in fear of the people closest to them. Presumably Donna Shields had once thought she loved her husband. What had been going through her mind as she walked down the aisle towards him on her wedding day? Had she known then what he was capable of? Had she wilfully buried it so she wouldn't lose the big day, the white dress? Or had it begun after that, the repeated belittling, the numerous tiny daily brutalities?

She gazed across the room at the desk where Pete sat whenever he was in this office. Marriage was a killer, all right. One way or another, it got you in the end.

27

It wasn't that Rory expected much from his home life. All his mates had complaints about their parents. Jack W.'s dad was old. Ancient, even compared to his mum and Simon. He kept a stash of Viagra in the back of his sock drawer. Jack claimed he'd tried one and had a boner from Friday night till Monday lunchtime but Rory wasn't convinced. And Sam P.'s mum was bipolar and either buzzing around the house like a malfunctioning robot or lying in bed for days on end. Rory had once gone round there after school and she'd come lurching out of her bedroom wearing a grey dressing gown and then cried because there wasn't any milk.

But Rory couldn't remember when the atmosphere in his own house had been worse. Granted, it must have been pretty bad right after Megan was killed, but his memory of those days and weeks was blurry – an endless round of police and relatives and people telling him he mustn't blame himself, and being able to eat cereal whenever he wanted to because there was no one to tell him that it wasn't a proper meal and that if he ate any more there wouldn't be any left for the morning. And it hadn't exactly been a laugh a minute that time a couple of years ago when his mum had found out something about Simon that made her stop speaking to him for a few days and describe him as a 'selfish fat pig' after two glasses of wine.

But this was different. The last few days, it was as if all of them were walking around with individual black clouds over their heads but no one was mentioning them. Simon had been bad-tempered and short with everyone, picking Rory up on everything he did. If he even so much as left his school bag on the kitchen floor for a nanosecond Simon would launch into a rant about respect and collective living. Rory always switched off as soon as Simon started speaking anyway, so he didn't tend to hear the rest. Meanwhile, ever since the last Megan's Angels meeting, his mum seemed to have been sucked down a black hole she couldn't get out of. Talking to her was just like shouting down into the void from where her voice would come back faint and echoey.

Rory himself hadn't been on top form lately either. He'd been getting more texts. *How does it feel to be a killer?* the last one had said. It had got so bad that the pinging noise of an incoming message on his phone now made him go rigid with anxiety. One time he'd confided in Jack H., who had put a hand on his shoulder and shrugged, which had been strangely comforting. But still he couldn't bring himself to open up to his mum.

He was on his way home from school. The first part of the journey, to the clocktower, was always a bit of a laugh. There was a gang of them who usually walked together, devouring crisps and Haribo sweets his mother would never allow in the house. They used to call into the chippy on the way home, but that had gone the way of every single other useful place that had ever opened in Crouch End – namely been turned into a gourmet coffee shop full of double buggies and Eastern European au pairs. When Rory was little there used to be a Woolworths there, right in the centre, where he and Megan would buy pick 'n' mix on a Saturday morning, but now that was a Waitrose.

He'd passed the clocktower and said goodbye to his friends,

dodging a guy with a clipboard wearing a tabard and a fixed smile as he tried to sell charity to shoppers who resolutely refused to meet his eye. All the way home, Rory was thinking about the texts. They were really getting to him now.

That's why he had finally given into Jack H.'s nagging to get Sanjeev involved. He'd held out against it for ages, not because he had anything against Sanjeev, who was actually OK for a geek and whose older sister was downright hot, but because he didn't want everyone knowing about the texts. He was enough of a freak as it was. But Sanjeev, who in addition to being the cleverest in the year could also, allegedly, hack into any computer or mobile phone on the planet, read the texts without comment. Then he told him to leave it with him, and Rory had walked away feeling momentarily lighter.

It was a muggy day – the air was hot and heavy and smelled of overripe fruit. Rory had his blazer scrunched up in a ball in his bag and his white school shirt untucked, sleeves rolled up past his elbows.

As he made his way up the familiar street, he did the usual litany in his head: number 13, where he used to go to nursery as a baby, now remembered only in snapshots – a brightly painted animal mural, wedges of apple on a plate. Number 29, where his best friend from primary used to live before his parents got divorced and he had to move to Hertford with his mum. No, not Hertford, *Hereford*. His mum kept trying to explain the difference and turn it into an impromptu geography lesson, but as far as Rory was concerned it was exactly the same thing. Far was far. The hedge at number 42 where once a burglar had dumped the stolen bike he'd escaped on and Rory's friend Hannah, who'd witnessed it all from her bedroom window, had had to give a statement to the police – to Rory's then acute envy. His neighbourhood was as familiar and comforting to him as the sight of his own hand on the end of his arm. After Megan died, he remembered how everything inside him used to loosen up when he got to these few roads around his house, and he'd be surprised to realize how rigidly he'd been holding himself in.

Turning the corner into his road, he slowed down as he always did, trying to gauge the emotional temperature of his home through its red-brick façade. There had been times in the past when the house had stopped him dead in his tracks before he even reached the front gate, something about it telling him to turn round and go back the way he'd come, to knock on a friend's door and pretend to be locked out, so he wouldn't have to face whatever was there. But today the house was blank and uncommunicative, giving nothing away.

As he was heading up the path, Rory remembered it was his mum's half-day, which could either be a very good thing, or a very bad thing. Sometimes on his mum's half-day he'd open the front door and the whole house would be smelling of freshly baked bread and cakes. Other times she'd be shut off in her study doing God knows what, and when starvation pangs compelled him to go in to ask what was for dinner, she'd blink at him as if she wasn't really sure exactly who he was. And then there were the times he'd come home and a big wave of sadness would come rushing out to meet him like a tsunami. *Thwack.*

Today though, there was neither the baking smell nor the wall of misery. Instead, he heard voices coming from the kitchen.

He hovered in the hallway, his heavy bag still on his back. He was tempted to tiptoe upstairs to his top-floor lair without having to be paraded in front of whoever was in the kitchen, but on the other hand he was starving. He hadn't eaten since lunchtime – he didn't count the bag of salt and vinegar crisps on the way home. He needed proper food. He thought about the packet of bagels in the bread bin. He was sure there was a new jar of peanut butter in the cupboard.

'Rory, is that you? Come through to the kitchen and say hello.'

He dropped his bag to the floor and made a face in the hall mirror before proceeding slowly down the hallway.

'Ah, there you are. Darling, say hello to Susan.'

The woman sitting at the kitchen table gazed at him as if she was having trouble focusing. She had long black curly hair that looked like it needed a wash, and green eyes which were pink around the edges. Her face looked too wide for the amount of skin which was stretched very thin and almost see-through in places. Her hand when he shook it was shockingly cold, despite the mugginess of the day, and lay limply in his like a foreign object.

'Would you like some tea, darling? Biscuit?'

He looked more closely at his mother. She had that unnatural brightness that usually came from being with . . . Oh. Now he knew who this woman was. The knowledge was a dull thud in his stomach. Susan Glover. The mother of the latest victim.

'Kieren just dropped Susan off. You remember Kieren, don't you, the Glovers' lovely FLO? He thought it would do Susan good to get out of the house. Did you have a good day at school?'

His mum was bustling about the kitchen pouring water into the kettle, opening cupboards, rustling biscuit packets, but all the time it was like she was play-acting, as if the stage directions had called for a 'normal family scene'. Rory guessed it must be because of the woman. Mrs Glover. Probably his mum wanted to show her that life did get back to normal and the Glovers could look forward to being an ordinary family again. Yeah, right.

'Are you taking your GCSEs this summer?'

Mrs Glover's voice was like a child's. It made Rory feel un-comfortable. Adults should sound like adults. Otherwise it was just creepy. But then maybe that wasn't her real voice. Maybe it was just the voice she'd been landed with since what happened to her daughter. Maybe they were all walking around using voices that weren't really their own.

'Yeah. That's right.'

'He's about to retake maths for the second time!' his mum chimed in. Rory hated it when she did that – used his abysmal academic record to try to prove something about herself. *Oh, look how relaxed I am, no hot-housing here. See how tolerant I am? What a good sport?*

'Third time lucky, they say.' The soft voice cracked as Mrs Glover tried to laugh.

'Better go. Got loadsa revision.'

He grabbed the tea that had just been poured and started backing out of the room.

'Catch!' A packet of biscuits sailed through the air. His mum was smiling, her cheeks flushed. Susan Glover looked on as if watching the scene through a thick pane of glass.

As he scurried up the stairs he heard his mum say something – probably at his expense – and giggle. At least she seemed to be pulling out of the dark mood she'd been in for the last few days. He sighed, remembering how Susan Glover's cheekbones looked like they might tear through the thin skin that covered them. He thought about how his own mum had been two weeks after Megan's death.

Life was shit sometimes. No word of a lie.

28

So now I've seen the template for how it will be. I've seen how life becomes possible again. I've seen how I can be a mother of a murdered child but also a mother of a living child, and a wife of a living man. I've seen how I can move about my kitchen as if I care about whether there are biscuits in the cupboard and teabags and coffee. Or whether the dishwasher needs emptying or the cat needs to be fed. And how much. And is he getting fat.

In Helen Purvis I've seen my future smiling nervously and darting about and putting a warm hand on my arm. Playing the part of a mother, a friend, a wife. I've seen how I can accommodate even this most unaccommodatable thing, and still keep on living and breathing.

Two weeks ago I weighed myself in the morning. Ten stone seven. I'd never been so heavy except during pregnancy. All day I was preoccupied with my body, feeling myself to be swollen, enormous, whale-like. I remember Poppy put her arms around me and squeezed and I moved away because I didn't want her to feel how my tummy squidged beneath her fingers. I put on the skinny jeans that I'd bought so proudly after I lost my Mia baby weight and felt constricted and stupid, like people would look at my legs and see two sausages bursting their casing.

It mattered to me then. What I looked like.

Just fourteen days later I've lost sixteen pounds. I stood on the scales this morning, and saw the needle at under nine and a half stone and felt nothing. Losing my daughter has made me thin. I can't bear the sight of my ribs poking through my skin because I know what has revealed them. I hate my cheekbones and my hip bones, all the hard nubs of me that have appeared since Poppy went. I want to wrap the fat back around me, winding it like a bandage until time is reversed and she is back.

Helen warned me about the pills. She said I would be tempted but that I must hold firm. She said I must do it for Mia and for Oliver. She showed me her son, a great big boy-man who had nothing to do with my little girls and my life. She wanted me to see how it is possible to re-form into a different type of unit, with new skin growing over the gaping hole, and things gradually shifting to make a new family shape. Her son looked embarrassed, like he wanted to be somewhere else.

I want to take the pills. All of them. And when they're gone I want more. I want a rolling prescription that never runs out. I want to shovel them into my mouth, handfuls at a time, until my throat is clogged with them and I can no longer breathe.

I didn't cry when I was with Helen but she did – a steady stream of tears to show that it was all right to cry, that it was better that way. I didn't tell her my tears are calcifying inside me, forming a solid layer of salt over my heart and veins. She says the girls are all together now. She wants me to find consolation in that. She showed me photos of Megan, a little girl frozen in time just as Poppy will be from now on. 'Don't worry, Megan will look after her,' Helen said. 'And she'll be with Tilly and Leila. They're all together. Doesn't that give you some comfort?'

She wanted to help, I know, but it doesn't help.

Two weeks ago I had my life and my girls and my petty worries about my weight and whether Oliver would still fancy me now I was fat. Now I have Helen Purvis and her laying on of hands.

I am in mourning for the life I never fully appreciated, for the future I wasn't even aware of.

For her.

For me.

For us.

29

KENWOOD KILLINGS: POLICE FOCUS ON VICTIM'S FAMILY

Leanne read the headline in the Thursday edition of the *Chronicle* with a growing feeling of dread. The story that followed was brief but to the point.

> A source close to the investigation has revealed that in the wake of the latest tragic discovery police are now very interested in the movements of a family member of one of the victims. The source wouldn't reveal any more details but says the police are acting on a tip-off from a member of the public.

Leanne closed her eyes momentarily.

'Well?' Desmond was standing by her desk, so near she could see where the static on his polyester-mix trousers was trying to make them adhere to the laminate surface. His face, when she finally glanced up, had the rigid expression of someone holding themselves back from saying what they really mean.

'I know how it looks, sir, but this isn't down to me. I have no idea how this got out.'

'You're the closest person to the Reids and the only officer who knew the full story of that teacher's information about Guy Reid.'

'Yes, but it wasn't me, sir. I wouldn't—'

'How much do you trust your new boyfriend, Leanne?'

'*Pardon?*'

She was genuinely dumbfounded. Desmond never got personal. It wasn't his style.

'Look, Leanne, I don't give a monkey's what you get up to in your private life, as long as it's legal, obviously, but I can't ignore the facts. You *are* in a relationship with a journalist, and suddenly all these confidential stories start appearing in the press, and ding-dong.' Here Desmond tapped the side of his head with a thick finger. 'Alarm bells start ringing.'

'Will is a features editor on a marketing magazine read by just a handful of people. He's not a news reporter. And he wouldn't. He just wouldn't. And anyway, I never talk to him about work stuff.'

She and Will never had those sorts of conversations – well, only in as much as she'd have the odd moan every now and then about something that had happened. He wasn't interested in her work except to support her if things were going badly. But already she could feel her nerve endings start to prickle with doubt. How well did she know Will, in the final analysis? Could he have a side to him that she'd never suspected? As soon as the thought crossed her mind she batted it away again. She'd met his ex, she'd met his mother. She knew his friends, his brother. One time when he had to work over a weekend and she, for once, didn't, she'd spent a whole day alone in his flat rifling through his things. He had nothing to hide. She was sure of it. He was – as much as such things existed – a regular nice bloke. Last Christmas he'd got a card from his barber. And one from the guys at the local Indian takeaway. Will wasn't like Pete. He had no hard edges.

'Just be careful, Leanne.' Desmond had pulled himself upright as if someone was tugging on an invisible wire stretching from the top of his head to the ceiling. 'You have a good record on the force. Don't blow it. Obviously we're conducting urgent inquiries into where this latest leak came from. I would hate for the evidence to point your way.'

After he'd gone, Leanne tried to slow down her racing heart by breathing in deeply like she'd learned at the yoga classes she'd started but had to give up owing to never being able to make the times.

'Want to talk about it?' asked Ruby Adjaye, scooting her chair over to Leanne's and gazing at her through her ridiculously long black eyelashes.

Leanne shook her head. Ruby had been a good friend, particularly after Pete left, but she adored Will, and Leanne knew she wouldn't entertain a word of doubt about him. Ruby couldn't understand why Leanne and Will weren't living together properly yet. She kept sending Leanne links to features on adopting babies from abroad.

'Cool. In that case you'll have plenty of time to deal with the charming Mrs Donna Shields.'

Leanne groaned. 'She's not here again, is she? Please tell me she's not in reception.'

Ruby hesitated before putting her out of her misery: 'No. She wanted to wait for you but I said you were in a meeting and might not be out for hours. She's got quite a tongue on her, hasn't she?'

'Did she say what she wanted?'

'She wants to know what happened with the hair sample.'

'Blimey, does she think we have no other cases at all? She's only just left it. It's just a breach of RO, not a bloody terrorist alert.'

'She's convinced they'll match whatever we've taken from

the latest Kenwood Killer scene. She says you're dragging your feet.'

'She wants the reward. That's what she's after. Her and the other gazillion callers we've had to the information line.'

Still, after Ruby had gone back to her desk, Leanne couldn't stop thinking about Donna Shields. She was scared of her ex, there was no doubt about that. And having looked through his file, Leanne could see why. Disturbed childhood – abusive mother, absent father. A couple of serious incidents in adolescence involving aberrant sexual behaviour with young girls, and several reports of domestic violence as an adult, but no criminal convictions. Yet.

Sighing, she got to her feet and retraced her steps to Desmond's office.

'So you want to run a test just to prove a breach of RO?' Desmond said after listening to her garbled explanation. He sounded dubious, and she didn't blame him. Those tests didn't come cheap.

'I've been through his file, sir, and I think he's dangerous. I just think it might be worth building up evidence against him. Just in case . . . The thing is, we don't want another Melanie Banks.'

Desmond's head snapped up as if yanked on a string. Even a year after her death, Melanie Banks was still a very sore subject. The woman had come in repeatedly before she died to report her estranged husband for threatening behaviour, but though two other officers had spoken to him once or twice, there had seemed little about the case to mark it as a priority. Until Melanie and her two little kids were found with their throats cut. Unsurprisingly there'd been a massive public outcry; a women's group had got hold of the figures for the proportion of the annual police budget that had been spent on protecting and recovering property and compared it to the proportion spent on investigating domestic violence and accused the Met, and Desmond in particular, of not valuing women's lives. It had been the biggest PR disaster of his career to date.

'We're not going to start squandering our resources just to pander to public pressure,' he said, fixing Leanne with a hard look.

'I understand that, sir.'

'However, in view of the fact that there's a young girl involved, I give you the authority to exercise your own judgement.'

Leanne blinked, grappling for the meaning behind his words.

'So I can submit the sample to the lab?'

'Isn't that what I just said?'

Back at her desk, Leanne called up the first of the many forms she was going to need to fill in, already regretting sticking her neck out. It wasn't as if she didn't have enough other stuff to do. When, almost as an afterthought, she made a note to have the test result cross-referenced with the Megan Purvis sample, she felt a twinge, knowing it wasn't strictly protocol. Yet afterwards there was a feeling that she had done the right thing. Donna Shields was hard and brittle and indistinguishable from all the other downbeaten people who passed through the station, but still there was something about her desperation that stayed with Leanne, like when you listen to music and the last note hangs in the air long after the CD has finished. This job had given Leanne a tougher skin but still she never lost sight of how differently her life could have turned out if she hadn't had the support of her family and the basic ingredients every child needs – food, shelter, love. Sometimes, particularly on days like today when everything was going wrong, it was good to remind yourself that things could be a whole lot worse.

Leanne tried to get back to work, only to find herself going over and over the earlier scene with Desmond where he'd probed her about the newspaper leak. She knew the information hadn't come from her but she couldn't help looking around at her fellow officers and wondering what they were thinking. Did they really think she was giving information to the media? What for? Money? The idea of it gave her a tight feeling across her chest and she put her head down to avoid catching anyone's eye.

When a buzz of noise went up from the other side of the room she stiffened, pretty sure she could guess what lay behind it. Unable to resist glancing up, she saw she was right. Pete had arrived. Catching sight of his dark head across the office set off a physical reaction that travelled from her eyes to her brain to her heart and then outwards from there. She knew exactly how that black hair felt under her fingers, the thick bounce of it. She knew how it looked when he flicked it back out of his eyes, how it tickled her face when he was above her on his elbows . . .

Leanne switched her eyes abruptly back to the computer screen.

'You can stop pretending now. We all know you're not really working.'

He'd come up behind her so close his breath was warm in her ear.

'Ah, well, that's where you're wrong, o ye of little faith.' She angled the screen so he could see the form she was filling in with its usual unnecessarily complicated layout. She was conscious of his face just inches from hers. If she just turned her head . . .

She didn't turn her head.

'So how are the Reids?'

Pete had dropped into the empty chair at the desk opposite Leanne. His voice was louder now, less intimate. Well, good. Hopefully he'd got the message. He was a father now. Everything was different.

'They're pretty shit, as you'd expect. I saw Emma on Monday, and she was . . . well . . . Did Desmond tell you . . . ?'

'About Guy loitering around primary schools? Yeah, he did. This morning. And even if he hadn't I could always have read about it in the paper.'

Leanne felt her face burning. 'That wasn't me. I would never . . .'

216

'Relax. I was winding you up. I know it wasn't you. But what do you think about Guy? Have you ever had any doubts?'

Leanne shook her head slowly. 'He's a bit uptight and can come over a bit full of himself. Plus I think he's probably clinically depressed, though I'm sure he'd never admit it. But I've seen him with his own daughters and with other people's too and he never gave the slightest indication—'

'Not that people like that always do. Does Emma know anything's up?'

'I don't think so. Not in that sense anyway. I feel awful though, because she's convinced herself Guy is seeing someone else. Apparently his secretary let slip he's been leaving work early. He told her he was working at home, and she put two and two together and made five million. I felt horrible letting Emma carry on tormenting herself when I knew it wasn't true.'

'Yeah, but the truth could turn out to be a whole lot worse.'

'Maybe. But don't try to downplay how crap it is to find out your husband is cheating on you.'

Why had she said that? And worse, said it in that stupid squeaky voice that he'd recognize immediately as her upset voice.

Pete was staring at her. 'I wouldn't downplay it. I'd never—'

Leanne cut him off before he could say anything more. 'Anyway, I don't think that's the only reason Emma's acting a bit weird. She's become obsessed with the idea that these hair bobbles are important somehow and she's furious with us for not doing anything about it.'

She explained to Pete about Tilly's personal effects, and how Emma was convinced they held the key to the whole case.

Pete's face softened. 'I've had the same thing with Fiona and Mark. Not about hair stuff but they were sure we'd missed something. One of Leila's friend's mums was convinced a kid who'd been doing teacher training at the school had done a suspicious flit, so Fiona and Mark became absolutely certain he was the killer. When we finally traced him, he was teaching English as a foreign language in Thailand.'

Leanne sighed. 'The hair bands seem to have lodged in her brain and I know I've disappointed her by not following it up, but I wouldn't know where to start. I mean, what do you think?'

Pete ran a hand through his own hair.

'It does sound like she's grasping at straws, but then she's never said anything like this before, has she? Not in two whole years. Why would she start letting her imagination run riot now?'

'Yes, but *hair bobbles*, Pete? I told Desmond and he just looked at me like I was mad.'

'But she knows her own child, Leanne. That's the thing.'

Leanne had to check her phone again then, so that Pete wouldn't see how much that hurt. Sometimes when she was talking to him, she forgot what had happened before, forgot that he wasn't hers any more, forgot he'd had a baby with someone else. And then something would happen, like him talking about what parents know with such authority and, *wham*, it hit her all over again. She remembered how it had felt the first time she'd seen him again after the baby – Daisy – had been born, how she'd forced herself to go up to him and congratulate him and asked to see a photograph of her and smiled even though the sight of the tiny creature gazing up at the camera almost tore her heart in two. Ruby had been incredulous afterwards. 'Why would you do that? What kind of masochist are you?' But she knew it was something she had to get out of the way so that she could keep her pride and they could both carry on working alongside each other, though thankfully not at the same station most of the time.

'But what could it mean? Realistically? That this guy, whoever he is, has a fetish about little girls' hair?'

'Well, think about it. Let's suppose Emma is right and Tilly would never in a million years have been wearing mismatched elastics when she got snatched. So, one of her hair thingies comes off somehow. So why doesn't he just leave it off or, I don't know, put all her hair in the remaining band, or just not have any at all? Why replace it, and where would he get a replacement from anyway? None of it makes sense.'

She was interrupted by her phone vibrating in her hand. The caller ID said 'withheld' and she was just about to dismiss it when something tugged at her memory.

'Howard Walsh here. Can you talk?'

She looked up at Pete and did a 'sorry, what can you do' shrug. He nodded once and got to his feet, giving a small wave before turning away. She saw the new female crime-data analyst track his progress back to his temporary desk with a kind of greedy intensity.

'Yes, Howard, how are you?' Too late she remembered he didn't do small talk.

'I've more news on Nemo.'

Leanne, still preoccupied with Pete who was now perched on his desk, talking to someone on the phone, was having problems remembering what she and the strange, nervy undercover cop had talked about that day on the Heath.

'Remember my initial contact? The one who told me the group was actively involved in the whole Kenwood case? Well, he now tells me one of the four members is Bobby Jarvis.'

'You mean *the* Bobby Jarvis?'

'That's right, the original Lion of the North.'

Now there was a phrase Leanne hadn't heard in a long time. Immediately she was transported back to her teenage bedroom in Kent, listening to the radio on interminable Sunday afternoons, the voice of the DJ booming across the airwaves in his broad Yorkshire accent. She could still remember seeing him for the first time on television, with his shock of dyed-blond hair. He'd fallen out of favour after a few years as people like him tended to do. His blokey style of innuendo and low-level misogyny went out of fashion during her teens. She seemed to remember a few seasons in panto and the odd TV appearance but she hadn't heard anything about him in years. And now, after all this time, after all those children's TV shows and all those backstage meet-and-greets with young fans, he'd resurfaced in a paedophile ring.

'How does he know so much – your contact? Is he in the ring himself?'

'No. But he has some sort of hold over one of the other members – some evidence that would link him to a crime. This guy in the ring is a professional of some sort. Teacher maybe, or lawyer. Something like that. Anyway, he wouldn't be too keen for anything like that to be made public.'

Leanne didn't ask Howard what hold *he* had over this contact to make him share his information so freely.

'They were definitely involved. Nemo, I mean. I'm still not sure how, or to what degree, but at least one of them came into contact with Poppy Glover.'

Leanne glanced over at the board at the other end of the office where Desmond had pinned photographs of the four murdered girls. Even from metres away she could see Poppy Glover's shy, gap-toothed smile. She shut her eyes.

'Into contact? In what way?'

'I still don't know. Obviously I've kept my boss updated but he's very anxious we don't do anything to jeopardize our own in-vestigation.'

'But surely we should at least pick up Bobby Jarvis? We've got the semen sample from near Poppy's body. We could run tests and—'

'And what if it isn't him who was there? As soon as you pick him up, Nemo will shut down completely. You'd never trace the others. What if it was one of them?'

'But we can't just leave them to carry on. They might be target-ing their next victim as we speak. You know the gaps between murders have been getting shorter.'

'Obviously your guv'nor will have his own views, but I think it's a risk you're going to have to take – for now.'

Howard's voice had grown weary and clipped, as if he was already detaching himself from the conversation. Leanne got the impression he'd only called her because his superiors had told him to keep her in the loop but that he now felt he'd more than discharged his duty. She pictured him fidgeting with his wire-framed glasses while his Adam's apple bobbed up and down like a gobstopper caught under the thin skin of his throat. She sensed that he was about to hang up and felt a wave of panic.

'One more thing. Have you ever come across someone called Jason Shields?'

'No. I don't think so.'

But Howard Walsh's quiet, contained voice was even more hesitant than usual.

'Are you sure?' Leanne pressed.

'No. Well, there's something ringing a bell somewhere but I can't really be sure.'

'Could you maybe ask around?'

'Look, I'm already sticking my neck out asking around about Nemo. I start throwing out other names, I'm going to blow my cover. Three years of work down the drain.'

She felt stupid now and wished she hadn't opened her big mouth. Howard clearly had her down as some kind of clueless amateur. She'd got the feeling when they'd met that he didn't much like women. Mind you, maybe he just didn't like people. Who could blame him after all the things he must have seen.

The call left Leanne feeling unsettled and needing to clear her head. She headed for the women's toilets, which meant going past Pete's temporary desk. She saw him look up and deliberately averted her gaze.

In the loo, Leanne discovered her period had arrived. That was all she needed. 'Give me a break,' she said out loud. She wondered when she might turn magically into one of those proper women so in tune with their bodies they made a note in their diaries of the dates they were due so they were always prepared, instead of being ambushed by it month after month. Emerging from the cubicle, she glanced at the ancient dispensing machine in the corner. Out of order. How did she guess?

By the time she re-entered the office, she was in a foul temper. Brushing past Pete's desk again without even a glance, she strode back to her own, snatched up her bag and headed out, pretending not to hear Ruby's 'There's someone waiting—'

In the corridor outside she rifled through the contents of her bag, but though she found plenty of old receipts and dog-eared flyers she'd accepted from people in the streets – she never could walk past an outstretched hand, that was her problem – there was nothing remotely useful. She'd have to nip out for something. It was a right pain. Still, at least it would give her a chance to call Will. There was something she needed to talk to him about – without Ruby and Pete and all the rest listening in. She pressed the green exit button and pushed through the heavy door that led to the reception area, hearing the click as it locked behind her. So intent was she on her mission that she didn't notice the blonde woman sitting in a chair to the right of the duty officer's desk.

'Leanne!'

Leanne liked to think she was a pretty tolerant sort of person, but there were some voices that really grated, and Sally Freeland's was one of them.

'I was hoping you'd have time for a coffee. That woman who picked up your phone said you were busy but I thought it was worth hanging around anyway, and here you are!'

Too late Leanne remembered that Ruby had been trying to tell her about someone waiting.

'Actually, it's not a good time, Sally. I've got something urgent I

222

need to do.' For a brief moment she considered asking Sally if she had a tampon but thought better of it.

'Well, I'll just come along with you to your car.'

Leanne thought about saying no, but she didn't want to get into a discussion with the journalist in the lobby. After all, she was already under suspicion of passing on information to the press.

'Free country, I suppose,' she said, striding on.

As ever it was a shock to step out into the daylight and realize there was a whole world going on outside the police station. Sometimes if you stayed in there too long it was as if that was the only reality there was, and when you thought about the 'outside' it was like thinking about the billions of stars and planets in the solar system. You knew they existed in theory but you couldn't fully believe in them.

'I really am pushed for time,' she said as she headed across the forecourt.

'Oh absolutely. Me too. There simply aren't enough hours in the day. So I'll just come straight down to it. I was thinking maybe you and I could do a bit of information sharing. I mean, we all want the same end result, don't we, to find whoever is doing these terrible killings and stop them? So it makes sense to pool what we know.'

Leanne stopped and glanced at her unwelcome companion.

'If you are withholding any information that could help solve a crime, you could be up on a charge of obstructing the course of justice or impeding a police investigation. I would advise you to think very seriously.'

Sally made a dismissive gesture with her hand as if the prospect of a criminal charge was a minor irritation.

'I'm not withholding anything. It's just information that *might* prove to be helpful, but I won't be able to tell without seeing how it fits into place with other pieces. It's like a jigsaw. Do you see? One piece in isolation is next to useless.'

Leanne wasn't in the mood for this. It didn't help that the other woman's immaculate all-white outfit – tight-fitting linen trousers, silk shirt, high wedge sandals – was making her feel so crumpled and scruffy in comparison.

'If you have any information, Sally, then you can pass it on to me or to someone else on the investigation, but I can't enter into any tit-for-tat information sharing, you know that. Now if you'll excuse me.'

She turned her back and walked off, smoothing the creases out of her too-tight navy-blue skirt as she moved.

'So you don't want to know about Nemo then?'

Leanne stopped in her tracks before slowly turning round, her mind racing. What did Sally know about Nemo? How had she found out?

'I don't have time to talk to you,' she said, before adding grudgingly, 'At least not now.'

Sally Freeland smiled like she'd won a victory and Leanne pinched the inside of her wrist to stop herself saying something she'd regret.

'How about later this afternoon?'

'Yes. OK. But it'll have to be north – Hampstead or Highgate.'

Sally's eyebrows rose as if Leanne had given something away.

'No probs. Whatever suits.'

The skin on Leanne's wrist smarted as she turned and walked away.

30

Emma clicked on the link that was minimized at the bottom of her laptop so that it sprang once more into life.

A source close to the investigation has revealed that in the wake of the latest tragic discovery police are now very interested in the movements of a family member of one of the victims. The source wouldn't reveal any more details but says the police are acting on a tip-off from a member of the public.

Movements of a family member of one of the victims? What did that even mean? Ever since Fiona Botsford had texted her at eight thirty-five that morning asking if she'd read the *Chronicle*, the questions had been going round and round in Emma's head. Which victim? Which family member? Her unquiet brain ran through them all, over and over. Simon Hewitt? But then why not Daniel Purvis? How come he never came to any of the support meetings? She'd always found that strange. Mark Botsford. He was so quiet, almost preternaturally self-controlled. She'd never seen him cry. She kept running through the list of people, afraid to stop thinking for fear of what she'd then have to face.

The one man she hadn't included in her list. Guy.

She kept remembering how Leanne had asked all those questions about Guy when they'd met at King's Cross. And what about this woman he'd been sneaking off early from work to see? Could that have anything to do with it?

She had a flashback to the first time she'd ever seen Guy, when she was helping her friend Ade move into a shared house in Brixton and the door of the neighbouring room had opened and there had been this man in an old T-shirt and a pair of tartan pyjama bottoms. Struggling under the weight of a cardboard box she'd hardly noticed him and then he'd looked at her with those green eyes and something had dropped away inside her. And now the memories were coming faster. Their first holiday where they'd borrowed his cousin's ancient camper van and they'd broken down somewhere in the Dordogne and had to spend three nights in a *pension* that smelled like cabbage soup and there'd been nothing to do but lie in bed on the bobbly nylon sheets and laugh and fuck and eat croissants smuggled in from the bakery down the road. The day after Jemima was born, when he'd arrived, red-faced and out of breath, bursting through the door of the ward the very second visiting hours started, having run all the way from the tube, desperate to see them both again.

Those memories weren't lies. That Guy existed. He still existed. So why wouldn't these doubts just leave her alone?

By 11.30 that morning she couldn't bear it any more. She picked up the phone and dialled the number that still produced a tight, painful knot in her stomach. By one o'clock she was in the car and by twenty-five past, she was sitting under an umbrella in the cramped courtyard of a pub. At the next table a group of medics from the sprawling hospital up the hill were drinking Jägermeister shots. Emma hoped they'd just come off shift rather than being about to start.

'Sorry I'm late. It's been a pig of a morning.'

Leanne burst into the courtyard, her cheeks the exact shade of pink as the short-sleeved cotton top which had come untucked from her navy skirt.

'I got you an orange juice. I assumed you wouldn't be drinking on duty.'

Leanne glanced wistfully over at the Jägermeister table and Emma wondered whether she should have got her a glass of wine after all.

'Look, Leanne. I'm just going to come straight to the point. I—'

'I think I can guess what prompted this, Emma. You read the snippet in the *Chronicle*, didn't you?'

Emma nodded, her mouth suddenly dry.

'I have to know. Is it Guy you're investigating?'

Leanne put down the orange juice she'd been sipping through a black bendy straw so that she could reach out and put her hand over Emma's.

'I knew that's what you'd be thinking, after our conversation the other day. I'm going to be honest with you, Emma, in a way I couldn't be the last time we met because I was under orders, but my boss now thinks you have the right to know, and maybe you can even help us get to the bottom of what's going on. Do you mind if I tape this?'

Leanne was already reaching down into the outside pocket of her bag from where she eventually produced an old-fashioned mini tape recorder.

'I have got one of the digital ones, but I can't work it out,' she explained.

Then she caught sight of Emma's face.

'It's just a formality, Emma. This isn't an official interview, but I need to record it just in case it becomes part of our investigation. Do you understand? Otherwise, I'm afraid, I won't be able to give you the information you need.'

'OK,' Emma said, but her voice was hoarse and gravelly.

'Righto. Let's just make sure this thing is working. Can you say something?'

'It feels like I'm stuck inside a made-for-TV drama or something.'

Leanne smiled and clicked the machine off, rewound and played it back.

Feels like I'm stuck inside a made-for-TV drama or something, came Emma's tinny voice.

'Perfect. The thing is, Emma, as you know, Guy has been finishing work at peculiar times and going AWOL, only he hasn't been seeing another woman. He's been sitting in his car outside primary schools. Mostly one in St John's Wood, but we've also found out he's been spotted at a couple of others in the area.'

'I don't understand. That's nowhere near where our daughters go to school—'

'Exactly. That's why I was hoping you'd be able to shed some light on what he might be doing?'

Emma shook her head slowly. She swallowed, suddenly afraid she was going to vomit right there and then. Something occurred to her. 'Have you asked him? Have the police talked to Guy?'

The thought that he could have been called into the station and hadn't told her was unbearable.

'We're talking to him right now as it happens.'

'So that's why you insisted on meeting here rather than at the station?'

Leanne nodded. 'It shouldn't take too long. We just need him to clear it up for us.'

But Emma's thoughts were whirling around in her brain and she could hardly focus on what her companion was saying. Why would Guy be lurking outside primary schools?

'Emma.' Leanne leaned right in so she was inches away from Emma's face. Her eyes, close up, were tinged with pink as if she hadn't been sleeping. 'You know that when Tilly died we tested Guy's DNA against the sample found at the scene of Megan Purvis's murder. It wasn't a match. Keep bearing that in mind. Guy is not suspected of anything. This is just a formality.'

But on the way home the doubts built up in Emma's head until she thought she would explode. What if the thing that had come between her and Guy wasn't grief but guilt? Paedophilia was a compulsion, wasn't it? A disease? Maybe he couldn't help himself. The sudden pain that shot up her side at the thought of her two surviving daughters stopped her in her tracks.

By the time she reached her house, Emma was having difficulty breathing. Though she was panting, she didn't seem to be able to draw enough oxygen into her lungs. At first she assumed Guy wasn't back from the police station yet as she couldn't see his car anywhere, but then she spotted it further down the street.

Approaching the front door, she wondered if she had the nerve to go in. There was a painful stitch in her side and her heart was pounding uncontrollably. But she knew it was less than an hour until the girls were home from school so she forced herself to take out her keys.

Guy was sitting at the kitchen table with his head in his hands. Emma noticed with a shock how grey his hair was getting at the back. He still had his work clothes on – his shoulders in his grey suit jacket were slumped.

He didn't look up, though he must have known she was standing in the doorway. For a moment there was a silence that settled over the two of them like a net.

Then: 'I've been with Leanne. I know you were called in by the police.'

Silence.

'Tell me. Tell me why you've been sneaking out of work to go and lurk outside primary schools.'

More silence.

'You owe me an explanation, you bastard. I need to know if you did something to our daughter.'

That got a reaction all right. Guy's head shot up.

'What? What did you just say?'

'You heard.' But the conviction was already draining from her voice. 'I just want to know what's going on. It was bad enough when I thought you were seeing another woman but now I know you've been hanging around watching little girls come out of school. Day after day after day. Why were you there?'

'Because I miss her!' The words tore from Guy's throat as if ripped out of him against his will. To her astonishment, Emma saw that he was crying, tears that fell messily from his reddened eyes, splashing on the blond-wood table.

'I go and I sit and I watch the gate and I imagine that she's going to come through it any moment. And I watch the girls and the way they talk and laugh and carry their paintings so carefully to show their parents, and I imagine she's one of them and for five or ten minutes I convince myself it never happened.'

'So why not go to our daughters' school? Why not go and watch the children you still have instead of a whole bunch of strangers?'

'Because I don't want Caitlin and Jemima to see me like this. I don't want anyone to see me like this. I don't want you to see me like this. It's been two whole years. I'm supposed to be coping.'

Emma looked at her weeping husband and felt something shifting and dissolving inside. The feeling panicked her. The barrier between her and Guy had been there so long it was part of her emotional framework. How would she keep holding herself upright without it?

'Who says you're supposed to be coping? Who do you think will judge you if you fall apart?'

Guy gazed at her through his overspilling eyes. And then a noise came from out of nowhere like the cry made by foxes that occasionally woke them up in the dead of night. A terrible, inhuman roar, and then she was across the floor and standing beside him and he had his arms around her waist and his face buried in her stomach and she was stroking his head and telling him it was OK, it was OK, it was OK. And for the first time since it had happened, for the first time in two years, she forced herself to believe this might be true.

31

Suzy's house was in the Bermuda triangle where three different North London districts met. They all had Green in their name, though there was nothing green about any of them. The terraced houses on Suzy's road were either greyish brick or painted the maroon colour favoured by Greeks of a certain age or done up in fake stone cladding. A double mattress had been dumped on the corner. Jason wrinkled up his nose at the sight of the large brown stain in the middle. People were disgusting.

The houses in this street were mostly rented out and carved up into bedsits. Next door to Suzy's house one lot of tenants had clearly recently moved out. The front yard was piled with black bin bags, many of them split, the contents strewn all over the path. There was a bright-orange flannel slipper on the pavement just outside and Jason kicked it back in through the gate.

Outside Suzy's door, he paused before ringing the bell. He squinted at his reflection in the diamond-shaped panel of the white plastic front door, with its fake leaded glass. His mouth was dry and he tried to swallow. The palms of his hands felt damp with sweat.

Suzy's house was a riot of soft furnishings in various vibrant colours and prints. The cushions on the sofa they passed were red, as was the kettle, while the toaster and the pedal bin were bright blue. Sitting at the kitchen table he could feel the beginnings of a headache throbbing at his temples.

'Shame you couldn't get here earlier,' Suzy said, perching on his knee and putting her arms around his neck. 'Bethany is about to get home from school. I thought I told you she gets home later on Thursdays on account of street dance. We could have . . . you know . . .'

She nuzzled into his neck. The pain in his head intensified.

'Sorry. I got held up at the gym.'

'Show us your muscles then.' Suzy pushed her hands with their bright-yellow nails up the sleeve of his T-shirt and squeezed his biceps with her fingers.

'Yeah. I can see you've been busy,' she said. 'Wanna see mine?'

She bent her left arm and made a straining face as if trying to flex her non-existent muscles. Just then there was the sound of a key in the lock followed by an explosion of high-pitched giggles.

'Sounds like Emily is here as well,' said Suzy, not moving from Jason's lap. 'Sometimes I'd swear that girl lives at our house. Her mum's on her own, like me, and she's got three other little ones. I think Em comes round here for a bit of peace and quiet. It's not easy for her back home.'

Jason's heart was pounding as the two girls came into the kitchen, looping the straps of their bags over the chairs.

'Oh, all right, Jase,' said Bethany, hardly registering his presence. 'Mum, what's there to eat? I'm starving.'

Jason waited for Suzy to tell them it was nearly dinner time, but she just reached over for the packet of chocolate digestives on the sideboard and tossed it at her daughter.

'How did you get home?' Jason asked, hoping his voice was steady. He directed the question at Bethany, not daring to look at Emily who was leaning awkwardly against the fridge.

'Bus,' she said airily, licking the chocolate off the top of her biscuit.

He got up, tipping Suzy off his lap.

'They're too young to be getting the bus on their own.' He could feel the anger working its way up his body, through his arms all the way down to his fingertips. It felt good. 'Do you know how many nutters there are out there? Anything could happen.'

Suzy stared at him, an ugly flush creeping over her chest and neck – red to match the kettle.

'It's fine. Loads of them get the bus together. I don't want to fall out with you, Jason, but please don't start telling me how to raise my own kid. Not when I've been doing it just fine on my own for three years, thank you very much.'

For a few seconds they stared at each other. He snatched a glance at Emily and saw she looked nervous, as if she was about to cry.

'Course you have. I'm sorry, love.' He reached out to take Suzy's hand. 'I'm just a bit over-anxious. It probably comes from having a daughter of my own I'm not allowed to see and lying awake at night thinking of all the terrible things that could be happening to her. Course you know what's best.'

Suzy squeezed his hand and her body relaxed.

'You're missing your daughter. That's natural. It still winds me up that your ex is keeping her from you. I haven't always seen eye to eye with Bethany's dad, but I'd never stop him seeing her. Children need their fathers.'

She raised her face up to his and touched his cheek with a yellow nail.

'Our first row,' she said softly. 'This is getting serious.'

She was joking and yet not joking.

All the time, Jason was conscious of Emily standing to his left. He wanted to unhook Suzy's arms and turn to look at her, but he worried his face might give him away.

'We've been planning my birthday on Saturday,' Bethany said, spraying biscuit crumbs all over the kitchen surfaces. 'We were going to go bowling, but now I think we'll just chill here with pizza and movies. We're going to stay up all night. Aren't we, Emily?'

Finally Jason turned to look. The girl had her long dark hair in a plait which she'd pulled forward over her shoulder so she could play with the end. Her narrow face looked paler than ever in contrast to the bright pink of the bread bin she was standing beside. Her strangely colourless eyes were fixed on her friend as if looking at either of the adults would be too scary. Jason noticed the individual hairs standing up on his arm and he felt curiously light-headed.

'Mum's giving me One Direction tickets for my present, aren't you, Mummy, lovely beautiful Mummy?'

'Just you wait and see, Miss Nosy.'

Suzy snuggled into Jason and he had to stop himself from pulling away. She was wearing some kind of cloying perfume that was catching in his throat.

'How many you got coming to your sleepover, Bethany?' he asked.

'Dunno. Four? Five if I'm talking to Tasha by then but she was such a cow in maths. She told Mr Tenby that I'd told Josh Perriman the answer but I never did. I didn't even know the answer.'

Jason stiffened at the word 'cow', waiting for Suzy to call her out on it, but she seemed to think the whole thing was funny. If that had been Keira . . . No, he mustn't think about Keira. But now that the thought was in his mind, it was making him antsy. Anger was prickling at the soles of his feet, the palms of his hands, the soft flesh of his inner wrist. He glanced again at Emily and had a flash of another dark-haired girl, the smell of apple shampoo. Blood rushed to his head and he closed his eyes. Suzy, misinterpreting his actions, stood up on tiptoe to kiss him on the mouth.

'I gotta go,' he said, moving abruptly away. 'Tell you what, though, Suzy, I'll come back the day after tomorrow for the sleepover. Help you with sorting out food and all that stuff.'

Suzy's expression now dissolved into the kind of look she might have given a kitten that had just done something unbearably cute.

'Aw, that's so sweet of you. But honestly, don't worry. I can sort out the sleepover. I'm used to it. Better for you to come round when it's just the two of us, if you know what I mean.' She gave him an exaggerated wink.

'Eww, gross!' Bethany was grinning in a way that was all too knowing for an eleven-year-old, if you asked him.

'No, I'd like to help. It'd make me feel, you know, part of your life.'

Suzy reached up and kissed him on the cheek.

'You are a sweetheart. You know that? You look all hard on the outside, but you're just a big softie underneath, aren't you?'

He forced himself to look up and hold her gaze.

'I'd love it if you helped,' she said, then she gave him a playful pinch on the arm. 'Just wanted to check you're real.'

32

'You a writer then?'

The man had sat himself down on the opposite side of the table before Sally had a chance to tell him she was waiting for someone. She took a deep breath in, then exhaled slowly until her flare of anger was under control.

'The computer,' the man went on, nodding towards Sally's MacBook Pro. 'I saw you were deep in thought, tapping away there. I write myself actually.'

Sally's heart, which was already in free fall, plummeted further.

'Yes,' he continued as if she'd evinced the slightest interest, 'I write fantasy mostly – only it's a bit different, a bit cross-genre.'

'Don't tell me. *The Hobbit* meets *Fifty Shades of Grey*?'

'Haha. That's very funny. No, mine is about a group of Nazi-hunting vampires. It's actually a bit of an allegory of the dichotomy at the heart of modern society between our opposing desires for justice and for retribution. It's four hundred and fifteen thousand words long at the moment.' He looked expectantly at Sally.

'Well, you know what they say? Everyone has a book in them – and in most cases that's exactly where it should stay.'

The man's smile slipped and Sally went back to her computer screen where she was trying to force a new angle on to the Kenwood Killings, to disguise the fact she was actually just trotting out the same rehashed facts and conjectures. When she looked up again the man had gone and Leanne Miller was slipping into his recently vacated seat.

'Thank you for coming.' Sally smiled in what she hoped was a warm way.

She tried not to stare at the creases in Leanne's pink top. What was it about plain-clothes policewomen and irons?

'I haven't got long,' said Leanne, waving aside Sally's offer of a latte. 'I've already been out of the office much longer than I'd planned.'

'Right. Well, the thing is, like I said before, I thought it would be a good thing for both of us if we pooled our resources on this case. I'm not suggesting you tell me official secrets or anything, just that we help each other a bit.'

Leanne looked like she was stifling a sigh, and Sally felt her hackles rising.

'You mentioned Nemo this morning.'

'Yes. But before we talk about that, I do need to know what might be in it for me, supposing I was to have information that might turn out to be useful to you.'

Leanne didn't even try to stifle her sigh this time.

'I've talked to my boss. He'd be prepared to offer you the first exclusive interview once the case is solved. Depending on what you have to say, of course.'

'I want to be involved as the case unfolds. I want to be included in the investigation.'

Leanne started to gather her things together. 'Uh-uh, not going to happen,' she said, perching a pair of sunglasses on her head.

Sally put up her hand in a gesture of surrender. 'OK, OK. But

238

I want exclusive interviews with all the officers involved, not just DCI Desmond.'

Leanne nodded – just the slightest of movements.

'And I want an interview with Emma Reid.'

'You know perfectly well I can't force Emma to talk to you.'

'Not force. *Persuade.* She'll listen to you. Especially if you tell her I've helped with finding Tilly's killer.'

Leanne glared at her, and Sally forced herself to hold her gaze.

'I'll talk to her. That's all I can do.' Leanne looked pointedly at her watch. 'Nemo?'

'Right. So I have a contact, anonymous naturally, who is a member of this online paedophile chatroom which was formed basically to fantasize about the Kenwood Killings. Hideous, isn't it, what turns some people on? One of them even used to be quite famous, my contact says, though he wouldn't give me any details of who it was.'

'Wait. This man you know is a member of this chatroom? He's actually in it?'

'Yes. Have you heard about it then?'

'I'll tell you at the end. Carry on.'

'Well, like I say, the group was formed to swap fantasies and photographs. At least that's what my contact thought when he joined, but then he went offline for a while. He has issues with his conscience, my contact. Keeps wanting to go straight, as it were, but then gets dragged back into it. It's an addiction, you know. Child pornography. Anyway. When he went back to the chatroom he got the sense something big had happened, only no one was saying anything. But then, from little comments here and there, he realized the others were talking to each other privately, so no one else could see. They'd formed their own private group. When I spoke to him the first time, he didn't know anything about it except they were calling it Nemo. But then somebody in the group sent round a photo by mistake. *Of the body.*'

Sally had lowered her voice for the last sentence.

'Of which body?' Leanne prompted urgently.

'The last one. Poppy Glover. Apparently they used that app where the photo disappears after a few seconds, but he swears that's what it was of.'

'And where did they get the photo? Did he say?'

'No. Apparently the others all got angry with the one who had sent the photo and they tried to tell the others that he'd got the picture from another case entirely. An American case. But my contact swears it was the Glover girl. He recognized the Heath Extension in the background and the description of the clothes she was wearing when she disappeared.'

'So where does he think the photo came from?'

'Well! He thinks they were there, obviously, when she died. And if that's the case, maybe they were there when the others died too. Maybe the whole group thing wasn't built around fantasies but is a way for them to relive something that actually happened. Maybe Nemo is the Kenwood Killer.'

Leanne leaned back in her chair and blew air out from her cheeks.

'We'll have to have your contact's name, of course.'

Sally was already shaking her head. 'No. He stays anonymous. That's my deal with him. He hasn't committed any crime. He's just someone who has a compulsion he can't help. He's deeply ashamed of it. I've told you the name of this ring. It won't take much for you to track them down, surely?'

Leanne pulled her mouth into a tight line. 'No way. If this gang might be responsible for the murders, you are legally bound to tell us what you know and that means the identity of your source. If he's really just an observer and a fantasist, he won't have anything to worry about.'

'The others will kill him. His life won't be safe.'

'We can try to sort out some protection. But obviously our main priority is the children out there who could be at risk from these people if what you say is true. You *have* to give up your source, Sally. Or else you might find you're going down with him.'

33

'Are you completely positive?'

Shock was causing Rory's voice to come out several notches higher than normal.

'Yeah, bro, I checked the number against your addy list in your phone. Her name's Jemima Reid. She's the one been sending you all that shit. You know this nutter? You gonna get the police involved?'

'Nah, man. I'll deal with it. Listen, how much do I owe you?'

'It's on the house, bro.'

For a horrible moment Rory thought he might cry at this simple act of generosity. Sanjeev looked a bit overcome too. He started scrolling intently through his phone which is exactly what Rory did whenever he was trying to avert a public display of emotion. Rory toyed with the idea of slapping him on the back, but in the end kept his hands firmly wedged in his pockets, while all around them in the playground kids in black blazers streamed past on their way back into the school building.

'Nice one,' he said.

'Yeah, all right.' Sanjeev didn't look up.

Rory should by rights have been heading in for double

geography but the thought of two hours revising flood plains and river basins was insupportable. A few weeks ago they'd been on a school trip to the Thames Barrier. Some schools got to go to Madagascar and the North Pole for their trips, but they went on the tube to see a great big concrete wall. He started towards the school doors, but at the last minute swung round and walked quickly in the opposite direction towards the gates. He'd never cut classes, not even in the worst time just after Megan died when he would have had an excellent excuse and no one would have made a fuss, but weirdly that was when he had most wanted to be in school, listening to stuff about recurring numbers and Shakespearean fatalism. Today, however, he just couldn't stomach it.

He dodged out of the gate unnoticed while a bunch of sixth-formers were pushing their way back in from their lunch break and set off up the hill. He still couldn't process the idea that Jemima Reid was behind the poisonous texts. True, he'd always thought she was weird, but weird in a normal sort of way, not in a full-blown psycho way. He remembered how she always stared at him across the room and he'd thought she might quite fancy him and though it had annoyed him, it had also been pleasing in a way. And now it turned out that all that time she'd been sending him those nasty, threatening messages, trying to make him feel guilty.

His stomach twisted itself into knots, forming a hard painful mass as he walked further up the hill, growing more and more angry.

He would go and confront her. He knew she went to the private school up by the Heath. He'd go there and wait for her to leave and have it out with her. What gave her the right to make him feel worse than he already did?

Reaching the gates of her school, on the outer edges of the Heath, he stood on the opposite side of the road and waited for the school day to end, realizing too late that a) he was going to have to wait a long time and b) chances were she would be picked up by a parent and he wouldn't get to talk to her anyway. Frustration and the painful knot in his stomach made him feel suddenly like he was either going to burst into tears or scream out loud, right here on his own in the street. He thought about going home, but then had a mental image of Jemima sitting in her bedroom – he pictured it with posters of Justin Bieber and One Direction on the wall – typing out all those sick messages, and he knew he couldn't leave without finding out why she'd done it.

A group of kids came along, tipping the remains of their lunch into their open mouths from brown-paper bags. Stuffing his blazer into his backpack, Rory marched across the road and slipped through the school gates alongside them. He had no plan in mind, he just knew he had to confront Jemima Reid and he had to do it there and then before his nerve failed.

Once inside, he headed for the school office where a woman in a bright-red dress and those canvas shoes that lace right up your legs eyed him suspiciously.

'Jemima is in class,' she said. 'What did you want with her?'

Rory recognized the protectiveness similar to that of the teachers at his own school who'd had four years of practice of shielding him from pushy reporters pretending to be uncles and cousins. 'I'm Rory Purvis,' he said, for the first time ever using his unwanted celebrity to press home an advantage. The woman's eyes, which were outlined in black so that the blue irises kind of sprung out at you in an alarming way, widened and Rory could see she knew his name.

'Look, I just need to have a few words with Jemima. There've been some, well, developments and I need to talk them over with her. We've become quite . . . well, close.'

He forced himself to keep looking her in the eye.

The woman stared at him, deliberating.

'OK. It's a bit irregular, mind. I mean, imagine if we let all our students come out of classes every time one of their friends had something they wanted to talk over. But as there are special circumstances, I'll have a word with the Head.'

She disappeared through a doorway, from where Rory could hear the sound of murmuring voices, and then the woman with the red dress reappeared, accompanied by an older woman who held out her hand.

'Rory, isn't it? I understand you're here to see Jemima. While I wouldn't wish to encourage you to make a habit of this, on this one occasion I will make an exception. I have tried to contact Jemima's mum to get her approval, but she isn't responding, so I'm just going to have to trust that you are who you say you are and that this really is urgent.'

As if they hadn't just been on Google Images in the Head's office, checking him out!

'Sureya here will fetch Jemima and the two of you can go into my office and have a chat.'

Too late, Rory saw that his idea of taking Jemima Reid outside for a bollocking had never been realistic. Schools were more like prisons than prisons were, in his opinion. He had a vision of Jemima being called out of class and being told who was waiting for her and throwing a hissy fit, but there was nothing he could do about it now.

Installed in the Head's office, he fidgeted with his bag, wishing he'd never come. The righteous anger that had propelled him here had all but fizzled out and he was left with a prickling feeling of apprehension. He looked around the room. There was an abstract painting on the opposite wall that looked like someone had inhaled a load of paints through their nose and then sneezed them out over a canvas. Through the window, he could see a green lawn sloping away towards a red-brick building with brightly coloured ceramics on the window sills that looked like it could be an art block. It was a world away from the concrete and tarmac of his own school.

Finally the door opened and the Head walked in followed by Jemima, her round face betraying no emotion at all.

'You two know each other, don't you?'

The Head looked as if she'd love to be invited to stay, but eventually she said, 'Well, I have plenty of admin to be getting on with,' and backed out to the secretary's office, leaving the two of them standing in silence.

'I know you've been sending me texts.'

Jemima, who was leaning against the wall with the abstract painting, staring at the floor, with the cuffs of her long-sleeved T-shirt pulled over her hands, glanced up and caught his eye and then looked down again.

'Oi! I said, I know it's you who's been sending me those nasty texts. Not cool. I want to know why. What have I ever done to you? *Well?*'

Jemima kept her eyes trained on the ground.

He got out his phone and called up the last message. The 'murderer' one. Then he crossed the room and thrust the screen under her nose. 'Read that. Go on, read it. How do you think that makes me feel? Was it your idea of a joke? Did you think it was funny? Is that it?'

'No.'

The sound was so quiet, it might almost have not been a word at all but a cough or the scrape of a chair leg.

'Well, what then? Why are you trying to make me think it's my fault? If it's my fault Megan died, it's just as much your fault that Tilly died.'

'No!'

Again that odd sound. Rory looked again. Jemima's face was scrunched up and she looked as if she was about to cry – or else give birth or something painful like that.

246

Then he understood. 'That's it, isn't it? That's what it's all about. You feel guilty yourself and you're just trying to make me feel the same so you don't have to face it. What a shitty thing to do.'

Jemima covered her face with her hands and tried to say something.

'What?' Rory was angry. He didn't have the patience for this. 'I can't hear a word you're saying.'

'I said I'm sorry!'

Now she was crying for real. You'd have thought, after the last four years, that Rory would be used to the sight of female tears, but he found himself growing horrified all over again.

'Don't you ever think about it?' She was gazing at him wild-eyed, her cheeks bright red, her curly hair all mussed up.

'About what?'

'What more you could have done? We're the older ones, right? We should have been able to do something.'

'That's just dumb.' Rory didn't want to listen to any more of it. There was that familiar tight feeling in his chest and a noise in his head like an engine starting up.

'No, it's not. They blame us, you know. Our parents. They think it's our fault.'

'It's not true. You're talking shit.'

But now he could see his mum's face in his head, the way it sagged when she thought no one was watching, as if pulled down by hundreds of tiny weights.

'It is. You know it is. That's what's turned your mum into a nutter.'

And instantly, Rory could see that it was so. His mum had been nuts ever since Megan died. She went to work and had meetings and did whatever it was she did in her job. She chatted with her Megan's Angels group. She sat on the sofa next to Simon with her feet in his lap. But underneath it all there was something broken.

'I didn't . . . She wasn't . . .'

But the noise in his head was louder and the tightness was like wire cutting into him and now he was crying too. He wiped his hand across his eyes.

'Oh my God! You're literally crying!' Jemima was staring at him open-mouthed.

Shame flooded through him, but he couldn't stop. 'I should have stayed with her. I shouldn't have been playing football.'

The words came out without him even being aware of what he was saying. He'd never even allowed himself to think this stuff before, let alone say it out loud. He was shocked but at the same time he felt strangely lighter.

'Yeah, well, Tilly only went to the shop on her own because I refused to go with her, and then she just nagged and nagged until Mum gave in and let her go.'

'It's not a bloody competition, you know. A who-can-feel-the-most-guilty competition.'

They glared at each other for a moment and then, to his surprise, Rory found himself smiling.

'We're both fucking nutjobs. Do you know that?'

Jemima tried to scowl, but he could see that something had given way inside her.

'Yeah, whatever. I am sorry though. About the texts.'

Thinking about the encounter as he started on the long walk home, Rory felt hot with embarrassment. He couldn't now believe he'd cried. And yet something about the exchange had also left him strangely buoyant. For years his mother and various nut-doctors had been telling him it wasn't his fault, but it had taken that weird thirteen-year-old kid to get him to admit that he'd ever thought it was.

He decided to take a walk across the Heath. Usually he avoided going anywhere near it but today something had changed. It wasn't his fault. He didn't need to feel guilty. And why shouldn't he go anywhere he bloody well wanted to. It being a dry, early summer day, the Heath was crowded with dog walkers and joggers and groups of Japanese tourists filming the trees on their iPads. As he followed the footpath between two of the bathing ponds, he took out his phone again and scrolled through the text messages Jemima had sent him. His phone was an old one that had belonged to Simon. He'd had an iPhone once but he'd left it on the bus and his mum had refused to fork out for a replacement so he was stuck with the most embarrassing phone in the northern hemisphere. On an impulse, he clicked the phone shut and then hurled it into the brown waters of the mixed pond, at the far end of which he could see a mass of sunbathers crowded on to the wooden jetty. For a second he felt euphoric, but by the time it hit the surface he was already regretting his spontaneity.

For a moment he stood gazing out at the water, frozen in an agony of regret. *His phone!* Then he shrugged and moved on. Sometimes shit things just happened. And there wasn't a bloody thing you could do to change them.

34

The girl had long thin arms that she wrapped around herself and bulging eyes that looked several sizes too big for her gaunt face. She was softly spoken and her accent, when loud enough to be heard, was boarding-school posh. Her long brown hair was messily hooked behind her ears and feathered with split ends. Leanne wanted to whisk her off for a haircut and a decent meal. What happens to people in their lives, she thought, to send them so off-kilter?

'I just need to know I'm safe, that's all. I want to help, don't get me wrong, but I can't go to prison, I just can't.'

The girl was scratching her arms with her bitten, jagged nails and Leanne tried not to look at the pink welts rising up on the unnaturally pale skin. She tried to guess. Heroin? Maybe with a bit of methamphetamine, judging by the state of her teeth. She glanced down at her notebook. So far all she knew for sure was that the girl's name was Lucy and she was twenty-two years old, though she looked thirty-two. She'd been caught shoplifting in a department store and had told the arresting officer she had information about the Poppy Glover case, about the day she went missing. But since she'd been brought in to see Leanne, she'd been refusing to give them anything more until she had assurances that all charges against her would be dropped.

'There's a killer out there who is preying on young vulnerable children. If you have any information at all that could help us stop him, I suggest you share it now before he chooses a new victim.'

It was the same line she'd used on Sally Freeland the day before but she could tell it wasn't going to work on Lucy.

'I get you. I really do. I just really need to think about myself and what's best for me. I hope you understand.'

'Do you think the parents of Poppy Glover would understand?'

Leanne had pretty well-developed antennae for when someone genuinely was sitting on useful evidence and when they were simply making things up to save their own skin, but with Lucy she couldn't tell. Junkies were inveterate liars. But still, there was something about this girl's body language, the way she kept darting a look at Leanne, then turning her eyes quickly away, that made her think maybe she was telling the truth. In Leanne's experience, if people were lying, they tended either to look away the whole time or to fix you with intense eye contact as if daring you to disbelieve them.

A knock on the door of the interview room startled her. Ruby was standing there with a computer printout. A quick analysis had revealed Leanne's companion to be Lucy Cromarty, originally from Richmond-upon-Thames, an upmarket area of south-west London, but for the last two years of no fixed abode. In and out of police custody for petty theft and drugs offences. One short stay in prison with the threat of an automatic longer custodial sentence should she reoffend. Periodic attempts at rehab, including several top-end private clinics, but fewer recently. Family grown weary of throwing money at the problem without seeing any lasting results, Leanne supposed. The printout made depressing reading, but there was no obvious connection between this girl and any of the Kenwood families. Leanne went back to the table and sat down heavily.

'So, Lucy Cromarty, how about we try it again.'

An hour and a half later, she was heading back to her desk feeling hollowed out. After the printout arrived, Lucy had clammed up entirely, answering 'no comment' to all Leanne's questions. She would have to talk to Desmond about the immunity issue. Not an avenue the DCI would be too happy about, but an instinct told her it might be worth it. Lucy Cromarty definitely knew something she wasn't sharing.

Leanne's heart sank when she saw someone had left today's *Chronicle* on her desk folded to one of the inside pages. She swallowed painfully and tried to ignore the hollow pit that had opened up in her stomach. What now? When she got close enough to read the print, she saw the words she had been dreading: KENWOOD KILLER INVESTIGATION: NEW EVIDENCE MEANS POLICE ARE NOW FOCUSING THEIR SEARCH OVERSEAS.

She put her elbows on the desk and rested her head in her hands and closed her eyes. Eventually she became aware of someone standing next to her and glanced up to see Pete.

'Want to talk?'

She shook her head.

'Surely you should be pleased. I mean, the latest info in the *Chronicle*'s all wrong, isn't it? That lets you off the hook.'

He was trying to cheer her up and Leanne had a flashback to how it had been when they lived together and he'd try to make it up to her for something or other – failing to show up for dinner when he'd promised to be back in time, missing her hospital appointments.

'I'm going home.' She stood up so abruptly her chair, weighted down by her bag and jacket, toppled over behind her.

Pete bent to pick it up.

'I'll take you. I'm heading over your way.'

'No.'

It came out louder than she'd expected, and Ruby shot her a questioning glance as she gathered up her stuff and made a hasty exit.

Letting herself in through the front door of her flat she was greeted by the drawling baritone of Johnny Cash. She could hear Will crooning along, and Leanne felt a pain somewhere to the left of her breastbone.

'Hello, honey,' he called at the sound of the door slamming behind her. 'I'm in the kitchen.'

There was a scent of spices wafting through the hall. Will loved cooking curries and stir-fries. She thought she could smell coconut there as well.

Leanne made her way slowly along the narrow hallway, her steps growing heavier until on the threshold of the kitchen she could hardly raise one foot in front of the other.

'There she is. There's Mummy.'

Will was holding Leanne's cat, Norm, in his arms and moving its paw to make it look like Norm was waving.

Clearly Leanne's expression wasn't what Will was expecting because he put the cat down and Norm stalked across the kitchen and disappeared through the catflap.

'What's up, sweetheart? Crap day at the office? Come here.'

Will crossed to Leanne and wrapped his arms around her. She stood rigid, hands glued to her sides.

Sensing her strange mood, Will drew back, keeping his hands on her shoulders.

'What?' he asked, his brown eyes serious for once. 'Talk to me. What's up?'

'There was another story in the *Chronicle* today. About the investigation.'

Will's face softened.

'Ignore it, darling. You know you haven't done anything wrong. They're just trying to find someone to blame for the fact they still don't have a clue who is going around killing all these poor kids.'

'It's completely wrong.'

'Well, obviously it's wrong. They should never have . . .'

'No, I mean the newspaper story. This one is completely wrong.'

'What do you mean? I don't—'

'I mean, the whole thing about the police looking abroad was total bullshit that I made up when I called you yesterday morning. It was a test, Will, and you failed. How could you do that to me?'

For a split second, Will's face remained frozen in an expression of total incomprehension, and then it crumpled in on itself, flushing wine-red.

'Oh God, Leanne, I'm sorry.'

He moved towards her again but she stepped backwards, so he stood awkwardly, his hands still semi-outstretched.

'I'm so sorry,' he repeated. 'It started as a stupid mistake. Something slipped out while I was on the phone to one of my contacts on the *Chronicle*. And then he kept asking me.'

'So why didn't you just say you didn't know anything?'

'Because I'm an idiot, because I liked feeling useful for once, because he hinted there'd be a job for me on the *Chronicle*, because I wanted to make you proud. I wanted to feel worthy of you.'

'You almost cost me my job!'

'No, love, I would never have let it get that far. You have to believe me.'

Leanne shook her head. 'I don't believe this. I really thought you loved me.'

'I do. More than anything. That's why I did it. I just wanted to feel like I was going somewhere. National papers – you know I've always dreamed of it. I wanted to be an alpha male for once. Like him.'

'Who?'

'Pete, of course. Who else?'

'Are you kidding me?'

Leanne couldn't remember the last time she'd been this angry. In a way it felt good to have a focus for all the emotions that had been building up over the past few days and weeks, ever since Poppy Glover's murder. She could see Will felt terrible. Guilt and remorse were written all over his face.

'How do you think it is for me being in his shadow the whole time? I know if he hadn't screwed up by sleeping with someone else, you two would still be together. How am I supposed to feel about that? I know you've been seeing him at work the last few weeks and it kills me.'

'Right, so you thought you'd leak confidential information you got from me to a national newspaper, knowing it could ruin my career, just so you could prove something to my ex. Smart, Will. Very smart.'

'Not to prove it to him. I don't give a shit about him. To prove it to *you*. To prove myself to you.'

Will's face was always boyish, but now he looked like a child caught out in a misdemeanour and protesting that it wasn't his fault. For a moment she softened towards him. He was still so naive. She knew he loved her and she supposed she could see how he might convince himself he was acting for the greater good, but really, what did he think was going to happen when she found out?

'Leanne, sweetheart, I'm so, so, so sorry.' Will reached out his hands so he was gripping the tops of Leanne's arms. 'I'll make it up to you. I promise. Just give me a chance. OK?'

There was a film of water over Will's eyes so the brown irises looked like they were fraying softly at the edges. It would be so easy to take a step forward and lay her head against his chest and feel his arms closing around her, his face nuzzling her neck.

But even while she was imagining how that would feel, she was already distancing herself, wondering how long it would take him to clear his clothes from her bedroom wardrobe and his toiletries from the bathroom. There were a few odds and ends in the kitchen that he'd brought over. A set of digital scales, a Le Creuset oven dish. He was a much better, more committed cook than she was. She'd miss that. Already Will was receding into her past, even though he was right in front of her.

'Please, Leanne!' He was like a drowning man determinedly clinging on to her hand even while slipping further and further into the water. 'Give me another chance.'

He looked so young, standing there in her kitchen with his stricken expression and his pooling tears. For a split second she wondered if it might be possible to retract the last few hours, like cancelling a credit-card transaction, and go back to the way things were.

'Sorry, Will,' she said, remembering too late that she wasn't the one who should be apologizing.

But sorry was exactly what she was.

35

All day he'd been feeling funny. That restless feeling like he just wanted to be moving all the time never left him alone and he found himself pacing around his flat, unable to sit still. But the worst thing was the flashbacks. Usually he had a lie-in on a Saturday. But today he couldn't stay in bed. The closer it got to the time he was due at Suzy's for Bethany's sleepover, the harder it was to ward off the images that flashed relentlessly through his mind. Hair that smelled of apples, peach-soft skin. Heart beating like a baby bird. No. No. No. He couldn't, wouldn't think of it. Today was different. Emily was different. It wouldn't end up the same way. He hadn't meant to hurt anyone. That's why he'd written 'SORRY'. Because he was. And afterwards he'd been so careful. Gloves. Black waterproof nylon jacket. Plastic sheeting in his car. Yet still he'd found blood on his best trousers and something sticky and disgusting behind his ear.

Focus on something else. Fifty more push-ups. Twenty-five pull-ups on the bar hooked over the living-room door.

But when he approached Suzy's house, it felt as if all his nerve-endings were jangling. He'd dressed carefully. He didn't want it to look like he'd made too much of an effort so he'd worn his new jeans – light-blue stiff denim – and a white polo shirt that showed off his tan and clung just tightly enough to the muscles of his chest and upper arms.

Shame Suzy hadn't made as much of an effort. When she came to the door she was wearing denim shorts that she really didn't have any business wearing at her age and a lime-green T-shirt. Her hair was piled loosely on top of her head and held up with an enormous claw-type clip. Flat sandals revealed metallic-painted toenails.

'All right, babe?' She pressed her lips to his. 'Honestly, you wouldn't believe the state Bethany has got herself into over this sleepover. It's all she's spoken about for days, I swear to God. It got to the point last night where I told her, if I hear one more word about the sodding sleepover, it's cancelled.'

'They here already?'

'Yeah. They're all in the garden. They wanted cocktails! The little madams.'

At the back door, Jason hesitated, momentarily immobilized by tension. He could hear the sound of girlish giggles coming from the garden and Bethany squealing, 'Oh my GOD!'

'Oh look, it's my mum's boyfriend,' she said as he walked outside blinking in the sunlight. She sang the last word as if 'boyfriend' was actually a code word for something else.

'Give over,' said Suzy, but she looked pleased and grabbed hold of Jason's hand.

'Jason, this is Katie.' She indicated a large blonde girl in a T-shirt dress who looked a lot older than the others. 'And this is Tara.' A mixed-race girl with a beautiful heart-shaped face and hundreds of tiny plaits raised her hand shyly.

'And of course you know Emily.'

Until that moment he hadn't dared look at her, but now he saw that she had dressed up for the occasion in a white dress with thin straps and a rosebud pattern. He wondered if she'd got dressed up for him and his heart started thudding painfully against his ribcage. Her dark hair was loose today and hanging down over her face so he couldn't see her eyes, but he knew they would be glued to the ground. She was so shy, so different from the others with their loud shrieking voices and cackling laughs. Before he could stop it, he had a flashback to another girl, also quiet and unable to meet his eye. Instantly his skin was damp with sweat and his face was hot and he had to dig his trimmed nails into his palm and count backwards from ten in his head until the heat ebbed away. He didn't know what was wrong with him. He thought he'd dealt with all that. This wasn't going to be the same. Emily was different. *He* was different. He'd learned, matured. He'd been doing a lot of work on himself. This time he'd keep himself under control.

'Jason's going to help me keep you lot in order, aren't you, Jase?'

Suzy looped a proprietorial arm around his waist and he had to stop himself shrugging it off. He sent a silent message to Emily assuring her she had no reason to be jealous.

'Yeah, that's right,' he said. 'So no trouble, right? No sneaking boys in here.'

Tara and Katie squealed in gleeful mock horror.

'No way,' said Bethany, but he could tell she was secretly thrilled at the idea. Give her a year or two and she'd be a right handful. Suzy would be better off laying down some firm ground rules now. Not that she would, of course. She was probably exactly the same when she was a teenager. Sneaking around with boys at thirteen. On the pill by fourteen. If Keira so much as . . .

But that was a thought too far. He forced himself to imagine a big red STOP sign, just as he'd been taught to by his anger-management coach. He pictured it standing between him and thoughts of his estranged daughter.

'Oh, they're too young for all that,' said Suzy. 'Bethany knows

I'm going to pack her off to a convent if she ever so much as mentions a boy's name.'

But Jason knew the truth. He knew what really went on in girls' heads.

'Who wants to go on the trampoline?'

Bethany had had enough of her mocktail and was anxious to be getting on with the next thing. Jason had noticed that about her before. How impatient she was.

There was a chorus of agreement from the other girls and they all jumped up and started racing towards the trampoline at the far end of the small garden. Jason swallowed noisily, his mouth suddenly dry as dust. The others kicked off their flip-flops but Emily lingered over unbuckling her sandals. Her shoulder blades jutted out sharply from between the straps of her dress as she bent over, carefully removing first one shoe then the other.

'Come on, babe, let's leave 'em to it.' Suzy tugged at his shirt.

'Yeah, coming.' But he remained rooted to the spot, his heart thudding. Any moment now she'd go up the ladder. She was smaller than the others, so she wouldn't be able to pull herself up without it, as they had. He wanted to stay to watch her jumping, her dark hair streaming out behind her. He could imagine it so clearly it hurt.

'Jase!' Suzy's voice was sharp and her fingers tightened vice-like around his arm.

'Sorry, love, I was miles away. Thinking about my Keira, and how much she'd love this.'

Immediately Suzy's grip relaxed and her tone changed.

'Oh God, I'm such a selfish cow sometimes!' She gave herself a playful slap to the forehead. 'I should have known being here would make you miss your daughter. I can't even imagine how I'd feel if someone tried to take Bethany from me. I'm going to help you take your mind off it though. Come on.'

She turned him round until he was facing away from the

trampoline and then started pulling him in the direction of the back door. 'This lot will be busy for a while and I've got a really good idea for distracting you from gloomy thoughts.'

She briefly rested her hand on his bum and Jason stiffened, fighting the wave of anger that swept over him, taking him by surprise.

But by the time he'd followed Suzy up the stairs, he was feeling calmer. There was no rush. He had all night, after all.

36

Leanne felt it the moment she swiped in through the office door –
a low-level energy like the whole place was humming. There was a
familiar prickle as the hairs on her arms stood up in anticipation.
Ever since Desmond had called her first thing to tell her they'd
arrested Sally Freeland's source and he'd given up the details of the
paedophile ring, she'd had that on-the-edge-of-your-seat feeling
which had almost, though not quite, made her forget about Will.

'We've got them. All of them.'

Desmond's deputy, Andy Curtis, didn't smile often so when he
did it was always a shock, taking ten years off him at a stroke.

'You did well, Leanne, and don't think it won't be recognized.
We're on the verge of cracking this one.'

'Don't tell me you can feel it in your water.'

'Oi, my water never lies, I'll have you know. Seriously though,
we've got all five of those bastards in separate rooms downstairs.'

'Five? Including Blake?'

A prick of conscience pierced Leanne's excitement. She'd
promised Sally Freeland she'd do her best to keep her source,
Julian Blake, out of things. After all, without his information they
wouldn't have had any grounds to pull the Nemo lot in.

'Yeah, he's here too. Crying like a baby apparently. Did you know he's a schoolteacher? Head of a sixth form apparently. Married as well.'

Leanne felt a wave of nausea. From what Sally had said, Julian Blake, aka 'Serge', was a man who battled daily against his compulsions.

'Don't lose any sympathy over that scum.' Curtis had noticed her expression. 'Anyway, if he wasn't involved and his information leads to an arrest then he'll get off lightly.'

'Has anyone fessed up?'

It was too much to hope, but there was always that faint chance of an instant, total cave-in.

'Not yet, but once they realize we've seized their computers, they might get more chatty.'

'How's the Lion of the North?'

Curtis smiled again, his face looking awkward as if the smiling muscles were protesting against the unfamiliar exercise.

'Yes, well, Bobby Jarvis is trying his best to roar, but actually it's more like a mewl. The boss is in with him right now.'

Leanne had wondered which of the men would get the dubious honour of the Desmond treatment.

'Pete's talking to one of the others. Stephen Lancaster. A barrister as it turns out, would you believe?'

Leanne remembered now Howard Walsh telling her about a teacher or a lawyer who had passed on secrets about the ring to one of his contacts who was holding compromising information about him. Instinctively she knew here was the weakest link. And it was Pete who had him.

'Here she is, the hero of the hour,' said Ruby as Leanne came to sit down.

Leanne made a face. 'Hardly,' she said.

Ruby examined her more closely. Leanne had taken time with her appearance that morning, smearing foundation over her blotchy skin and concealer under her dark-ringed eyes, but she still looked exactly like what she was – a woman who'd spent half the night crying.

'You OK?'

Leanne nodded stiffly.

'It's just that for someone who might very well have helped solve the most infamous murder case of recent times, you don't look very happy.'

'Is it that obvious?'

'Only to a person with a modicum of emotional intelligence – which rules out 99.9 per cent of the people in this place.'

Leanne sighed. 'I finished with Will.'

Ruby's perfectly shaped eyebrows shot up. 'But I thought things were great with you two.'

Leanne felt something tearing inside her as she remembered the myriad little kindnesses Will had shown her. She knew how it would look from the outside once people knew, yet she was convinced he hadn't been using her to further his career. He had been trying to impress her. He had thought that was what she wanted – a man with ambition, a man going places. He'd been trying to compete with Pete, not realizing that it was precisely for his un-Peteness that she'd first fallen for him.

'He let me down, Ruby. It was him leaking the stuff to the papers.'

'Oh. Shit. Sorry.'

Leanne held up her hand. She couldn't deal with anyone being nice to her at the moment.

'Leanne?'

She hadn't noticed Desmond until he was just yards from her desk. She was already clambering to her feet when he said, 'In my office, please.'

Pete was already in there. He looked as rough as she did. His hair was a mess and his eyes had that droopy hooded look she remembered from when they were together, mornings after they'd stayed up far too late, talking and having sex. Instantly heat surged to her face and she cursed herself for letting her thoughts get carried away. Still, she couldn't help glancing at him again. He was doing that thing he always did when he was excited, fluttering his fingers against his thigh as if playing an invisible piano.

'Sir?' The suspense was killing her. 'Have you got a confession, sir?'

'Not as such.'

Desmond loved this kind of scenario – having information that you didn't have, eking it out, revealing things little by little.

In the end it was Pete who explained: 'Lancaster admitted they were at the scene of the crime when Poppy Glover was killed – so that photo Julian Blake says he saw was authentic – but he says they got there after she died.'

'What?'

'These guys were obsessed with the case. They had a detailed online map of the area and they'd try to guess where the next victim would show up. One of them, a creep called Ben Gattis who lives in an apartment block just off the Heath Extension, became convinced that sooner or later the killer would dump a body there. It's separate from the main bit of the Heath, very quiet, completely open to the road all around its border and, crucially, far smaller and more manageable than the other part. Gattis walks his dog in the area every day so he knows all the likely places – where the cameras are, and aren't. It didn't happen with Leila Botsford, but still, the day after Poppy Glover disappeared he was up again before dawn patrolling the Heath Extension. Bingo. He came across Poppy's body and called the others.'

'But why?'

Despite her training and her months in Vice, Leanne couldn't or didn't want to get her head around what these men were hoping to get from stumbling across the body of a child.

Pete sighed. 'They're fantasists, Leanne. They've built a world around fantasizing about having power over children. A dead child. It's their ultimate fantasy.'

Leanne closed her eyes, feeling dizzy. Suddenly the emotion of the last few hours, combined with lack of sleep, made her feel she was going to keel over. Pete stepped across the room to put his hand under her elbow.

'Breathe,' he whispered in her ear. She took in a lungful of air. Her elbow burned where he touched it.

'Are you sure you can believe them?' she asked.

Desmond chipped in this time. 'Once Lancaster opened up, the others caved in pretty quickly and, separately, they all told the same story. They came across the body in situ.'

Leanne felt too weak even to mind about Desmond saying 'in situ'.

'And they didn't see who put her there?'

Pete shook his head.

'But we still have the semen sample from the dock leaf, right? We still have that much evidence to find the killer?'

'The semen came from one of the men. We're not sure which one at this time.' Desmond was clipped and to the point.

Leanne swallowed down the bile that had shot up into her mouth at the thought of what these men, these pillars of the establishment, had done when confronted with the body of a dead child.

'They are the ones who took off her clothes as well,' Pete continued woodenly, clearly thinking she might as well have it all in one go. 'When they found her she was fully dressed and laid out carefully as if asleep, just like Tilly and Leila.'

So now they were back at the beginning again. Four little girls dead, four families decimated. And the man responsible for it all was still out there, going about his business, picking his next victim.

37

There were empty pizza boxes piled on the coffee table, their bases soaked with grease. Jason tried not to look at them. Earlier he'd suggested to Suzy that she might want to get a bin bag and clean them up along with the empty Coke cans and Quality Street wrappers but she hadn't yet made a move.

They were all sitting around in Suzy's cramped, red-cushioned living room. Jason and Suzy were squashed into the armchair while the four girls shared the sofa. They'd changed into their pyjamas in readiness for the sleepover and Jason had had to look at a point on the wall, next to the blown-up photo of Suzy and Bethany in a photographer's studio wearing matching white outfits and in bare feet, so that he wouldn't stare as they trooped in. He hadn't been able to look at Emily at all, just the most fleeting glimpse of pale, skinny calves coming out of white cotton knee-length pyjama bottoms.

The flashbacks were coming almost constantly now – fragments that he batted away only to find another coming at him, and another. The curve of a bare shoulder, a sweep of dark eyelashes against a plump cheek, then a piercing scream, the kicking of a leg, his own voice shouting, the black fog of loss of control. Now panic. His breath being torn from him in strips of pain. Is she breathing? No. No, no, no.

He shifted in his chair, cursing Suzy who'd insisted on sitting on his lap and now lay across him like a dead weight, her head snuggled into his chest.

'You sure you want to watch this?' She raised her face up to whisper in his ear. 'I'm sure romcom isn't really your cup of tea. Why don't we slip off and leave them to it?'

She was stroking his cheek now with her long nail. It felt like a cockroach running across his face.

'No, you're all right. I like her. Jennifer Aniston. I could watch her all day.'

She folded her arms across her chest in a mock sulk. To his left, Emily, who was wedged between Bethany and the arm of the sofa, shifted position and Jason closed his eyes against the sudden image of his own hands, huge, around a slender throat.

'Come on, babe. Let's go.' Suzy was prodding him in the chest.

'I said no. All right?'

It had come out harsher than he intended and he felt Suzy stiffen on his lap. The girls on the sofa suddenly went quiet.

'Sorry. I'm a bit knackered and bad-tempered. Don't pay any attention to me.' He planted a kiss on Suzy's forehead and she appeared to relax a little.

All through the rest of the film, he worried that his outburst might have put Emily off. He didn't dare look at her, but he could tell from the way she'd curled up tighter, pulling her legs right up under her, that he had made her uncomfortable.

He worked his fingers into the pocket of his jeans and grasped his keys, then he deliberately pressed the sharp edge of one into his thigh over and over.

38

Leanne felt drained of everything – energy, hope, love. All seemed to have seeped away. Will had called her so many times she'd put her phone on silent. She'd listened to the first message – an incoherent ramble trying to explain why he'd done it. Endlessly begging her forgiveness. She was the best woman he'd ever known, he said. He couldn't face losing her. After that she didn't listen to any of the others.

The whole station had been muted since the afternoon's disappointment. For a moment they'd believed the Nemo gang were going to be the key that unlocked the Kenwood Killings case once and for all. But, after all, the body had been there when the men had arrived. Already dead. Now, hours later, they were all slumped at their desks as day dragged on into evening.

Back to square one. That's where the investigation was, and that's exactly where she was too. All the time she'd invested in Will, all the energy, all the trust. It hadn't been an explosion of fireworks or anything, not like with Pete, but rather a slow, gentle sliding from friendship into love. And now it had been all for nothing.

Her phone started vibrating, convulsing against the laminate desktop. She almost didn't bother checking it. Will again. It had to be. But when she finally gave in and flipped up the lid of the leather case, she saw an unfamiliar number.

'DC Miller?'

'Yes?'

'It's Gary Allison from the forensic lab.'

'Blimey, you're keen, aren't you? Working on a Saturday?'

'Yeah, well, I'm off on holiday on Monday and I had the ridiculous notion that if I came in on the weekend I might not come back to a mountain of stuff. Anyway, you asked me to run a DNA check for you?'

For a second her mind was blank, then suddenly it came to her: Donna Shields. Amid the emotional turbulence of the last twenty-four hours she'd forgotten all about the hatchet-faced woman and the hair sample she'd brought in for testing. Leanne's heart sagged as she thought of the paperwork she'd have to fill in now that the test had been completed. Her mind was so preoccupied that she failed to properly register what Gary Allison was telling her.

'What?' she asked. 'What did you say?'

'I said we have a match.' The man was trying to hide his excitement but there was a giveaway tremor in his voice. 'The sample you sent me is a match for the DNA found on the body of Megan Purvis.'

39

'Mum, Emily's not feeling well.'

Jason and Suzy were sitting downstairs on the sofa watching on catch-up a programme where people were filmed on a first date in a restaurant. Suzy had been laughing like a drain, which infuriated Jason because he couldn't hear what was going on in Bethany's room upstairs where the girls had been for the last hour. He'd been trying to control his growing anger, digging the key ever deeper into his leg, but he could sense it building up, so it was a relief when Bethany had burst through the door.

Suzy, on the other hand, didn't bother to hide her annoyance at the interruption. 'What do you mean, not well?'

'She's got a temperature and she says she feels sick.'

Suzy rolled her eyes. 'I did warn you, didn't I? All that pizza and Coke and then you lot would go outside on the trampoline in your jim-jams. Go and find her a paracetamol. You know where they are.'

'She wants to go home.'

Suzy's head, which was tucked under Jason's arm, started shaking from side to side.

'No way. Uh-uh. I am not calling Emily's mum. Poor thing doesn't even have a car. She can't be dragging her little ones on the bus to come here and pick Emily up. And there's no way I can give her a lift. I've already had two glasses of wine.'

Jason sat frozen, sure they must be able to hear his heart thudding against his chest. This was it. He didn't even have to think up a way to get her on her own. Yet at the same time as he was celebrating this turn of fortune, he could also feel the nausea rising. What if he messed up again? What if he lost control? Another flashback assailed him – carrying a roll of heavy-duty plastic sacking and noticing a little foot hanging out of the bottom. No. It wouldn't be like that again. He had changed. He'd worked on himself. He was different.

Emily was different.

'I'll take her.' The steadiness of his own voice surprised him. 'I've got the car. It won't take a minute.'

'You don't even know where she lives.'

That Bethany had an answer for everything.

'If she goes to your school it can't be far, can it?'

'You don't have to.' Suzy sounded dubious. 'I think we should just wait a while. Play it by ear.'

Luckily Bethany had an answer for that too: 'Aw, Mum. Please let him take her home. She's being a right moody cow. She's spoiling my birthday.'

'There you are. That's settled. We can't have the birthday girl getting upset, can we?'

Jason was rewarded with a smile from Bethany and Suzy caved in, as he'd known she would.

'Oh, all right. You win. You're a good man, Jason Shields. Bit soft in the head, but good. Go and tell Emily to get her stuff together, Bethany.'

Once the girl was out of the room, Suzy rested her hand on the crotch of his jeans.

'Don't worry, I'll make it up to you when you get back.'
Her splayed-out fingers looked like fat spider legs.

40

One minute Leanne had been at her desk feeling like nothing good was ever going to happen again, and now here she was on a shabby street outside a door sandwiched between a convenience store and a launderette with the whole place cordoned off by patrol cars and yellow tape, and feeling like her heart was about to explode in her chest.

'Back! Get back!' shouted the cop nearest the door who, like the others in the advance group, was dressed in full protective gear. There was a loud crack and then they were all streaming in through the dark, narrow hallway and up to the first floor where Donna Shields had told her Jason rented a one-bedroom flat. Pete tugged her arm, pulling her back on to the pavement to wait.

She hadn't yet had a chance to process it, this feeling of excitement mixed with anxiety. She knew that, without a confession, there might be an issue with the hair sample Donna had given her being used as evidence in court. The thought that they might catch him and then have the whole case collapse because she hadn't followed procedure made her feel giddy with dread. But at least they had him. And they'd find something. There was always something.

The advance group, which had already made it upstairs, was now thumping on the flat door. Then there was another loud crack and the sound of thudding footsteps.

'Not here!' the shout went up.

The adrenaline that had been coursing around Leanne's body for the last two hours dropped, leaving her able to breathe properly for the first time. By the time she, Pete and Desmond arrived upstairs, the cops in protective gear had gone back outside where they formed a guard around the main door of the building. Snapping on latex gloves and pulling covers over their shoes, Leanne followed Desmond into the small, neat, curiously impersonal flat, with Pete close behind.

'Right, we're looking for anything that gives us an idea where he's gone. Scribbled note, anything at all.'

Another team had already gone to the strip club where Shields ran security, but they'd called to say it was shuttered up. Not open on weekends, apparently.

The flat was bland. The kind of thin grey carpet beloved of landlords everywhere, magnolia walls, a boxy two-person sofa and matching armchair covered in a beige synthetic fabric. A wood-effect coffee table that looked like it would snap if you put anything heavier than a magazine on it. An old-fashioned television with a deep back on a black metal stand in the corner. No pictures on the walls, no books, no DVDs. On the table between the two windows overlooking the street, there was a pile of what looked to be men's fitness magazines, the corners all neatly lined up. There was nothing to say who lived here.

'Leanne, check the bedroom; Pete, the kitchen.'

Leanne had to duck her head under the pull-up bar over the living-room door lintel. There was no room in the cramped hallway and her arm felt seared where Pete's pressed against it as they opened the three closed doors. Tiny bathroom that stank of bleach and aftershave, a kitchen that wasn't much bigger into which Pete disappeared, and a small, square bedroom with the same grey carpet and a narrow double bed neatly made. A line of shoes at the foot of the bed in matched pairs. Black shiny work-style lace-ups, pristine white trainers, well-preserved Timber-lands, their laces neatly tucked into the boots.

She heard Pete cry out: 'Guv? There's a laptop in here!'

Then the sound of Desmond's footsteps heading towards the kitchen. Jason Shields would have everything password-protected, she was sure of it. How long would it take to get into his laptop? An hour? Two? And all the time he was out in the world, looking at children in the street, sizing up his next victim.

She fought back a shiver.

There were no clothes on the floor or flung over the back of a chair, no glass of water by the bed. She looked at the toiletries in their grey bottles lined up in height order on the chest of drawers and the skin on her neck felt cold and clammy. This man left no trace of himself, as if he wanted to be J-clothed away. Still she went through the drawers with their neatly paired-up socks and dazzling white trunks and the colour-coded piles of carefully ironed T-shirts. Navy, grey, white, black. The last drawer had exercise gear. Lycra shorts and tops. White vests.

A cursory look through the flimsy free-standing wardrobe produced a similar lack of results.

She crossed to the window and looked out. A back yard full of stacked crates and rubbish surrounded by other back yards full of the same. The window of the building straight across was half covered by a purple sheet. Leanne's heart stopped as a child's face appeared in the bottom right-hand corner. The child raised its hand to wave and Leanne ducked away.

In the kitchen she could hear the sound of Pete talking to some-one from IT on the phone.

'No, I've done that,' he was saying. 'It's not working.'

She knew they'd have to get going soon to take the laptop in for testing. She turned and her eyes swept again over the bed. Then, more from habit than hope, she bent to take a quick look underneath it – and saw a single piece of A4 paper, folded in half. As she picked it up, she saw it was a printout of a webpage. On closer inspection it looked to be from a dating website. Leanne's heart started pounding. There was a profile from someone calling themselves ButterfliesInMyTummy and a photograph of a chubby orange-skinned woman with curly blonde hair and comfy sheepskin boots sitting in an armchair. Leanne frowned. This didn't fit with the man who lived in this room and whose DNA had been found on the body of a murdered child. She stared down at the woman while her heart continued to hammer, and then slowly she turned over the paper at its razor-sharp crease and now there was a coldness in her head like her brain was freezing from the inside out as she saw that there was another part to the photograph. Now she saw the young girl with wavy blonde hair and blue eyes laughing into the camera. And she knew. She knew.

41

When Emily appeared in the living room accompanied by the others, she was wearing a cardigan over her pyjamas and wouldn't meet anyone's eyes.

'Jason says he'll drive you home. That's kind of him, isn't it?' Suzy was smiling, but there was a faint edge to her voice. 'Emily can be a bit of a baby sometimes,' she'd complained to him after Bethany had gone back upstairs. 'You can understand why – I mean, she never gets the chance to be babied at home, not with all those smaller brothers and sisters, but she's got to understand sometimes it isn't all about her. This should be Bethany's day.'

Now the girl stood uncomfortably in the doorway playing with her bag. 'But I thought you were taking me,' she said to Suzy.

'Sorry, sweetheart. I've had too much to drink, and I'm not someone who would ever drink and drive.' Jason guessed she was saying that for his benefit. Could she really not see the sweat breaking out on his forehead or the way his fingers were trembling in his lap? He remembered when he'd felt like this before and his stomach twisted.

But now the girl, Emily, was looking nervous, darting looks at her friends as if wanting them to step in.

'Actually, I'm feeling a bit better,' she said in a soft voice that he struggled to hear. 'Maybe I'll stay here with you guys.'

Jason froze, then he felt the anger pierce him like a bullet, exploding inside him into sharp shards of shrapnel. He was so close, so close. Was he really going to be thwarted now, after everything he'd done? Emily was his reward for these past weeks of laughing at Suzy's feeble jokes, and pretending to be interested in her petty arguments with people at work, and going to bed with her and imagining she was someone else. And now, after all that, it was all going to be snatched away?

'Er, no. Sorry, Emily. I'm afraid it's too late to change your mind.' Jason could hardly believe that Suzy had chosen now to grow a backbone. He could have kissed her. 'You said you didn't feel well. Jason's all ready to take you now and I've already called your mum.'

Emily looked as if she was about to cry, and Suzy visibly softened.

'The thing is, lovey, you do look peaky and I've got to think about the others, haven't I? I can't have you giving germs to Katie and Tara. So Jason's going to run you back home and, tell you what, if you're feeling better tomorrow your mum can pop you back again in the morning. OK?'

Emily nodded, but the look she shot in his direction was one of fear, which both thrilled and angered him. Could she really not see what he'd done for her, how he'd picked her out as the special one?

He tried to speak but his mouth was suddenly bone dry. He cleared his throat and swallowed, then tried again. 'Right then. Are you ready, Emily?'

And now he was moving towards her, and she was peeling herself slowly off the wall as if she was a frightened animal being led off to slaughter and he just wanted to shake her because she was being so ungrateful and had almost ruined the whole thing – and why did all of them have to spoil things? There was a burning feeling in his chest and his lungs weren't working properly. She was still wavering, fixing her pale eyes on Bethany like she was asking to be rescued or something. He put his hand on her arm and he felt her flinch.

He forced his fingers to remain resting gently on her arm, resisting the urge to grip hold of her and drag her through the door. He was so close he could smell on her breath the sickly Haribo sweets they'd been scoffing from a big tub up in Bethany's room.

'The car's just outside.'

He tried to make the words come out casual but his voice sounded false and high-pitched even to his own ears. Now the burning had reached his throat and he just needed to be out of there. He was so close, and this time he wouldn't blow it. He felt her shrinking under his touch, but still she allowed herself to be guided out of the living-room door, and she wouldn't do that if she didn't want to, right? Because underneath it all, underneath the shyness and fearfulness, she wanted this as much as he did.

'Wait,' Suzy called just as they reached the hallway. 'Maybe I'll come with you, just for the ride. Let me get my shoes.'

Jason stopped, his hand searing where it touched Emily's skin. The bitch. She was doing it on purpose. Playing with him.

The ball of anger ignited into a flame inside him. 'I don't believe you!' he snapped. 'You'd actually go out and leave three ten-year-olds on their own?'

'Oi, I'm *eleven* now!' yelled Bethany, but Jason paid her no attention.

'Do you realize you could be arrested for that?'

He'd swung around to face Suzy who had one foot strapped into its sandal, one still bare, and was gaping at him uncertainly.

'We'll only be gone a few minutes.'

'Yeah, well, how many minutes does it take for a fire to start or a nutter to break in? How many?'

He knew he should lower his voice but he couldn't.

'Fine,' she said, and started unbuckling the shoe. 'I'll wait here.' She looked upset.

'I just think you need to be a bit more careful. That's all.'

'I said I'll wait.'

She was glaring at him now and he had to get out of there. He had his hand on the small of Emily's back, guiding her out. He could feel the little nubs of her vertebrae through her thin cotton cardigan. His breath was coming out in short gasps and he steered her towards the front door before anyone else could notice.

'Nearly there,' he said in his new gruff voice. He thought she might reward him with one of her shy smiles, but instead she arched her back, pulling away from him. Another savage bolt of anger shot through him.

The burning feeling was no longer just in his chest but had now taken over the whole of him – face, head, even the soles of his feet were on fire, so were the palms of his hands and his scalp under his gelled hair. He'd tried, he really had, but it was getting to the point where he couldn't be held responsible any more. Not when she was being so ungrateful, and he could feel Suzy and Bethany and the others behind him watching them. Well, it was nearly over. Another minute and they'd be in the car.

He paused in the hallway and reached out for the front-door latch.

42

There were lights on in all the rooms, but no way of knowing what was happening inside. The wheelie bins in the concrete front yard obscured the window of what must surely be the living room and the upstairs curtains were drawn. As the car screeched to a halt, Leanne pressed her hands briefly to her eyes like she did when there was a horror film on the television she couldn't bear to watch. Perhaps Pete recognized the gesture because he turned to her. 'You OK?' he whispered. She had no time to do anything but nod because now they were getting ready to jump out.

But were they too late? That was the question that had been ricocheting around Leanne's head ever since she'd picked up the paper from the floor of Jason Shields' bedroom and seen the photograph of the child. Of course they'd got straight on to the dating website and it had been the work of minutes to find an address for ButterfliesInMyTummy, but who knew how long he had been going round to the house, in all likelihood grooming the daughter. From the messages they'd sent each other through the website, it had been weeks since their first date.

Looking at the white front door with its mean diamond of faux leaded glass, Leanne had a terrible conviction that they were too late, that they'd failed the girl in the photo like they'd failed Megan and Tilly and Leila and Poppy. Yet how could they have known? Jason Shields was an outlier, an anomaly. No criminal record, except for the restraining order. Not on the Sexual Offenders Register. There were no clues they'd missed.

The driver turned off the engine and Leanne flung open her door, her eyes fixed on the house. She had one foot out of the car when the white front door suddenly flew open, revealing a very slight young girl wearing cut-off pyjamas, a cardigan and sandals. Right behind her, so close he must have been pressing on her back, was the man she recognized from his website profile as Jason Shields.

43

Emma replaced her phone gently on the bedside table and sat completely still, trying to absorb what Leanne had just told her. The light filtering in through the ivory curtains was grey and weak and she reckoned it must still be very early. Leanne had clearly been up all night. Her voice had that tightness to it as if it had been stretched to breaking point.

'We've made an arrest,' she'd said. 'I didn't want you to hear it from anyone else.'

It wasn't anyone known to the police, at least not in that context, Leanne told her. He hadn't confessed yet but the evidence against him was pretty conclusive.

Emma had listened to Leanne without saying a word, speaking only to thank her at the end. Guy hadn't stirred throughout the whole thing. She always set her phone to silent overnight and she'd only woken up because she'd heard it vibrating against the glass of water on her bedside table.

It was over.

The words formed in her head, but still she couldn't process them.

Tilly's killer had been caught. They could get on with their lives.

So why didn't she feel more euphoric? Surely she ought to be leaping around with joy, or at least waking Guy up to tell him the news.

She glanced over at him. He lay half under, half out of the duvet, one arm up at a right angle above his head, his face turned to the side so that his neck was long and straight.

How could she have thought he had anything to do with Tilly's death? Her treachery made her feel giddy with shame. That she should have doubted this man who'd stroked her back and held back her hair when morning sickness sent her hunching over the toilet bowl, who'd sat on his own in his car outside strangers' schools day after day to weep for his dead daughter because he still felt he had to be the strong one at home, the one who didn't show weakness and protected them all, left her saturated with guilt.

She climbed back under the duvet and lay down. Guy looked so peaceful there, his arm flung up like a baby. Once she told him the news he'd want to be up making phone calls, doing things. And then the girls would be up and upset, just when Jemima had seemed in the last few days to be coming back to her at last, even allowing Emma to cuddle her the evening before as they sat watching television on the sofa. No, Emma wanted to leave him sleeping, just a little longer.

She turned over on to her side and shuffled carefully towards him, in small movements. There was a moment of hesitation when she wondered whether she had the right any longer to touch him. She was so out of practice, she could hardly remember what it felt like to have someone else's skin against her own. Tentatively she reached an arm across Guy's body and he shifted slightly in his sleep. She moved closer and then gently, hardly daring to breathe, she laid her head on his chest. Instantly his arm that had been flung up by his pillow came down and settled around her like a shawl.

44

Sally knew, before she was even fully awake, that she'd made a terrible mistake. Her mouth tasted like it had been coated with something sour and furry and there was a horrible fermenting smell in her nostrils. She opened her eyes and immediately shut them again, not wanting to believe what she now knew incontrovertibly to be the case. Self-loathing crawled all over her like a grubby hand.

Would she never learn?

She swung her legs over the side of the bed and slipped out of the bedcovers, disgustedly kicking off the knickers that were still hooked around one of her ankles. She was going to have to do some serious work on herself. Perhaps she'd take herself back to that luxury retreat on that island in Thailand. She hadn't been sure about some of the stuff there. Who needed a breathing workshop, for goodness sake? Breathing was one of the very few life skills she'd managed to master. But she was sure the not-drinking had done her some good, and the meditation and the disgusting green juices. Slipping on the hotel dressing gown that was hanging over the chair and unhooking her handbag from the chair-back, she crept around the foot of the bed in which Simon Hewitt lay spreadeagled like a beached starfish.

Locking the door of the en suite bathroom, she looked at herself in the mirror and winced. She tried to piece together what had brought her to this dismal personal low, but piecing together the night before was like trying to work out a Sudoku – no sooner had she got one line of memory to fit than another burst right apart.

She knew she'd been feeling bad about Simon ever since she first found out about the existence of Nemo and realized for sure that he'd had nothing to do with the murders, and so when he called her yesterday afternoon to ask her if she wanted to go for a drink, she hadn't declined, and besides she'd been lonely, with only the prospect of a Saturday evening on her own in the hotel bar. So she'd said yes, and they'd met for dinner and he'd made her laugh, and she'd remembered what she'd liked about him after all. And they'd shared a second bottle of wine, and then a third.

She slid down the tiled wall on to the bathmat she'd complained about on the first day after she'd slipped on it. She tried to guess how many hours she had until she had to present herself – all bright-eyed – at the house of the wife of the man in her bed, for the interview with Emma Reid that Leanne had managed to arrange in return for information. There was no doubt about it, she was a horrible person and she was going straight to hell. Unzipping her bag, she took her phone out of the inside pocket to check on the time, sliding it free from its smooth leather pouch. She saw she had a voicemail from Leanne Miller and cursed herself for having missed the call. Her lifecoach Mina had once accused her of self-sabotage. At the time Sally had been furious, but now she could see exactly what Mina meant.

'Hello, Sally,' came Leanne's voice, sounding tired and slow. 'I promised to keep you in the loop with developments on the

Kenwood Killings case, so I'm calling to let you know we made an arrest last night. I thought you should know.'

An arrest. Sally sat up on her heels. She needed to be showered and out of there and down the police station before Ken Forbes and all the other arseholes got wind of it. She wished Leanne had been more forthcoming. An arrest could mean anyone.

All she knew for sure was that there was one person who could definitively be removed from the list of suspects, and that was because he was currently snoring away in her bed.

45

For the last few days, Rory had had a little residual glow thinking about the meeting with Jemima Reid in her Head's office. But by Sunday morning, his good will had evaporated leaving just one thought in his head. *Why?* Why had he thought it was a good idea to throw his mobile into the pond? It had felt symbolic and life-affirming and liberating at the time, and it was just a crappy old thing, but still it was a phone.

What if Georgia Reynolds had rung him? She'd said she'd call him if she got stuck with the physics revision exercises they'd been set for homework. He couldn't bear to think she might be imagining he was ignoring her. Getting a replacement phone was now a top priority. He knew he'd seen an old Nokia somewhere around the house. He ran through all the possibilities in his head. Basket on hallway dresser? No. Tray on the desk in Simon's study? No. He'd gone through it just a couple of days ago looking for loose change that Simon wouldn't miss. Got it! His mum's bedside cabinet. That was where she kept her knickers and socks, but also where she kept the occasional ten-pack of cigarettes. She'd given up years before but still had the odd one, even though she thought no one else knew. He was sure there was a phone in there.

He crept down one flight of stairs and hovered uncertainly outside his mum and Simon's room. He knew his mum wouldn't be there. She always went to yoga on Sunday mornings, followed by a trip to the crematorium garden where there was a rosebush planted in Megan's name. His mum insisted it calmed her to go there, although Rory had never noticed any evidence of this. She'd probably also call in to the supermarket to pick up cakes for this afternoon when that journalist was coming here to interview Emma Reid. Rory wondered whether Jemima would come too. He wasn't sure how he felt about that. Simon's whereabouts were another matter. Rory knew he'd gone out the previous evening. In fact, there had been a bit of a row about it, Rory now remembered. Simon was supposed to be at home but had called to say he was going out drinking with some old friends and didn't know when he'd be back. His mum hadn't been happy, but it happened pretty much all the time and she never seemed to get unhappy enough to do anything about it.

The bedroom door was slightly ajar and Rory nudged it open. Phew. The room was empty, bed neatly made, curtains pulled back. Looked like Simon hadn't made it home at all last night.

Dropping to his knees next to his mum's side of the bed, Rory pulled open the bottom drawer of the bedside cabinet. There was a jumble of tights in there – mostly black but some brown and some disgustingly flesh-coloured. The tights were all tangled together in knots and he pushed them gingerly aside, trying to touch them as little as possible. Finally, his hand closed around a hard rectangular object. Eureka! He pulled the phone out. It was dead, of course, and even older than he'd thought, though it had probably been a decent enough phone whenever she first got it. He wondered when his mum had stopped using it. If it was anything like her other phones, it was probably when she lost the charger. His mother couldn't seem to grasp that you could get replacement chargers for phones or that there was a good chance a charger from the same manufacturer might fit several models. She still believed her laptop would work only with the specific lead it had come with.

Rory had a drawer full of chargers in his desk. Surely one of them would fit.

He slipped back out of the room and up the stairs just as the front door opened and his mum burst in.

Yesssss! His luck was definitely on the turn.

46

How was Leanne going to cope with going round to Helen Purvis's this afternoon? She could hardly see straight. Slumped over a now-tepid coffee in the canteen, she toyed with the idea of ringing Emma to cancel, but she felt responsible. It was she who'd persuaded Emma into an interview as a return favour to Sally, and she'd promised to be there. No doubt they'd all be questioning her about Jason Shields, but she had nothing to tell them.

So far Shields had answered 'no comment' to everything they'd asked him, including his name. They'd been up most of the night, then he'd had a couple of hours' sleep and now he was back in the interview room with Desmond and Pete, but as far as she knew there was no progress. Soon the solicitor he'd been assigned would get there and that would mostly likely be that. She was trying not to think of the ramifications if there was no confession and no further evidence. If the sample taken by Donna Shields was deemed inadmissible because Leanne hadn't followed procedure in getting it tested, might the whole case against him collapse?

'Got any speed?' Pete dropped into the seat opposite her. His skin looked grey and there was a deep furrow above the bridge of his nose that she'd never noticed before. 'Coke? Uppers? Pro Plus?'

'Paracetamol?' Leanne offered.

'That'll do.'

He'd brought over two coffees and drained his in one go.

'You given up on Shields?' Leanne tried to keep the note of panic out of her voice.

Pete shook his head. 'On a break. He isn't giving us anything at all in there, though you can see it's costing him. There's this little muscle in his neck that keeps spasming and you can hear his teeth grinding.'

'Have you told the Botsfords?'

'Yeah, I rang them earlier. It's weird – I thought there'd be more of a sense of elation when we finally got him, but it feels a bit like an anti-climax. Do you know what I mean?'

Leanne nodded. She knew exactly what he meant. Maybe it was simply because they were so tired, or because Shields was so unforthcoming, but there was something about the man they'd brought in last night that felt too ordinary, too tawdry for the amount of damage he'd done.

'Right, you two. I thought I'd find you here. There's been a development.'

For someone who'd been up all night, Desmond was looking surprisingly chipper. Leanne wondered if he kept a supply of toiletries in his office for emergency spruce-ups.

'Development, sir?' Pete was gazing at him blearily.

'We're going to agree to immunity from prosecution for Lucy Cromarty – the girl Leanne interviewed the other day who says she has information about the Poppy Glover abduction. With Shields in custody her evidence might be crucial in having something to charge him with. Pete, I want you to take a break, and then go in there and find out what she has to say.'

'But, sir, what about Shields?'

'I'm going to take Leanne back in with me – see how he reacts to a woman asking him questions. And we're going to hit him

293

with the photographs of the crime scenes. He's really on edge. Did you see how he was when you were grilling him about Leila Botsford? His whole body was tense, like a coiled spring.'

You could say this much for Desmond. Exhausted or not, he never missed a chance for a cliché.

'I'm going to go and get the files. Leanne, you meet me downstairs in ten minutes. Give him time to stew a little.'

After Desmond left, Pete leaned back in his chair and closed his eyes.

'You're not peed off, are you? That I'm going back in there instead of you?' Leanne was excited but also nervous and her voice betrayed her tension.

'A bit. Nah, not really. I was dying in there by the end. Couldn't wait to get out, to be honest.'

'You could always nip home for a bit. Kelly and Daisy will be happy to see you, I expect.'

She'd kept her voice deliberately neutral. Pete leaned forward again and put his head in his hands.

'I miss you.'

He wasn't looking at her so at first she thought she must have misheard.

'What?'

'I said I miss you.'

And now he did look at her with those green eyes. Her stomach caved in, her ribcage sliding open. She was too tired for this. Too tired for the resistance she needed to find. It would be too easy to get up and step round to the other side of the table and sink down on to his lap and feel his arms around her.

'Don't, Pete,' she said so quietly she wondered if she'd even uttered the words.

'I've got to say it, Leanne. I know I cocked up, and I know I've got to deal with it. And Kelly's sweet and nice and she deserves better, and Daisy's adorable and I'd give my life for her and I want to be there for her, but I'm fucking lonely and I miss you and I can't bear that I hurt you. And I know I should feel happy that you've found Will and you're happy, but I can't. I want to come back. I want to come home.'

Leanne got up so abruptly the plastic chair she'd been sitting on scraped across the vinyl floor.

'Look, Leanne, I didn't mean—'

'I know. It's OK. I have to go.'

When she arrived at the interview room downstairs, Desmond was already waiting outside. 'Are you sure you're OK, Leanne? You look upset. I know you're close to the Reid family. I hope this isn't going to be too difficult?'

'No, sir. I'm good to go, sir.'

Good to go. Where had that come from?

'Excellent. After you.'

Up close, Jason Shields was smaller than Leanne had thought. It was all that body-building stuff that made him seem more intimidating. His arms where they came out of his polo-shirt were the size of one of her thighs – and that was saying something. He had the same hardness in his face as his wife, only without that same ex-addict look. She'd seen his file: violent father, neglectful mother, in and out of care. Stint in the army including a tour in Iraq. An early disciplinary warning for fighting with another squaddie but then a commendation for bravery. Yet until now he'd had no criminal record, no history of substance abuse. Held down a security job in a City club for the last seven years. Clearly he was someone who had learned to keep himself under the tightest control. But the thing about people who kept themselves so locked in was that sooner or later they had to break out. And Jason Shields had the look of someone who was very close to breaking point. His thin lips were tightly pressed together and, as Pete had said, there was a clearly visible tic in his neck and also, now she looked closely, at his jaw. His hands where they rested on the table in front of him were trembling.

'We've got some photographs we want to show you, Jason,' Desmond began. 'These are the victims in the Kenwood Killings case. I want you to take a close look at them. Tell me if there's anything you recognize. First we have Megan Purvis.' He flung down some photographs on the table.

Leanne made sure her eyes stayed fixed on Jason Shields. She'd seen the pictures, of course, but that didn't mean they didn't affect her. Over the years, she'd perfected a technique of blurring the thing that she didn't want to see, even while staring right at it.

Jason Shields glanced down at the photographs of Megan Purvis without giving anything away, but Leanne saw the muscle spasm in his cheek go into overdrive.

'Have you anything you'd like to say?'

The man in the chair opposite shook his head. The tiniest movement.

'And now Tilly Reid. Here's how Tilly looked when we found her.'

Again Desmond carefully laid the photographs down. But this time there was no mistaking the struggle going on inside the man in front of them. The tremble had moved up from his hands through his arms and chest and now his whole body seemed to be shaking.

Come on, Leanne urged him silently. *Come on, spit it all out.*

The confession was close enough to taste.

47

On and on and on, one right after the other. Jason felt like he was being buried under a hailstorm of questions. He tried to keep in control, practising a few techniques that stress doctor, Dr Ancona, had taught him. You had to take your mind to your happy place. Well, Jason hadn't had that many happy places. Nothing from his shitty childhood, that was for sure. Him and Donna had gone to Crete one year when Keira was little – a beautiful resort near a little rocky cove – but they'd had a big row on the second day and she'd made him so mad he'd picked up the ceramic lamp from the bedside table and smashed it against the wall.

But then they started with the photographs. The woman was there by then – he could see her judging him the minute she walked in the door. Her type always did that. Looked at his muscles, found out what he did for a living, thought they had him sussed. Well, she didn't have a fucking clue. He wasn't who they'd decided he was. You couldn't judge a person by the lowest point in their life or the worst thing they'd ever done. But that was exactly what that woman cop was doing. He could see it. And as soon as he saw it, the flashbacks started. Normally he'd have been able to fight them off, but then they started with the photographs and it was just like it was all happening again.

He was walking through the park trying to kill time before going to work. He was early but he'd had to get away from home as Donna was doing his head in. They were arguing all the time at that stage and he only had to look at her to feel the rage building in his veins. So he'd parked the car on a whim right by the park gates and gone inside. He hadn't been planning to case the playground. He hadn't, he hadn't. And when he'd seen the girl playing there alone, he'd just been worried about her. He'd been taking her to find help. That's all he had been doing. But now they were showing him photographs of her body, dead, and he was remembering how his mouth had gone dry and the blood had been pounding in his ears so he couldn't hear anything except the roaring of his own heart. And she hadn't wanted to come and that had made him so angry because he was trying to help, and why couldn't she see that? And it was nearly dusk and no one was around except the boys playing football in the distance and they hadn't noticed when he picked her up with his hand over her mouth and carried her to the car. People should be more careful with their kids. He'd never have let Keira . . .

But now they were showing him other photographs and no, no, no. That wasn't right. He'd tried so hard not to think about it, not to dwell on it. But now he couldn't hold it in any more. He knew he should wait for his solicitor to arrive but the anger was building and building inside, heat searing his lungs until he could hardly breathe, and that woman cop was staring at him like she knew all about him even though she had no fucking clue, and now everything was red and there was no happy place and that woman had better stop staring at him and it was no good, he'd buried it so long he was about to explode with it.

'You lot think you're so fucking clever, don't you? You haven't got a fucking clue . . .'

48

It hadn't taken long for Rory to find a charger that fitted. His mum and Simon were always droning on about the state of his room but the truth was he knew exactly where everything was.

At first he'd thought the phone might be a goner as there was no sign of life at all when he plugged it in, but after a few minutes a light had come on and they'd been up and running, which was a relief, as he had a night out to arrange.

While he waited for the phone to charge, he opened up his laptop and scrolled through his Facebook page. He was on the bed leaning back against the pillows with the computer resting on the duvet. Simon always had a go at him about that too. He said the laptop would overheat and very possibly explode. Yeah right, because the news was full of people dying from exploding laptops.

One of the boys in his year had had a party the night before and there was the predictable run of photos. Rory had thought about going but he hardly knew him and hadn't been invited, and anyway he'd spent too many Saturday nights standing around with his mates outside houses where they weren't welcome. That was the kind of thing you did in Year 10. Now he was nearly at the end of Year 11 – don't think about the exams coming up after half-term – he was over all that.

This morning there were a load of posts from people who were in the middle of revising. Rory always felt a pang of guilt when he read about how much work other people were doing for their GCSEs. He knew he should be doing more. It was just that there was something in his brain that stopped him from being able to concentrate when a book was open in front of him.

He saw Jemima Reid had posted something – a YouTube clip of a dog biting its own paw thinking it was about to steal his bone which was actually pretty funny.

Fingers poised over the keys, he started a post: 'Gave my phone a bath lol. Need numbers so txt me on—' What was his new number? He rifled through a drawer in his desk until he found the SIM card he'd got the last time his mum had bought him a cheap phone.

Downstairs he could hear someone arriving for the interview. From the loud, posh voice he guessed it was that blonde journalist and was glad he was up here so he didn't have to go and face her. The couple of times he'd met her in the past she'd done that thing of putting her head on one side while she looked at him and screwing up her face, which is what people who had no actual feelings did when they wanted to look sympathetic, because they couldn't think of any actual sympathetic words.

He finished his Facebook post and got up and checked the screen on the phone. Four per cent charged. Could it actually be any slower? Still, soon it should be enough for him to make a few calls. He just had to be patient.

49

It was all Leanne could do not to turn to Desmond open-mouthed. Jason Shields wasn't just talking, he was practically spewing words from his mouth – and what he was saying beggared belief.

'You lot think you're so fucking clever, don't you?' he'd opened with. 'You haven't got a fucking clue.'

And, if he was telling the truth, he was absolutely right. They hadn't had a clue. Yes, he'd killed Megan Purvis. But, and here was the thing she still couldn't get her head around, he was denying he'd ever gone near any of the other three girls. Tilly, Leila, Poppy. What was the point of a partial confession? Why admit to what had always appeared to be the most brutal of the killings but deny the rest? It didn't make sense.

As Jason Shields rambled on, unstoppable as though someone had opened up a valve in him that could not now be shut off, Leanne thought again about the murder of Tilly Reid and how it had surprised them all because it was so different from the first murder, even though there was still that telling detail – that blue biro 'SORRY' written on the leg in awkward left-handed writing. Tilly had been fully dressed, peaceful, carefully arranged. No sign of a struggle or of any sexual activity. They'd been able to tell from the hairs on her jumper that her hair had been brushed and re-styled. Same with Leila Botsford. Poppy Glover had been different. Partially unclothed, with that semen sample found nearby. But the Nemo gang had been responsible for that. Without them the body would have been in the same condition as the previous two.

It seemed incredible. And yet she was convinced beyond all shadow of a doubt that it was true. Jason Shields might be guilty of the first murder, but there was a copycat killer out there. And they had no idea who it was.

50

It was only two weeks since they'd last been at the Purvises' house for the Megan's Angels meeting, but it felt to Emma as though everything had changed as she, Guy, Jemima and Caitlin stood waiting outside the front door. Then they had seemed like a random group of unhappy individuals, but now they felt like a family, maybe for the first time in years. Not a happy family, she wouldn't go so far as that, but a family nonetheless. She and Guy were standing shoulder to shoulder, and neither was pulling away as they would have done even a few days ago. Since the scene where he'd broken down and admitted to lurking outside schools to feel closer to Tilly, something had shifted between them. They were talking to each other, not around each other. Sometimes they even looked at one another when they spoke.

The news that the police had made an arrest had put an electrical charge through all of them.

She'd been nervous of telling Jemima the police had a suspect, thinking it might send her spiralling backwards into that wordless rage, but the change she'd noticed in her oldest daughter over

303

the last few days was still evident this afternoon. She hadn't even made a fuss about coming to the Purvises'.

But Emma was not looking forward to the afternoon. She couldn't stand Sally Freeland. She understood why Leanne had put forward Sally's request for an interview, and to give her credit, she hadn't put pressure on her. She'd made it clear it was completely Emma's own choice. But obviously Emma wanted to do anything she could to help the investigation, which had seemed at that point to have stalled – even if she privately thought this smacked of blackmail. Emma couldn't see why they didn't just threaten to charge Sally with withholding information, but Leanne had tried to explain how useful it would be to keep Freeland 'on side', as she called it. And Emma had been really grateful when Helen had volunteered to act as go-between, offering up her home as neutral territory.

When Helen came to the door, she looked taken aback to see Emma had brought an entourage.

'Sorry to arrive en masse,' said Emma, observing that Helen had that strained, over-bright look she sometimes got, as if she was trying that little bit too hard.

'Oh, no problem at all. Welcome, Reids! Actually I'm not long home myself. I always go to the crematorium on a Sunday morning. Megan and I always spent Sunday mornings together. It was our girly time.'

Emma couldn't imagine Helen having 'girly time' but then other people's families always were unfathomable, weren't they?

'Sally is here already,' Helen said in a low voice as she led them into the hallway.

'You don't mind then?'

Emma had never talked to Helen directly about what was rumoured to have happened between Simon and the blonde journalist, but she felt she had to say something.

'This isn't about me and what I mind and don't mind. This is about Megan and what's good for Megan and what I can do to help find the person who took her.' Helen always said 'took her' rather than 'killed her'.

'But they've already got someone. Didn't Jo ring you?'

Helen turned her gaze to Emma and once again the younger woman had a sense of something not right about her friend's mood.

'Yes, of course, but you know how it is. Mistakes can happen. Simon? Simon!' She was standing at the bottom of the stairs, shouting up to the floor above. 'The Reids are here. Come and say hello.'

'There's no need.' Guy looked uncomfortable. Emma tried to remember if she'd told him about the rumours.

Simon Hewitt appeared at the top of the stairs looking cloudy-eyed and puffy.

'Sorry. Had a heavy night last night, out celebrating a mate's birthday. Only been home an hour, so still trying to digest the news. An arrest! Have you any more information?'

Emma shook her head. He looked shocking. And please let him not come any closer – he absolutely reeked of alcohol. Next to him Guy was a picture of clean-living and health.

'I thought we could all go out in the garden. Sally is out there already.'

There was something pointed about the way Helen said 'Sally'. Emma could only guess how much it was costing her to remain polite.

'Actually,' Helen continued in that bright, varnished voice, 'the Botsfords are on their way over too. They've also had that call from the police about the arrest. No doubt they want to see if any of us know anything more.'

Emma wasn't sure she was in the mood for Fiona Botsford's prickliness but she didn't blame her for wanting to come over.

305

'And don't forget Leanne's coming as well,' she added. 'Maybe she'll have something more to tell us.'

But when Leanne finally stepped out into Helen Purvis's overgrown jungle of a garden twenty-five minutes later, pausing a few feet from the back doorstep to brush a couple of wayward honeysuckle petals from her wrinkled purple top, Emma could tell straight away there wasn't any good news. By this stage the village fête atmosphere they'd all been trying to cultivate for the sake of the children was starting to implode. Fiona and Mark Botsford, as usual, had been intense and unsmiling since they'd arrived, while it wouldn't even have taken a knife to cut the atmosphere between Sally Freeland and Simon Hewitt and Helen Purvis.

'Can you tell us anything more? Is it definitely the right guy? Has he confessed?'

Fiona Botsford hadn't even let Leanne sit down in the folding canvas chair Simon had fetched from the shed before bombarding her with questions.

Leanne looked exhausted, but not exhausted in that exhilarated way Emma would have expected if she'd been up all night getting a confession out of whoever they had locked up in their cells. There was a sag to her shoulders and her normally rose-flushed cheeks looked grey and sallow. But it was her eyes that most gave her away. Leanne was one of those rare people who look right at you, really at you, when they talk to you, but this afternoon her gaze slid off everyone as if they were coated in oil.

'I'm afraid I really can't tell you anything more than you already know.'

Emma felt herself slump with disappointment.

Sally Freeland, who'd been sitting to attention (in the best chair, the one with the faded floral cushions on it), couldn't hold herself back any more.

'Come on, Leanne. There must be something you can tell us.

Have a heart – these poor people are in agony waiting to find out what's going on.'

Leanne shrank back into the chair.

'I'm really sorry, folks. I know this is hard for you all but you just have to bear with us. All I can tell you is that we have someone in police custody who is helping us with our inquiries. This person has been able to give us certain information relating to the case.'

'Leanne, can't you be more specific? Look what you're doing to us! It's torture.'

Simon Hewitt put his hand on his wife's shoulder as he spoke and Emma saw that Helen did indeed look as if she was going through hell. Her face was pale and her shoulder was shaking under his fingers. Emma's own heart dissolved in sympathy.

Leanne shrugged. 'I'd love to be able to tell you more. Believe me, nothing will give me more pleasure than when I can stand in front of you and tell you it's all over. We've got them. But—'

'Them!' Sally almost barked the word. 'You said "them". Does that mean there's more than one? A gang?'

'No. No.'

Leanne was shaking her head, her eyes closed. 'I didn't say that. Please, please don't jump the gun.'

Her voice cracked.

51

Voices wafted in from the garden through Rory's open window. Sounded like they were all there. The whole merry gang. He'd heard Jemima Reid's voice a while ago asking for an orange juice. Now they were all getting agitated about something. Simon's booming voice clearly said the word 'torture'. Rory wished the windows of his room weren't Velux which meant he couldn't see anything unless he stood on his chair, which tended to swivel around precariously. He wouldn't mind knowing what they were all getting so worked up about. Once he'd sorted out the mobile he'd go outside.

Rory had the new SIM ready, but thought he'd better test the phone out first with the one already in there. No point going through the hassle of changing the SIM without being sure the phone definitely worked.

When he switched the mobile on, his heart sank. This thing must be ancient. The graphics were so bad. He could have done better himself. How long had his mum had this thing anyway? He clicked on the address-book icon looking for clues. Not one name he recognized. Was this even his mum's phone? He went back to the menu and found the messages icon. The inbox didn't shed any more light. A message from a plumber it looked like, giving a quote on some new radiator. Another message from someone called Mel saying could they make it 8 instead of 7.30. Puzzled, he clicked on the sent folder and suddenly everything in the room started spinning.

52

All Leanne wanted to do was lie down in her bed with the curtains drawn and close her eyes and try not to think. Not about Will or Pete or Jason Shields or any of it. She couldn't remember ever being this tired. Her phone, stuffed into the side pocket of her handbag, was buzzing almost non-stop. She hadn't checked it since arriving at Helen Purvis's house, but she guessed it would be Will. She'd had twenty-eight missed calls from him the last time she'd looked. She didn't have the energy for it – neither for his remorse nor for the effort it would take to forgive him and move on.

'Can you at least tell us if the suspect you have in custody is someone known to us.' That was how Guy Reid spoke – measured yet imperious. At least that's how he'd spoken when she'd first met him. After Tilly's death, he'd been different, defeated. But today some of that old arrogance was back. She scrutinized him more closely – he was perched awkwardly on the arm of the teak garden chair Jemima and Caitlin were both squeezed into, nursing a mug of coffee. There was definitely something different about him today.

'I can't give you any more details, Guy. I'm really sorry.'

And the thing was, she really was sorry. She was more sorry than any of them could know. She couldn't look at Helen in case she gave away the fact that she knew who'd killed her daughter. And she couldn't look at the others in case she gave away the fact that she didn't know who'd killed theirs. Instead, she kept her gaze fixed on the overgrown lawn like she was trying to mow it with her eyes.

'Should we get on with the interview?' she suggested.

She made the mistake of glancing at Emma who looked appalled.

'Surely not here – in the middle of everyone?'

They all looked towards Helen who would usually be fussing about trying to organize everything, but she hadn't moved from the rickety wrought-iron chair she was sitting on. This house must be worth a million, but Leanne couldn't help thinking the garden looked like a junk shop.

'We could go inside if you like, for a private chat.' Sally had on her journalist voice, but now Leanne could see her close up, she noticed that she too looked totally wrecked. Her face was heavily made up as normal, but the skin looked clammy under the layers of foundation and the hand that clutched the strap of her leather bag was trembling.

Leanne was trying not to catch Emma's eye because she knew if she did something would be required of her. She'd have to get up out of this chair and move somewhere else and doubtless be pestered with more questions that she couldn't answer. Jason Shields was a rock in her gut, weighting her to the floor. She dropped her head into her hands as her phone buzzed again. She wasn't supposed to switch her phone off, not in the middle of a live investigation, but she'd had just about all she could stand. Pulling it out of her bag, she glanced at the screen and frowned. Above the numerous missed calls from Will and one from Pete, there was a missed call and a voicemail from Desmond. She felt adrenalin beginning to kick in once again. Had Jason Shields changed his story?

While Sally Freeland outlined her vision for the interview, Leanne pressed her phone to her ear.

'Leanne, there's been a development you need to be brought up to speed on.'

She couldn't be sure, but wasn't there an edge of something in her boss's voice?

'Lucy Cromarty, the shoplifter with information about the Poppy Glover abduction, has finally come clean. Seems it was her who nicked a purse from a woman's bag in the ice-cream queue the evening Poppy disappeared. Lucy had strolled off and was a few yards away when the woman started kicking off, which is when she noticed Poppy Glover being led away by—'

'Rory. Dude. Come and sit down.'

Simon Hewitt's artificially jolly shout cut across Leanne's concentration, drowning out the message. Heart racing uncomfortably, she pressed the option to play the message again.

'Rory? Mate? What's up?'

Leanne looked up as the message started again: 'Leanne, there's been a development . . .'

Rory was standing on the back doorstep where she herself had stood earlier on. His face was whiter than the woodwork around the door. His arm was outstretched and he was holding something in his hand. A phone, she now realized.

Simon was heading towards his stepson, but the boy's eyes were fixed on a point past Simon's shoulder.

In her ear, Desmond droned on: '. . . Was a few yards away when the woman started kicking off . . .'

'Mum?'

Rory was moving off the step towards Helen, ignoring Simon who stood awkwardly in the middle ground. Without his habitual cynical expression, Rory looked suddenly like a needy young child, and yet Helen didn't make a move towards him. In fact she looked like she was frozen to the spot, staring not at her son but at the phone in his hand.

From Leanne's own phone came the sound of Desmond's voice repeating, 'Which is when she noticed Poppy Glover being led away by . . .'

Leanne pressed the phone against her ear so she wouldn't miss the next word, but even so it took her a while to process what he'd said. Her attention was distracted by Rory saying, 'Mum, I found this phone in your drawer and the thing is, I don't think it's yours. I think it's Mrs Botsford's. I think it's the phone she sent that last text to Leila on. The one telling her to go out the back exit not the front.'

Only now did it sink in. What Desmond had said. A woman. Poppy Glover had been led away from the ice-cream van by a *woman*.

There was a sharp cry to Leanne's right and Fiona Botsford darted forward to grab the phone from Rory's hand. 'But this is mine!' she said frantically, scrolling through something on the screen. 'This is the phone that was stolen. I don't understand.'

Leanne was up on her feet before her mind even caught up with her body.

'Let's go for a chat,' she said, hauling Helen out of her chair and bundling her past Rory. Without stopping to think, she propelled her down the hallway and straight through the front door. Her heart was slamming against her ribs as she manoeuvred the strangely compliant woman into the passenger seat of her car and then threw herself behind the wheel and pulled away from the kerb. At the next corner she stopped, realizing she had to call in ahead to get officers round to the Purvis house and to alert Desmond to what was going on.

'She just looked so lovely, you see,' Helen said when Leanne had finished her call to the station. In contrast to her earlier tenseness, Helen was now sitting quite serenely, almost as if they were friends going out for a drive.

'Who?'

'Leila Botsford. I saw her and Fiona in the café they went to after ballet and I just knew she'd be a good friend for Megan. I followed them home. Then after that I followed them a few more days until I knew where Leila went to school and what their routine was. It wasn't hard to swipe Fiona's phone from her bag in the organic shop. When you get to my age, you're largely invisible. It comes in handy sometimes.

'I didn't hurt her though, Leanne. I would never have done anything to hurt any of them. It's just that I didn't want Megan to be lonely. And obviously it was nice for me not to be so lonely either. You don't know what it's like. People would say they understood how I was feeling, but they didn't. There was never anyone who knew *exactly* how I felt. Not until Emma.'

'You followed Tilly as well.'

'No, no. I saw her walking to the shops on her own. It was fortuitous, that's all.'

Fortuitous. Helen was mad. How had Leanne not noticed it before?

Except she had noticed it, she just hadn't been able to process it. Because mothers of murdered children were expected to be mad, weren't they? And how were you supposed to assess the correct form for that madness to take?

'I'm taking you in to the station, Helen. You'll have your rights read to you there and be formally questioned. You don't have to say anything else now.'

'But I want to. It's a relief really. I know all the families will hate me but they must see that the girls are all together now. They have each other, just as we have each other. That's why I couldn't understand how Fiona and Mark could bear to move away. How could they even think about breaking up the group when we bring

314

one another so much comfort? And I did take such great care of their girls. I really did. I do hope you'll tell them that. When you think of all the awful ways they could have died – like my poor Megan did – to go peacefully off to sleep, with a new, sweet-smelling hankie pressed to the nose and no fear. It's a kindness. I always told them I was a friend of their mum's. I had little things belonging to Megan in the car so they'd know I was a mother too, and wouldn't be afraid. I couldn't have borne for them to be afraid. And afterwards I treated them like princesses. I brushed their hair.'

Now Leanne understood about the hair bands Emma had become so obsessed by. A normal killer wouldn't pay attention if a hair elastic came loose when a body was being carried, but Helen had not only noticed but had cared and had replaced the missing band with one that presumably had once belonged to her own daughter.

'Of course I didn't like leaving them alone in the car boot overnight – sometimes more than one night – once they were peaceful—'

'By peaceful, I'm guessing you mean dead.'

Helen winced, as if Leanne had said something obscene.

'If you like. But even though they were, as you say, dead, I did my best to make it comfortable in there until it was safe for me to drive them somewhere quiet. It was padded with a duvet. Warm and cosy.'

'And Simon never thought it was odd – you getting up in the middle of the night and going out?'

'He sleeps like a log. Anyway, he's used to me getting up at weird times since Megan died. Grief plays havoc with your sleep cycle.'

The two women sat in silence. There was really nothing more to say. In a moment, when she had recovered herself enough, Leanne would switch the engine back on and drive through the empty Sunday-afternoon streets to the station. She didn't worry about Helen escaping. There was no fight left in her, she could tell. Besides, where would she go now? Leanne thought about the people she'd left behind at the Purvises' house – the Reids, the Botsfords, Rory. So many lives ripped apart.

As if she could sense Leanne's thoughts, Helen broke in. 'Please tell them I looked after their girls as if they were my own, as if they were Megan. That's why I took it so badly when Poppy was found in that state. You must catch him.' She was looking straight at Leanne now with those intense eyes. 'You must catch the monster who did that to her.'

Leanne looked at Helen and wondered how it would feel to be inside her head, to believe killing children was justified as long as they didn't suffer.

'I was so lonely after Megan died,' Helen said again. 'If it hadn't been for Rory I would have gone to be with her but I couldn't do that to him. You wouldn't believe how much it helped to meet Emma and Guy and Fiona and Mark and now Susan Glover too. We've been such a support to each other. I hope they won't forget that. It feels so wrong to have just left them all at home like that, so rude.'

Leanne turned the key in the ignition and pulled away from the kerb. As they drove up the hill towards the police station, they passed two young girls, ten or eleven, eating ice creams and giggling. Helen turned her head and watched until the girls were out of sight.

'They shouldn't be out walking on their own,' she said, and Leanne saw that the hands that rested on her lap were clenched tight. 'Anything could happen.'

53

A year ago one life ended and a new one began. The life before had Poppy and it had innocence and it had joy. There's still joy in this new one, but I'm not so careless with it now, I store it in a memory bank in case it should all be taken away. Because life, I now know, hangs always by a thread.

A year ago Helen Purvis (I can even say her name now) was free and walking the streets and parks and she came upon Poppy just as there was a commotion, a purse stolen, something meaningless and yet . . . The wrong place, the wrong time, that's what the police said. We couldn't have known.

And now Helen is in a secure psychiatric hospital and Rory lives with his dad. They moved to escape the publicity. Devon, I think, or Cornwall. Emma says Jemima keeps in touch with him. Rory's taken up surfing, she says. He's older but not broken. He will be OK. I'm so glad of that. Sometimes I close my eyes and send him goodwill – more often now I'm to have a son myself.

Emma was the first person I told about the pregnancy, before Oliver even. Funny how the group that Helen so arbitrarily put together has finally gelled in her absence. Even Fiona moving to Australia hasn't made too much difference. The three of us chat on Skype. Emma and Guy celebrated their fifteenth wedding anniversary last week. They're the couple Oliver and I look to whenever things get rocky, which they sometimes do. We say, if Emma and Guy can come through it . . .

A year ago the world changed but the sun is still out and it is the same sun, just like the jasmine growing on the back fence is the same jasmine, filling the air with the same heady, sweet smell, and the neighbour playing jazz loudly through the open window of the top-floor flat is the same neighbour.

And just for this moment, it is beautiful.

Acknowledgements

As ever, my thanks to the dynamic team at Curtis Brown, particularly Felicity Blunt, Emma Herdman, Vivienne Schuster, Alice Lutyens and Sophie Harris, and to Deborah Schneider in New York. Thanks also to the talented crew at Transworld – Jane Lawson, Marianne Velmans, Suzanne Bridson, Sarah Harwood, Elisabeth Merriman, Kate Samano, Claire Ward, Lynsey Dalladay, Laura Swainbank. And to Jeanette Slinger for her much-appreciated support.

I'm constantly amazed at the generosity of other writers. Thanks to all the writers I've met on Twitter and in real life who continue to help keep my neuroses (largely) at bay, particularly Louise Millar, Amanda Jennings, Lisa Jewell, Louise Douglas, Emma Kavanagh (and her very useful policeman husband) and the criminally clever Killer Women crime writers.

Thanks also to the bloggers, like Anne Cater, Liz Barnsley and Pan McIlroy, who spread the book love with such energy and passion. And to the indefatigable Tracy Fenton, founder of The Book Club on Facebook.

It takes a particularly dedicated kind of friend to be still cheerleading by the time book six comes around, so thanks to Rikki Finegold, Roma Cartwright, Juliet Brown, Fiona Godfrey, Renata Barcelos, Steve Griffiths, Sally Thompson, Ed Needham, Jo Lockwood, Helen Bates, Ben Clarke, Maria Trkulja, Mark Heholt, Jos Joures, Snai Patel, Mark Hindley.

Thanks to the Cohens – Gaynor, Sata, Simon, Emma; the Halls – Colin, Ed and Alfie; and the Fawcetts – Paul and Margaret. And lastly to Michael, Otis, Jake and Billie. Sorry for monopolizing the kichen table.

Tammy Cohen (who previously wrote under her formal name Tamar Cohen) has written several acclaimed novels about family fallout: *The Mistress's Revenge*, *The War of the Wives* and *Someone Else's Wedding*. *The Broken* was her first psychological thriller, followed by *Dying for Christmas*.

She lives in North London with her partner and three (nearly) grown children, plus one badly behaved dog. Chat with her on Twitter: @MsTamarCohen.